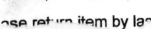
The

Underworld

Jessica Sorensen

For information:
http://jessicasorensensblog.blogspot.com/

Cover Photograph by Shutterstock
Cover Design by Mae I Design and Photography
www.maeidesign.com

The Underworld — Book 2
ISBN 978-1463756970

Chapter 1

I wasn't sure whether I was dead or alive. Perhaps alive in the sense that I was still breathing, but was I even breathing? I wasn't sure. I wasn't sure of anything.

Blackness swallowed me whole, and not the kind of blackness that comes from being in a dark room. No, this darkness was heavy and thick, and it wove into my body, making my skin damp and my limbs heavy.

Where this dark place was, or how long I'd been here, I didn't know. I might have been here for years, month, days, or even just a few seconds. Time felt nonexistent.

After awhile, I started to convince myself that I must be dead. That the memoria extracto—or whatever the heck that memory removing rock Stephan had used on me was called—had taken my life instead of wiping away my mind. But how could I tell for sure if I'd died, or if I was still thriving? I mean, was there really a difference between death and losing every ounce of who you are?

The only problem with my "I was dead" theory was that if I was dead, then why could I feel pain blazing in my leg—the exact leg Stephan had stabbed me in? Was feeling pain possible after you died? But if I wasn't dead, and instead my memory had been erased, along with my emotions, then why did my heart ache from Alex's betrayal?

The ache hurt so bad that I thought my heart was going to actually stop beating. How could Alex do this to me? Yes, I knew what the circumstances were, and I knew what I was—a girl who had gotten stuck harboring a world-saving star's energy inside her. But this wasn't just about the energy; it was also about Stephan, the leader of the Keepers, collaborating with the Death Walkers and quite possibly with Demetrius, a man who wanted to let a portal open on December 21, 2012. A portal that, if opened, would release hundreds and hundreds of Death Walkers, causing the world to end in a sheet of ice. And yet, despite all of the previously mentioned facts, Alex still let Stephan attempt to wipe my memory away. No questions asked.

Betrayal.

I knew all too well how much the feeling hurt.

But how could I feel the hurt?

How could I still feel?

It didn't matter how many questions I asked myself, because no answers ever came to me. All I had to pass the time was the blackness that suffocated me. Nothing but me and the darkness.

I was alone.

The pain in my leg shot up a notch, taking a toll on my ability to stand. So as carefully as I could, I lowered myself toward the ground, but a sharp pain fired up in my neck, and I froze. I let out a whimper as my fingers brushed the back of my neck, reminding me of when my Foreseer mark had appeared, and how Alex had kissed me. Then, right after the kiss, he'd betrayed me.

I sighed as I sank down on the ground, wondering if this was how it was always going to be. If I'd always be trapped in the dark, alone, just like when I couldn't feel. Although I may not have been surrounded by darkness back then, I was as lonely as I was now. The only difference now was that I could feel emotion. Scared, nervousness, pain—these were just a few things pouring through me at the moment.

And then, suddenly, my head began to hum, and my skin felt as if it were sparkling. I gasped as I was yanked backward. Something was dragging me through the blackness, leading me to…I had no idea. I kicked and tried to throw my weight forward, but it was useless. My heart raced as I squeezed my eyes shut and waited for whatever was coming next. The disappearance of my mind? My death?

And then I felt it; a faint electric spark kissing at my fingertip. But wait. No. There was

no way I could be feeling *that*.

There was no way I'd feel that again.

Was there?

Chapter 2

Buzz....buzz....buzz. My eyes flew open, and I was instantly blinded by a bright light. Light everywhere. Radiating throughout the room.

Room. Huh?

My head was buzzing as I shot upright in the bed. A bed? I was now in a bed, with a blanket draped over me. Pale purple walls surrounded me, and there was a small window next to the bed where I could see colorful lights flashing all over and strange shaped buildings that stretched up toward the sky. Wait. I knew this place. It was....Vegas?

"What the...?" I squinted my eyes toward the outside window, not believing what I was seeing. Vegas? How could I be in Vegas? I'd been in Colorado when I'd...well, I wasn't sure what had happened to me yet. Maybe I was dreaming or something. Perhaps my mind was creating this room as a sort of comfort from being trapped in the dark.

I did my classic pinch-myself-to-see-if-I'm-awake thing, and yep, it hurt.

So I was awake.

The buzzing in my head dropped down a notch, now only as loud as a faint whisper. Hmmm…so what was I supposed to do? There was a door on the wall right in front of the bed. Should I get up and go see what was out there? If there was one thing I'd learned, it was that there was no such thing as being too careful. For all I knew I'd open the door and a thousand Death Walkers' would come swarming in, their yellow eyes glowing with the hunger to kill me. Or even worse than Death Walkers, what if Stephan came in?

On my "Things That Terrify Me" list, Stephan now held top rank—one step above the Death Walkers.

Shows you how scary he is.

I decided the best way to approach the situation was to get up and go over to the door. Perhaps when I got close enough, I'd be able to hear something that would give me a clue as to what was out there. And if I did hear anything that sounded threatening or dangerous, like say a deep voice belonging to a man with a very distinctive scar grazing his left cheek, then I'd move on to my next plan. And that was to escape out the window. It was going to be a little tricky, though, since it looked like I was up on the second floor of the building. But I could always try the whole tying-the-sheets-together-and-making-a-rope trick.

Sucking in a deep breath, I tossed the blanket off of me and slid my legs off the edge of the bed. I was no longer dressed in the clothes I'd been wearing back in Colorado. I had on a pair of plaid pajama shorts and a tank top. Both had pink on them so there was no way they belonged to me. Across the top of my leg—right in the spot Stephan had stabbed—a bandaged was wrapped. Someone had fixed me up.

Who, though?

Good question.

My leg throbbed as I stood up, the grey carpet feeling warm against my bare feet. I limped over to the door. So far, I hadn't heard a single noise. Wherever I was, it was quiet.

Dead quiet.

I stood hesitantly in front of the closed door. Did I dare open it?

My heart knocked in my chest, and with a trembling hand, I reached for the doorknob. But before I could get my hand around it, it started to turn on its own, and at the very same time electricity whipped through me.

I jumped back, but instantly regretted it because my legs gave out on me and I toppled to the floor.

I grabbed hold of my injured leg. "Damn—"

The door swung open.

Ignoring the scorching pain in my leg, I scrambled to my feet and searched frantically for another way out of the room, other than trying to jump out the window.

"Gemma," Alex said in a guarded tone, as he walked through the doorway. He inched himself toward me, taking each step carefully, as though he thought walking too fast would spook me. But him just being here was spooking me.

He was wearing a black t-shirt and a pair of jeans, and his hair was scattered messily in its intentionally-done-perfect-yet-messy kind of way. He looked like a normal guy—completely harmless. Yet I knew he wasn't.

"Stay-y away f-from me." I stammered, my heart pounding insanely in my chest as I backed away from him. "Don't come any closer."

"I'm not going to hurt you." His voice was as soft as a feather. He continued to step toward me, his bright green eyes locked on me, just like when he watched Stephan try to take my emotions away. "I promise I won't hurt you."

"You promise!" I cried, anger raging through me like a boiling kettle of water. "Your promises are worth nothing." I mean, he'd promised me how many times that he wouldn't let anything happen to me? And yet, in the end, he'd let his father attempt to erase my mind and take my emotions away.

Alex stopped dead in his tracks, his expression filling with annoyance. "What the heck is that supposed to mean?"

My back brushed the wall. I was cornered. "It means your promises are worthless. At least the ones you make to me. You promised me you wouldn't let anything happened to me and look where it got me."

He raised his eyebrows, a slight mocking expression teasing at his lips as he spread his arms out to the side of him. "It got you here, safe and sound."

"Safe and sound," I repeated, glancing around the room where no potential danger was evident. I looked down at my hands, my arms, and except for the bandage around my leg, everything appeared to be fine. I could still *feel* as well, my emotions resting somewhere between confusion, anger, and longing. But I blame the last feeling on the sparks.

"Gemma," Alex said, and I looked up at him. "You're okay, right?"

I eyed him warily. I wasn't sure what to do here. I didn't trust him at all, despite the fact that I did seem to be alright. "I don't know...Am I?"

He cocked an eyebrow at me. "I'm asking you."

"Why? You're the one who knows what happened to me." I crossed my arms. "I mean, what's going on here? Am I supposed to feel? And where's Stephan? Outside the door waiting for you to come check on me and see if the memoria extracta—or whatever that stupid memory erasing rock is called—has wiped out my mind?" My anger simmered hotter as the painful memories of what had happened to me resurfaced.

"*Memoria extraho*," Alex said.

I gaped at him. "What?"

"The memory erasing rock is called a *memoria extraho*," he said.

10

I glared at him. "That's not important right now. All I need to know is what the heck is going on."

He hesitated, running his fingers through his dark brown hair, probably trying to conjure up some lie to tell me. I couldn't take this. I couldn't take anymore lies. I needed to get out of here and away from him, even though the electricity was telling me to do otherwise.

I darted to the side, starting to swing around him.

"Gemma," Alex warned, matching my move with cat-like reflexes. He blocked my escape. "Just listen to me for a second. If you'll settle down, I'll explain what's going on."

I let out this unnaturally high pitched laugh. "Will you?" I asked. "Because you never have before. Not fully, anyway."

"Gemma," he started, but I was already hopping up onto the bed, overlooking the pain igniting in my leg as I dodged around him, and headed for the door.

He stuck his arm out, attempting to catch me in mid-air as I leapt off of the bed, but he missed me by a sliver of an inch, and I was able to escape out of the room.

I wasn't exactly sure where I was planning on going, or what would be waiting for me down at the bottom of the stairs, but I knew I had to get away. Run. Find Laylen or someone else who would tell me what was going on.

My bare feet hammered against the stairs as I charged down them. There was a door just at the bottom, and the sunlight spilled through a small window at the top of it. If I could just make it outside, then I could run away to...Well, I really hadn't gotten that far in my escape plan. All I knew was that I was going to run away from this madness. I was sick of the lies and the secrets. I was sick of monsters and people trying to harm me.

I reached the bottom of the stairs, my hand extended out to the doorknob. Just a few steps and I'd be overtaken with the warm Vegas air and sunshine.

"Gemma," a voice said from beside of me.

I jumped, my heart racing. For a split second I thought I was dead. That the person who'd said my name would be Stephan.

But thankfully it wasn't.

"What the heck?" Laylen said breathlessly, his hand pressed over his heart. "You scared the heck out of me."

"You scared the heck out of me," I told him, equally as breathless.

His bright blue eyes stared at me in astonishment, almost as if he couldn't quite believe I was standing here.

Trust me, I felt the very same way.

For a moment I just stood there, taking in the sight of him. His blonde hair, the tips dyed bright blue. The dark red shade of his lips with a silver ring looped through the bottom. The mark of immortality tattooed across the pale skin of his forearm. It was such a relief to see him. I had so much I wanted to tell him and so many questions I wanted to ask.

"Are you alright?" He eyed me over as if he were checking to see if I was broken. "What were you running from?"

"I was—"

"From me," Alex's voice drifted up from behind me.

I spun around and scooted closer to Laylen.

Alex, in typical Alex style, strolled lazily down the stairs, as if he had thought I'd never actually run away. "I don't understand why you have to be so difficult," he said, his eyes locked on me like a target, the sparks reacting with such eagerness that my legs felt a little weak. "I told you I'd tell you what was going on. There's no reason to try and run away."

"There's no reason to try and run away," I said exasperatedly. "Are you kidding me?"

He frowned as he reached the bottom of the stairs. As he walked closer to me, I inched myself closer to Laylen. So close in fact that my shoulder bumped into his.

Alex's eyebrows dipped down as he stopped just short of me. "What do you think I'm going to do to you, Gemma? Hurt you?"

I shrugged. "I don't know. I never know anything when it comes to you."

He glowered at me, and I glowered right back, the electricity heating hotter and hotter the longer our eyes stayed on one another.

"Gemma," Laylen said, and for the second time in just a few short minutes I nearly jumped out of my skin. "Everything's okay. No one here's going to hurt you."

I looked up at him. And I mean it: I really had to look up, because Laylen is like six foot four. "Everything's okay?" I asked with skepticism. "Really?"

He nodded. "Yeah. Let's go sit down, and Alex and I will explain everything that's happened."

I cast a quick glance at Alex, and then looked back at Laylen. "I want *you* to explain it to me."

"Gemma, I already said I'd tell you the truth." Alex sounded irritated.

I opened my mouth to tell him that I really didn't care what he said he'd do. And that he was a liar. But Laylen spoke before I got the chance.

"Alex, you really can't blame her for not trusting you." He paused, deliberating something very charily. "After what you did."

That, of course, pissed Alex off. "I didn't do anything. And you have some nerve for saying that I did."

Laylen got this look on his face that I could tell meant he was about to say something that might start a fight. And Alex looked completely ready to fight back. That's what these two did sometimes; they got into arguments that became more heated the more they opened their mouths.

But I didn't have time for this right now. I needed to know what went on back at the cabin, after I'd...blacked out?

"Can't you just tell me what happened?" I begged Laylen. "*Please. I trust you more than I trust him.*" *In fact, I don't trust him at all.*

Laylen glanced at Alex, who shot him a dirty look, and returned his bright blue eyes to me. "Yeah, okay. I'll tell you what I know."

"Thank you," I said, feeling slightly less anxious. But still anxious enough that my legs were wobbly.

Laylen motioned for me to follow him as he swept through a beaded-curtain doorway, which led us into a living room with dark blue walls that were decorated with shelves holding odd looking knickknacks. Black and white tile checkerboarded the floor, and a set of purple velvet couches centered the room, along with an apothecary table topped with black candles.

Hmm...I was getting a weird sense of *déjà vu* with this room. Then it dawned on me. "Is this Adessa's house?" I asked.

"Yeah." Laylen took a seat on one of the purple velvet sofas. "Which is actually attached to her store."

I sat down next to him, and Alex, looking annoyed, dropped down in the chair across from us.

"So, where do you want me to begin?" Laylen asked me. And I liked that he asked, instead of trying to evade my questions, like a certain someone with bright green eyes would've done.

Having options, though, was kind of confusing me. "So...um...what happened?" I shook my head at the ridiculousness of my own question. "I mean, what happened back in Colorado? And how did we end up in Vegas?"

Laylen stayed quiet for a second, and I started to wonder if he even knew the answers to my questions. Alex had made it clear that because Laylen was a vampire, he was no longer part of the Keepers' world anymore, making Laylen a little out of the loop on things.

Laylen brushed his blue-tipped bangs away from his forehead. "Well, I guess I'll answer the easy question first. You're here at Adessa's because Aislin transported us here."

"What?!" I exclaimed, making Laylen flinch. I lowered my voice. "Sorry. But how? I mean, the last thing I can remember is being surrounded by a ton of Death Walkers, and Stephan trying to use some creepy smoking rock to try and take my mind away."

"The rock's called the *memoria extraho*," Alex interrupted.

"Well, you'd know since you were going to let him use it on me," I snapped.

A condescending look rose on his face. "If you'd just listen to me explain, then you'd realize you're wrong."

"I said I want Laylen to tell me," I told him firmly.

16

He shrugged and leaned back in the chair, resting his hands behind his head all casual and everything. "Fine. Whatever you want."

I stared at him, entirely taken off-guard. Huh? Did he just say whatever you want? To me?

"What?" Alex said, with a blasé attitude. "I was planning on telling you the truth, but if you're more likely to believe it from Laylen's mouth, then it's better that he tells you. That way you won't have any doubts."

I shook my head, wondering why he was acting so cooperative, but figured I would worry about it later, so I returned my attention back to Laylen. "So how did you and Aislin end up in Colorado?"

"Well, I guess to make a long story short, after Aislin came back to get me in Nevada, those Death Walkers you and I saw marching through the desert had reached the house. They ambushed us, but after a big struggle, Aislin and I managed to escape in the car. But the Death Walkers' cold ruined Aislin's crystal again so we had to come here to Adessa's to get another one. Then we transported to Colorado."

"So how did you guys not get attacked by the Death Walkers when you showed up in Colorado?" I asked. "And by Stephan? Because the last thing I can remember was that there were a ton of Death Walkers around, watching Stephan try to erase my mind."

Laylen glanced over at Alex, and they both exchanged a look I couldn't quite figure out. My muscles tensed up as

17

the idea that maybe Laylen was keeping secrets from me flashed through my mind. Would he? I mean, I barely knew him. But from the moment I'd met him, my instincts told me I could trust him. Although I sometimes wondered how much I could trust my own instincts.

"When Aislin and I showed up there—" Laylen's bright blue eyes focused back on me—"Stephan and the Death Walkers were gone."

"What?" I said, baffled. "Why would they just leave?"

Laylen looked at Alex again, and I grew even more uneasy. Something was up. I could feel it through the sudden heaviness in the air.

"I think maybe you should explain that part to her," Laylen told Alex. "It's more your story to tell, anyway."

"No," I protested, shaking my head. "I want you to tell me."

Laylen shifted uncomfortably in the sofa. "Look, Gemma, I understand why you want me to tell you. But I really think Alex should tell you the rest, because I wasn't even there for most of it."

This was so weird. I mean, the last time I'd talked to Laylen, back when we were at his house, he'd warned me to be careful when it came to trusting Alex. And now here he was telling me trust him.

It didn't make any sense.

"I...um..." I trailed off, staring confusedly at Laylen.

"Gemma, relax. It'll be alright." Laylen got to his feet, and gave me a pat on the shoulder, which puzzled me even more. No one's ever given me a pat on the shoulder before. "Everything will be okay. Alex will tell you what happened."

And with that, he left, the beaded curtains clinking together as he ducked through them.

I watched the curtains sway back and forth, feeling so lost. My mind was racing wildly with ideas of what could be going on; ideas ranging from Laylen being brainwashed to Laylen not being Laylen at all, but a body snatcher that had possessed his body.

"Gemma." Alex's voice pulled me out of my own head.

Slowly, I turned and looked at him. My emotions were all over the place, and the electricity was sparking like a firecracker. Part of me was saying *run*, that something was off and I needed to get away. But the other part of me held me to the sofa, wanting to hear what Alex had to say.

"So are you going to listen to what I have to say," he asked, his eyebrow arching upward, "or do you want to try and run again?"

"I don't know...." And yes, I understood how dumb my answer was, but it was the truth, so...

Alex sighed. "Why do you always have to be so difficult?"

"How do you expect me to be?" I asked, staring incredulously at him. "You were going to let your father erase my mind."

19

"No, I wasn't." He was losing his cool. "And if you'd just quit being stubborn and listen, you'd know what really went on."

I crossed my arms and flopped back in the chair, debating what I should do. Keep being "stubborn," as he'd so nicely put it? Or hear him out? "Fine, then tell me what happened."

Shock flickered across his face, just like it almost always did when I decided to cooperate. "Okay...Well, where do you want me to start?"

I shrugged. Did it really matter? It wasn't like he was going to tell me the truth or anything. "Wherever you want."

"Okay." He seemed to be struggling on where to begin. "Do you remember that necklace I gave you?"

I nodded as I touched my neck, and I quickly realized that the locket was no longer there. "Wait. Where is it?"

"Relax. I have it."

That didn't make me relax at all. "Why do you have it?"

"I'm getting to that." He took a deep breath and let it out slowly. "When I gave you the necklace, I wasn't just giving it to you because it belonged to you. I gave it to you because it has sugilite in it."

I gave him a questioning look. "What's sugilite?"

"It's the purple stone in the center of the locket. It protects whoever is wearing it from certain kinds of magic." He paused. "Like the mind erasing kind of magic."

"But I thought you said my mother gave me the necklace when I was little?"

"She did, specifically because the stone is sugilite." He leaned forward and rested his arms on his knees. "She gave it to you because you have the star's energy in you. It was her way of trying to protect you from anyone who tried to use magic on you to get to the star's power."

"So why didn't it work when I was little?" My voice was sharp and full of bitterness. "When Sophia detached my soul from my emotions, why didn't it protect me? Is that not a form of magic?"

Alex shook his head. "No, it's a form of magic. But Stephan...well, he knew what it was and took it off of you before Sophia detached your soul."

"Stephan knows what the necklace is?" This seemed to make the possibility of it actually protecting me and the star not possible.

He nodded. "That's why I tucked it into your shirt. So he wouldn't see it and make you take it off."

I remembered how, right before Alex had climbed out of the Jeep back at the cabin—back when Stephan had shown up with the Death Walkers—he had reached over and tucked the necklace into my shirt. *Whatever you do, keep that hidden. Don't let anyone know you have it,* he'd said.

"But why would you do that?" I questioned. "Why give it to me at all if you knew it would stop someone from being able to detach my soul? I thought you said that my soul had to be detached to keep the star's power thriving enough so that it could save the world."

He gave a look that made my skin go electric. "Because I wanted to stop anyone from being able to detach your soul."

I stifled a laugh. "I highly doubt that, especially since you've told me a ton of times that my soul has to be detached."

"Yeah...but I..." He drifted off.

"But you what?" I pressed.

"But." He took a breath. "When I first gave you the necklace, I was still deciding whether or not I was going to let my father see you wearing it. If he'd seen it, then he'd have made you take it off before he tried to use the *memoria extraho* on you."

As unsurprising as this was—I mean, how many times had Alex lied and betrayed me?—it still made my heart hurt a little. "If that's the case, then why did you give the necklace to me at all?"

He shrugged, his eyes wide with confusion. "I have no idea."

I shook my head, the electricity nipping at me like invisible gnats that I so wished I could swat away. "Well, that's nice."

"Look, Gemma," he said, his voice very let's-get-down-to-business. "I know I've done some pretty crappy things to you, but can't we just move past it? The point is, I did hide the necklace from my father. I protected you from getting your mind taken away."

"Why though?" I asked suspiciously. "I mean, you were so dead set that Stephan was good and that I was completely wrong about him sending my mom into The Underworld. You were so determined that I needed my emotions to be taken away so the star's power could save the world. So why the sudden change of heart?"

He was quiet for a moment, which sent up a red flag in my mind that he was about to tell me a lie.

"Stephan showing up with the Death Walkers," he finally said. "There has to be something else going on—something bad if he is working with them."

I eyed him warily. "If that's what you really believe, then why were you acting like you were on Stephan's side? You just stood there while he hurt me and tried to take everything about me away. You didn't do *anything*."

"I couldn't do anything. I had to pretend that I was on his side. Besides, I knew as soon as he tried to use the *memoria extraho* on you, he'd black out."

"He blacked out?" I said. "Why?"

"Because that's what the sugilite does," he explained. "Those who try to use harmful magic on someone who has sugilite on them, automatically get magical harm done on them instead. It's how sugilite works."

"What kind of harmful magic gets done on them?" I asked curiously, wondering if there was a possibility that

Stephan could perhaps be dead and that my problems would be over.

"That all depends on the kind of magic the person is trying to use. In my father's case, since he was trying to harm your mind, the sugilite harmed his mind instead, to the point that it made him pass out."

"So, what happened to him? Did you...kill him?"

He struggled to speak. "Gemma...I-I...I couldn't...I mean..." He took a deep breath, regaining his composure. "I couldn't kill my father...when I'm not really sure what's going on."

I tried to understand this—understand where he was coming from. Laylen had told me when it came to Alex and his father, Alex was sort of brainwashed. So I think I was more surprised about him letting the sugilite harm him, instead of not being able to kill him.

"So where is he?" I asked. "Stephan? Where did he end up?"

"The Death Walkers took him with them," he said with this strange look in his eyes, as if he was trying to figure something out.

They just took him and left. It sounded so...unbelievable, especially since the stupid things had been working so hard to get a hold of me.

"They just up and left? And left you and me behind, unharmed?" I asked skeptically.

He nodded. "Yeah, I know, it's weird."

Weird was putting it mildly. "So is Stephan going to return to normal, then?" I asked. "Or is his mind harmed for good?"

A glint of panic flashed in his eyes, and I had my answer before he said it. "No, he'll return to normal eventually."

"And then come after me again," I mumbled.

Alex didn't respond as he got to his feet and made his way over to me. He pulled something out of the pocket of his jeans before sitting down beside me. "Here." He held out his hand. A silver heart-shaped locket with a small violet stone in the center of it rested in his palm.

My locket.

I didn't take it right away. Instead I stared at it, wondering if what Alex had just told me held any truth to it or not. Could I trust him?

"You can have it back." He urged his hand at me.

I still didn't take the necklace. "I still don't understand why you took it off of me to begin with."

He gave me a skeptical look. "You don't know why?"

"How would I?"

He still looked like he had no idea how I didn't know the answer to my own question. But how the heck was I supposed to know? I never knew anything.

"Because Aislin had to use magic on us to get us out of there," he said.

"Oh." Now I was catching on. "And if I'd been wearing the necklace, then the sugilite would have blocked her magic."

He nodded. "So I took it off of you while we transported back here." He reached for my hand, but I pulled back, and he frowned. "I'm not going to hurt you. I'm just trying to give you your necklace back."

I quickly snatched up the necklace, the metal warm against my palm. "Thanks." I wrapped it around my neck and fumbled with the clamp. If what he was saying was true, then I wanted the necklace on at all times.

"Want my help?" A playful grin played at his lips.

I shot him a dirty look. "No. I got it." The last time he had "helped me," we ended up kissing. And that was the last thing I wanted right now...I think.

It took me awhile, but I finally got the clamp on the necklace hooked, the chain now secured around my neck. It was then that a sudden thought occurred to me. "Alex."

"Hmm...?" He had been watching me struggle to put the necklace on and seemed a little distracted.

"What happened to the *memoria extraho?*"

"Aislin and Adessa destroyed it," he told me. "After we got back, they used some kind of spell on it that took its magic out of it."

"So now it's just a rock?"

He nodded.

Well, I guess that meant there was one less thing I had to worry about. Although, how many

26

mind/memory/emotional erasing things were out there, I had no clue. But with everything I'd seen lately, I was guessing there might be more.

Alex suddenly shifted the subject. "Why don't we go get you something to eat? You've been out for almost two days. You've got to be starving."

"I've been out for two days?" I asked with astonishment.

He stood up. "Yeah, it was the longest nap ever."

I got to my feet. Even though I still had a ton of other questions, I was also very hungry. Besides, I wasn't sure I wanted him to be the one to answer all of my questions. Although, there was one thing I was dying to know—I had to know right now, even though thinking about it made me sick to my stomach.

"Okay, but I have one more question." I paused, taking a nervous deep breath. "With my emotions…I mean, am I…is it okay for me to have emotions?"

"I don't know. I really don't anything right now." He looked at me funny, and I had the urge to bolt for the door as the fear raced through me that he might suddenly whip out the *memoria extraho* and wipe away my mind. "For now," he said, "we're not going to do anything. Not until we know what's going on."

I was in no way, shape, or form relieved by what he said. "For now?" I asked.

He didn't say anything else. He just turned away, calling over his shoulder, "Let's go get you something to eat."

I glared a fiery glare at the back of his head, suddenly wishing I possessed pyrokinetic powers. I refused to go through this again. Get left out of the loop. Be given vague answers. I'd find out what I wanted to know, before it was too late. I'd get to the truth, whatever the cost.

Before going into the kitchen to get something to eat, I decided to go upstairs to change out of the pajamas I was wearing. Alex had told me, when I'd asked him if there was something else I could wear besides pajamas, that there were some clothes Aislin had picked out for me up in the room I'd woken up in.

As I dragged myself up the stairs, I thought about everything I'd just been told. It felt like I hadn't been told anything really. Like always, I had a huge list of unanswered questions roaming around in my head. And I was worried. Worried about whether or not Alex had told me anything truthful. Worried about why the Death Walkers had just up and left. Worried that Alex would suddenly decide I wasn't supposed to feel anymore and try to take my emotions away from me.

I reached the top of the staircase and let out a heavy sigh. Lost. Was lost considered an emotion? Because that's how I felt.

I was half out of it, consumed by my thoughts, as I opened the door to the room. But right as I went to pull the door open, it swung open on its own, and someone grabbed me by the arm and yanked me inside.

I opened my mouth to scream, but another hand came down over my mouth, and all I could do was think, *Great. Now what?*

Chapter 3

"Gemma," a voice whispered in my ear.

I frantically tried to wriggle my way free from whoever had a hold of me. My heart pounded inside my chest as thoughts of who it could be blasted through my mind. Stephan? A Death Walker? Some other kind of monster?

Whoever it was had ice-cold skin, so I was leaning toward a Death Walker or another kind of similar monster.

"Jesus Christ, Gemma. Calm down."

This time my brain registered who the voice belonged to and, feeling kind of stupid, I stopped my pathetic fight to get away. Laylen let go of me, and I let my breathing slow down to a normal pace.

"*What* are you doing?" I asked, breathing heavily. "You scared the heck out of me." *Again.*

"Shhh…" Laylen put his finger up to his deep red lips, glanced around the room, and then shut the door. "Keep your voice down."

"Why?" My voice came out way too loud so I lowered it. "Sorry. But why do I have to keep my voice down?"

He glanced around the room again, seeming nervous, and then locked the door. "So what do you think about what Alex told you?"

Hmm…so had I been wrong about Laylen trusting Alex? "I don't know. What do you think about it?"

He tilted his head from side to side, wavering. "I'm not sure. It just seems a little too…"

"Simple," I finished for him.

He nodded. "Exactly. Aislin and I show up there and Stephan and the Death Walkers are conveniently gone. It just doesn't make any sense."

"Yeah, that's what I thought too." I paused, considering what it could mean. But in my typical confused style, I felt as lost as ever. "So what do you think really happened?"

He shrugged. "I have no idea. But I know the chance of the Death Walkers just leaving when they know you have the star's energy in you, is slim to none. And I think it's really suspicious that Stephan just passed out like that."

"Well, Alex told me that Stephan passed out because of this." I lifted up my locket, the purple stone reflecting sharply in the light of the room. "That this little stone is sugilite and that because I was wearing it, and Stephan tried to use harmful magic on me, it made him black out."

Laylen took the locket in his hand, rubbing the purple stone with his thumb. The necklace was still attached to

31

my neck, so I had to crank my head forward, putting my neck in an awkward position.

"That's interesting," he murmured, and let the locket go, releasing my neck from its uncomfortable position. "It's sugilite, but still..." His expression twisted with confusion.

"What? Does sugilite not protect people from certain kinds of magic like Alex said?" I mean, really, the odds were pretty high that Alex had been lying.

"No, it does." He paused. "But I don't get it. Alex gives you this necklace that has sugilite, knowing if someone uses magic on you— to let's say, take your emotions or mind away—that it won't work. And that it'll end up doing harm to whoever is using the magic on you. Yet, supposedly, at least according to the Keepers, you're not supposed to have any emotions. So what would be the point of Alex protecting you from the thing he's been telling you has to be done?"

I frowned, not at Laylen, but at the mention of my emotions. "So Alex told you everything then?"

"Yeah, but it doesn't mean I believe every part of what he said."

"Me neither," I agreed. My leg was killing me, so I went over and sat down on the bed, and Laylen followed, sitting down next to me. "So what else did Alex tell you?"

He gave me a sort of amused look. "Well, he told me that you guys took a little trip to the City of Crystal, where you found out that you're a Foreseer."

I swallowed hard. "Did he tell about the vision I had to go into while I was at the City of Crystal?"

"He did," Laylen answered with hesitance.

I hated to be reminded of that vision, and just talking about it shoved the memory of it into my mind; Stephan forcing my mom to go into lake—the entrance to The Underworld—where she'd been tortured to insanity by Water Faeries.

"You okay?" Laylen asked.

"I'm fine." My voice sounded choked. There was a gap of silence before I asked, "Do you think there's a way she can still be alive? My mom, I mean."

Laylen sat there, looking at me, not in a feeling-sorry-for-me kind of way, but more as if he was seriously contemplating what I'd asked him. Part of me grew eager that he might say yes; that there was a possibility that my mother, who I hadn't seen since I was four years-old, and could barely remember a thing about—thanks to the detachment of my soul from my emotions, causing my memories to be erased away as well—might still be alive.

"I don't know, Gemma," he said softly. "She's been down there for a *really* long time."

My eagerness dropped to the floor and shattered like glass. "Oh. Okay."

"Now hold on one second before you go getting that sad look on your face. All I said was that she's been down there for awhile, not that there was no way she could be alive."

33

I tried to keep my excitement to a bare minimum. "So, are you saying that there might be a chance she still is?"

He twisted his lip ring from side to side. "Maybe. There've been some people that have survived the Water Faerie's torture for a long time without going too insane. And there have even been a few people that have escaped The Underworld before."

"There have!" I shouted, and then made an oh-crap face at the loudness of my voice. We both stayed silent for a moment, making sure no one had heard and had decided to head upstairs to check on me. The house was quiet, as still as the hot desert air, the only noise coming from the humming of engines from the cars passing by. "Sorry," I whispered. "But I'm just really confused. The way Alex made it sound, it seemed like there was hardly any way that anyone could ever escape The Underworld. That once they were sent down there, they were basically trapped there until they died from the torture."

Laylen's bright blue eyes twinkled mischievously. "Yeah, but Alex doesn't hang around with the same kind of crowd as I do, does he? You learn a lot of stuff when you're not just limited to the Keeper's circle."

Now I was letting myself get a little excited over what Laylen was saying. Well, except for the fact that he said "crowd." What kind of crowd were we talking about here? Vampire crowd? Witch crowd? Black Angel crowd? All were possibilities, and there were probably other possibilities that I didn't even know about.

34

"Is there any way we could find someone who will maybe help us find out if she's alive? And help us find out if there's a way we could get her out of The Underworld if she is?" I held my breath as I waited for him to answer.

It took him a second, but he nodded. "It won't be easy, though. And it'll be dangerous."

I should have been scared. But after you've faced a swarm of murderous Death Walkers, been hit by their Chill of Death, and stared into the eyes of a man who is trying to wipe your mind away, "dangerous" becomes a little easier to deal with. "So you're saying that maybe we could go and talk to someone about her?"

He mulled over my question for so long that I was sure he was going to say no. "Yeah, I think we might be able to do that."

"Really?" I was practically bouncing. "Are you serious?"

He nodded. "I think your mom may know more about what's going on than anyone does. I think that might be part of the reason why Stephan sent her there—so she couldn't tell anyone what she knew."

"I think so too," I agreed. "In fact, in the vision, she told Stephan that one day he'd get caught and that he didn't have everyone wrapped around his finger."

"Then I think the sooner we can find out if she's alive, the better. And maybe we can put all this madness together and get some real answers." He paused. "But I don't want you to get too excited, just in case things don't turn out the way...the way you want them to."

"I won't," I assured him, but I still couldn't help but get a little excited. Well, okay, I was beyond excited. In fact, I think I'd hit a whole new level of excitement and...yep, there it was. The prickle.

I know. I know. I was totally setting myself up for some serious heartache here. But I couldn't control myself at the moment. Just seeing my mother—it would be amazing. Especially after being raised by Marco and Sophia, who were two of the most cold-hearted people I knew. Well, besides Stephan.

Wait. Hold on. "Laylen, what happened to Marco and Sophia?"

"I have no idea," he said with a shrug. "No one does. They just up and disappeared."

Hmmm...very strange. So did that mean they were playing on the good side or the bad side?

I opened my mouth to ask Laylen this, but a knock at the door caused Laylen and I to jump to our feet.

"Gemma." Alex's voice floated through the door. "Are you in there?"

"Uh...yeah," I called out. "Just a second." I turned to Laylen and whispered, "Great. What am I supposed to tell him when he asks why you're in here?"

"You're not going to tell him," Laylen whispered searching for a place to hide. "If he knows I am in here, he'll know something's up. And if he knows what we're planning to do, he'll go out of his way to make sure it doesn't happen."

Excellent point. Alex would say it was too dangerous, at least for me anyway. Because that's what he always said. Besides, the question of whether or not Alex was lying about what had happened back at the cabin was still a big giant question mark. So for now, at least until we knew for sure what was going on, it was probably best to keep our plan a secret from Alex.

Laylen got down on the floor. "Just pretend I'm not here," he whispered. And with that, he slid underneath the bed.

I waited until he was completely under before unlocking the door and opening it. "Hey, what's up?" Real cool, Gemma. I sounded way too casual.

He gave me a suspicious look. "You've been up here forever. What are you doing?"

"Um...changing?" It sounded like a question, and I wanted to slap myself on the head for sucking so badly at playing it cool.

He looked down at the pajamas I was still wearing, and I realized my answer had been even more idiotic than I'd originally thought. I needed to think of something to tell him. And quick.

"Well...I was going to change, but I couldn't...um...figure out where the clothes are." Not my best lie, but hopefully it would do.

37

He looked unconvinced as he walked into the room and over to a dresser. He pulled open the top drawer and pointed inside it. "The clothes are in here."

Ignoring the heat the electricity caused by him being in the room, I made my way over to the dresser. "Oh. Okay. Thanks."

He gave me a strange look and then glanced around the room, as if he were looking for something that shouldn't be there. Like maybe a six foot four Keeper/Vampire hiding underneath the bed.

Finally, Alex gave up on looking for whatever it was he was looking for and stuffed his hands into the pockets. "Well, come downstairs when you're done. Adessa made dinner."

"Alright, I will," I told him, again sounding way too laid-back.

"Okay…" He raised his eyebrows at me, before heading to the door, shooting one last look over his shoulder before stepping out of the room.

I let out a breath of relief, shut the door, and spun around as Laylen army crawled from underneath the bed.

He stood up and dusted off his jeans "That was close."

"I know. It was like he knew you were here or something."

Laylen laughed, and I felt like I was missing out on a joke.

"What's so funny?" I asked.

He shook his head. "Nothing...so, yeah, I think we should sneak out tonight and talk to a few people I know. See if anyone has heard anything about your mom. You up for it?"

"I...uh...yeah?" Why did I suddenly feel hesitant? This was my mother we were talking about. But for some reason, it felt wrong—keeping what we were doing from Alex.

I shook my head at the absurdity of my own thoughts. I had to keep my head clear and not think about Alex. "Yeah, I'm definitely up for it."

He gave me a funny look. "Are you sure you want to go? I'm not going to tell you what to do—you've had that done to you way too much—but I feel I should warn you, it may end up being kind of dangerous."

I considered what he said, but still wanted to go. At this point in my life, I felt I needed to hear things for myself. "I'm still up for it."

"Then I'll come here tonight after everyone's asleep." He started for the door.

A thought popped inside my head. "Wait a sec."

He turned around. "What's up?"

"Why do you think Stephan wants the star's power?"

"I don't know. But if Stephan wants it, and he's working with the Death Walkers..." He trailed off, worry slipping onto his face. "Well, if our plan does work out, and we find out your mother's alive, maybe she'll have some of the answers to what the heck is going on."

***

After I'd changed into the most decent clothes I could find—a pair of shorts and a purple tank top—and pulled my long brown hair into a ponytail, I went downstairs. It took me a little bit to find the kitchen, which was a dimly lit room that had blue and black striped walls, black countertops, and indigo tiled flooring. Everyone was there by the time I entered. Alex and Aislin were sitting at a small oval table in the corner of the room, and Adessa and Laylen were over by the counter. Adessa was stirring something in a steaming pot on top of the stove.

Aislin's bright green eyes lit up when she saw me. She looked like her normal perfect self. Her golden blonde hair was curled up; a pair of diamond earrings twinkled in each one of her ear lobes. She had on a lacy pink tank top and her smile was as bright as ever. "Oh my God. It's so good to see you awake, instead of unconscious."

"I already told you she'd woken up." Alex rolled his eyes and shook his head. "I don't know why you're getting all excited about it."

"Because she's awake, Alex." Aislin gave him a firm look. "Need I remind you that for awhile we thought she wasn't ever going to wake up?"

If looks could kill, Aislin would have been dead by the invisible daggers shooting from Alex's bright green eyes. I don't know why he was getting mad at her, though. I'd already thought I was dead when I'd been trapped back in the black emptiness.

They continued to scowl at each other as I sat down in an empty chair at the table. They eventually stopped having their little stare down when Adessa came over and placed what looked like a pot of chicken noodle soup down on the table, her metal bangle bracelets clinking together as she moved her hands away. Like Aislin, Adessa is a witch, so I wasn't going to automatically assume what was in that pot was food. My knowledge about witches was limited, so whether or not they brewed pots of potions was beyond me. But in this new world I'd been thrust into only a few days ago, I was never going to assume things again.

Or at least try not to.

Adessa's golden cat eyes landed on me, and she gave me a welcoming smile. "Hello, Gemma."

I forced a small smile, just so I wouldn't seem rude. "Hey."

She smiled again, tucking a strand of her black wavy hair behind her ear, and then went back over to the stove.

Aislin grabbed the spoon in the pot, and began stirring it until Adessa took a seat at the table. Laylen did as well, carrying a stack of bowls in his hands. As I glanced around at the five of us, I couldn't help but think how strange this was. And I wasn't just saying strange because I was sitting at the table with two witches, a vampire, and a Keeper, but because I was sitting at a table, getting ready to eat. Something I'd never done before in my life.

"So, who's hungry?" Adessa asked, taking a bowl and scooping some—hopefully—chicken noodle soup into it. When no one answered, she set the bowl down in front of Alex, who slid it in front of me.

"Ladies first," he said with a charming smile.

How gentlemanly of him, which made it all the weirder.

"Thanks," I muttered. I stared down at the bowl of hot soup, watching the steam rise up as I thought of my mother and how, in just a few short hours, I might find out that she was still alive. After spending most of my life thinking she was dead, the idea seemed strange and unfamiliar.

"So, how are you feeling?" Aislin asked me.

I tore my gaze away from the soup, and my thoughts. "I'm fine."

Her forehead furrowed over. "Is something wrong?"

I shook my head. "No. Not really. I'm just a little confused still. That's all."

"About what?" she asked.

I shrugged. "Everything really."

She shot Alex a stern look. "Didn't you explain anything to her?"

"I explained to her that none of us know anything," he said, aggravated. "Not really, anyway."

Aislin's bright green eyes pierced into him as if she were trying to burn a telegraphic message into his mind.

Although I didn't mind Aislin—I mean, for the most part she'd been nice to me—I knew she was almost as good a liar as Alex, which put the count up to two people sitting at this table that I couldn't trust. And Adessa—well I knew nothing about her, and the whole trusting strangers thing had never gone that well for me. (Think City of Crystal, where an overly friendly half-faerie lives). The only person I felt I could rely on was Laylen.

I glanced over at Laylen, who was sitting there with no food in front of him, because…well, because he's a vampire and he doesn't eat food. Everyone else was slurping away, and I hoped they didn't notice when Laylen locked eyes with me. It was as if he was whispering a secret to me with his eyes. *Tonight.*

Yes. Tonight, I thought back. Tonight, maybe we'll get some answers.

Chapter 4

The rest of the conversation at the table consisted of a bunch of slurping. This was okay, though, because in just a short while, Laylen and I were going to be setting out on our endeavor to try and find out about my mom.

After I'd finished eating, I pretended to be tired and told everyone I was heading up to bed to go to sleep. And yeah, I got that saying I was tired sounded a little odd, since I'd just woken up from a two day nap. But I couldn't sit still, and I was afraid that all my bounciness was going to give away that something was up.

So for the sake of not getting Laylen and me busted before we even got the chance to try, I went up to my room to get some sleep. I never actually intended to fall asleep, but when I laid down on the bed, my eyelids suddenly felt heavy, and before I knew it, I'd dozed off.

It was dark. And I was cold. Water dripped on my head.

Painful screams filled the air. I shivered as I crept through the darkness, the air feeling damp against my skin.

"Gemma," a voice whispered.

I knew that voice. It was my mom's.

"Mom," I called out, turning in every direction, searching for her.

"Gemma." Her voice sounded so far away, and I started to run, my feet hitting the ground with a thud that echoed all around me. "Come find me."

"I'm trying," I said, searching through the dark for her.

Just then, a soft light filtered through the darkness, and I saw it. A figure, white and bony, floating in the air like a ghost. I screeched to a halt, a deathly feeling choking me so strongly it nearly sucked the wind out of me.

The white figure glided toward me. I spun around and ran in the opposite direction, my feet hammering against the ground

"Gemma!" my mother's voice screamed from somewhere behind me.

I kept running, contemplating what I should do. Turn around and face the ghostly figure—try to get to my mother. Or run like a coward.

I skidded to a stop and whirled back around, deciding I needed to try and save her. But I let out a scream at the sight of the hollowed out eyes that were only inches away from my face. The ghostly figure's bony hand reached for me, and I let out another scream, feeling more afraid than I'd ever felt in my life.

"Gemma, run," I heard my mother say. But I couldn't—I was too terrified to move.

This strange feeling passed over me as the ghostly figure's fingers moved to my mouth. I felt something being sucked away from inside me...and then I just felt empty.

***

45

I gasped for air as my eyes shot open, my heart hitting the inside of my chest about a million miles a minute, the fear I'd felt in my dream still rattling at my nerves.

It took my eyes a second to adjust to the blackness that had filled the bedroom, and for my heart to settle back down. God, I hated when I had nightmares like that. I could never be certain if they were *actually* nightmares. What if what I'd just seen was a vision? That couldn't be good. The strange ghostly figure had sent so much fear through me that I shivered, hoping that it was just a nightmare.

I climbed off the bed and flipped on the light. The brightness stung my eyes and I had to blink them into focus. I wondered what time it was and what time Laylen would show up. I didn't have a watch and couldn't see a clock anywhere in the room, but it had to be late since the sky was black, except for the silver specks of stars and the faint rainbow glow that Vegas' lights cast across it.

Perhaps I should go get Laylen. Of course, I had no idea where he was, and I worried that, if I went looking for him, I might run into the wrong person and end up having to explain why I was wandering around the house late at night.

So I decided to wait it out. Laylen said he'd be here, so he would.

I went over to the oval mirror hanging on the wall above the dresser. For it being so late, I sure looked awake, my violet eyes staring back at me all big and wide. Sliding

46

my ponytail to the side, I turned to look at the back of my neck where my Foreseer's mark was tattooed. It was the first time I'd seen it, and honestly, it was kind of strange to look at. I'd never even considered getting a real tattoo before, and now I suddenly had one, under no choice of my own. But I guess that just came with the territory of being part of a world where people's supernatural gifts mark them. It was almost like being branded.

I traced the black circle that curved around the S with my finger, my skin tingling beneath my touch. "So weird," I muttered.

A soft click came from behind me and I spun around as the bedroom door creaked open. I almost bolted for the window, but then I saw it was Laylen and I relaxed.

"Good. You're awake," Laylen said in a hushed voice and shut the door. He was dressed in a black long-sleeved thermal shirt, black jeans, and black boots, which made me wonder if we were going to the Black Dungeon, since almost everyone there dressed entirely in black. "You've been up here for so long I thought for sure you'd be asleep."

I had been, but I didn't tell him that. "If I'd stayed down there—" *around Alex*—"then they would've figured out something was up. I thought it'd be best if I came up here, where no one could see how bouncy I was."

"Well, I guess I don't have to ask you if you're ready to go then," he said with a smile.

47

"Yeah, I'm more than ready," I said, feeling both excited and nervous. Excited because what if I was told my mother was alive? And nervous because...Well, I had a feeling that even if we were not going to the Black Dungeon, we were probably going to a place that was a lot like it.

"Okay..." He hesitated, making me wonder if he'd changed his mind about going. "Here's the tricky part," he told me. "We're not going to be able to just walk out the front door of the house. Adessa sets up these magical charms at night so if someone tries to come in or go out, she'll know. It's her version of a security system."

"Okay, so how are we supposed to get out of the house?" I asked, and his gaze flickered in the direction of the window. My eyes widened. "You want us to *climb* out the *window*."

"It's the only way. All the downstairs windows have charms on them, and although I'm not sure exactly what Adessa's charms do if they get set off, I'd really rather not find out."

I glanced with uncertainty at the window. "But how are we even supposed to climb out.? Do you have some kind of special climbing-down-the-wall super-power or something?" Really, I wouldn't have been that surprised if he did.

He shook his head, seeming amused. "I'm a vampire, Gemma, not Spiderman." He paused. "No, you're going to get on my back, and I'm going to jump out."

48

I stared at him, waiting for him to deliver the punch-line of the joke, because he had to be joking. But the look on his face was dead serious.

"How's that even going to work without us getting hurt?" I asked, dumbfounded.

"We won't get hurt," he assured me. "That far of a fall won't hurt me at all. It's a vampire thing."

"Yeah, but I'm not a vampire," I made a point to say, even though it was obvious. "The fall *will* hurt me."

"That's why you'll be on my back, so I can break the fall for you."

I glanced back and forth between the window and him. Did I dare?

"And I promise I'll do my best not to drop you," he said, and then gave me a smile.

I rolled my eyes at him. "Alright...I'm in."

He went over to the window, clicked the latch open, and inched the window up, the hinges creaking and whining the entire time. After he had opened the window all the way, Laylen stuck his head out and looked down at the ground. Personally, I didn't want to look. I mean, it wasn't like I was afraid of heights or anything, but since I was about to jump out of a two story building, on the back of a vampire/Keeper, I thought it'd be better not to look.

Laylen ducked his head back in and turned his back to me. "Hop on."

I had never hopped on to someone's back before, but there was always a first time for everything, I guess. So, for

49

the first time that I could ever remember, I hopped up piggy-back style onto someone's back.

"You good?" Laylen asked as I moved around, trying to get comfortable.

I tightened my arms and legs around him, maybe a little too tightly. But he didn't complain. He grabbed onto my legs and stuck his head out the window. Then, with the balance of a tight-rope walker, he stood up on the window sill, giving me a full view of the glittery, rock hard asphalt down below. The warm air hit my skin as I tucked my head into his back, not wanting to look.

"It's really not that far," he told me.

I didn't say anything because I was too afraid to speak.

"It'll be over in a second," he assured me.

I shut my eyes, and then he jumped.

Chapter 5

I don't know if any of you remember, but the few times I've traveled through a crystal ball, it required a very long fall down a dark tunnel. And every time I landed, I ended up hurting myself. Jumping out the window was nothing like that. It was over by the time I actually acknowledged we were falling. Laylen landed with the gracefulness of a cat, his feet hitting the asphalt with a soft thud, and I barely felt the impact.

For a moment, neither of us moved. Even the air seemed to pause, as if we'd fallen so fast we were waiting for the rest of the world to catch up.

"You alive back there?" Laylen asked over his shoulder.

I slowly opened my eyes and looked back up at the window we'd just jumped out of. "I think so."

He let go of my legs, and I slid off of his back. The fall must have thrown off my equilibrium or something, because I felt off balance and dizzy. I started to tip sideways and Laylen caught me by the shoulder.

"What? Have you never jumped out of a window before?" he joked.

I shook my head, and we started off across the dark parking lot.

"So, where exactly are we going?" I asked

"To a place that's just up the road a little ways," he replied.

"So we're walking there then?" I asked, glancing up at the flickering lamppost as I walked by it.

He nodded. "It's not very far. Plus, my car got damaged during Aislin's and my little escape from the Death Walkers, so driving really isn't an option."

I looked around at the ominous-looking, graffiti-decorated buildings, the shadowed cars dotting the parking lot, and the giant garbage cans towering not too far away from us. All were perfect places for someone—or something to hide. And, okay, I know I made the choice to come out here, but now that I actually was, warnings were popping up all over in my head. And now that I thought about it, no one had ever said how high of a chance it was that Stephan and/or the Death Walkers would show up.

"Are we safe?" I asked Laylen as we reached the sidewalk that bordered the dark street.

"Hmm...Define safe," he said, fiddling with his lip ring.

I gaped at him. "What? So we're not safe?"

"Gemma, I already warned you it might be dangerous," he reminded me.

I shielded my eyes with my hand as a car driving by blinded me with its headlights. "Yeah, I know, but.... What are the odds of us running into a Death Walker?"

Out here?" he asked, and I nodded. "Probably lower than when we went into the Black Dungeon." He tucked his hands into his pockets and moved to the side as a homeless man, pushing a cart, passed by us.

"Well, what about the place we're going to?" I asked. "What are the odds of us running into one there?"

"Pretty low," he said.

"Well, what kind of place are we going to exactly?"

He raised an eyebrow at me. "The truth?"

I gave him a 'duh' look, but wasn't sure if he could see it through the darkness. "Always," I answered.

"A place where vampires hang out," he replied.

Maybe I should have asked this question beforehand, because going into a place where vampires hung out seemed kind of sketchy. "But isn't there going to be a problem with me going in there since I'm human?" Even Laylen himself had told me that other vampires—non-Keeper Vampires—were not really good. And then there was the whole humans-letting-vampires-bite-them thing that I'd seen going on back when we'd been at the Black Dungeon.

He shook his head and answered, "There'll be other humans there. It'll be like at the Black Dungeon, when you saw that man getting bitten."

53

I tried not to freak out. "So, there'll be a bunch of humans standing around, getting bitten by vampires because they want to..." *stimulate their desires.* Well, that idea was comforting. How was I supposed to walk into a room like that, when I couldn't even talk about it aloud?

"You'll be fine. Just make sure you stay by me at all times," he said, sounding just like Alex.

"Well, what are we going to do when we get to this place?" I asked, inching closer to Laylen as the door to a bar swung open and a group of men stumbled outside, talking rowdily.

"We're going to go see if we can talk to Vladislav," he told me. And when I gave him a confused look he explained further, "He's a vampire. A very important vampire."

Even though the air was hot, I shivered. An important vampire. What did that mean? Well, I got that it meant he was important—*duh*—but what did it require to be considered important in the vampire world?

I hated to even think about it.

We veered off to the right, away from the road. The already dark atmosphere shifted even darker. There were no lampposts and no lights on in any of the broken down buildings.

"Laylen, are you sure this is the right way?" I asked in a quiet voice. "There's nothing here."

"Yeah, I'm sure." He swung his arm around my shoulder, all buddy-buddy, which was the strangest thing ever. "Trust me."

And trust him I did, letting him lead me deeper into the shadows of the night, making me grow so edgy that I just about turned around and ran back. Of course, since it was almost pitch black and I could hardly see a thing, I'd have probably just ended up getting lost if did.

"Alright," Laylen muttered to himself as we came to a stop in front of a garage door belonging to an old metal warehouse.

"So this is the place?" I asked uneasily.

He nodded. "This is the place."

I glanced at the closed metal garage door. "So how do we get inside?"

"Like this." He turned around, guiding me with him, and he looked up at a camera perched on the wall above us. "Smile for the camera."

Okay, I highly doubted that whoever was watching the surveillance screen could actually see us — it was way too dark. Then again...I squinted up at Laylen. Did vampires have night vision or something?

I opened my mouth to ask him if he did, but I was cut off by the roar of the garage door lifting to life as it moved up from the ground. I was surprised to find that, on the other side of it, there was nothing. And I mean *nothing*, other than a concrete floor and a stairway leading up to a second floor, which also appeared to be bare.

"Umm...Where is everyone?" I asked.

Not answering, Laylen pulled me along with him as he stepped inside the warehouse. I was abruptly smacked in the face by an invisible wall of cold air. It was as if we'd walked into a freezer, and right away, I started to shiver, my low tolerance for the cold kicking into full force. Plus, I was wearing shorts and a tank top, so that didn't help.

"Are you cold?" Laylen asked. Then he shook his head. "Stupid question. Of course, you're cold. It's barely forty degrees in here."

"Why is-s it so c-cold?" I chattered.

"It's a vampire thing," he explained as he started to slip off the long-sleeved black thermal shirt he was wearing.

"What are you doing?" I asked, taken aback. Why was he taking off his clothes?

He wasn't, though. He had a black t-shirt on underneath it, and he handed the one he'd taken off to me. "Put this on. It might help a little."

I slipped his shirt on, smelling a hint of cologne lingering in the fabric. Putting it on did help a little, but the bottom of my legs were still exposed, and goose bumps spotted my skin. "So now what do we do?" I asked.

He nodded to the stairs. "We go upstairs."

He took me by the hand, and we made our way up the metal stairway, which shook with every step we took. The air grew colder the higher we got, which didn't make any sense. Wasn't warm air supposed to rise?

At the top of the stairs, there was a door; a red door—the color of blood—which seemed like an omen or something. I wrapped my arms around myself, trying to stay warm as Laylen opened the blood-red door. Instantly, the smells of smoke, rust, and sweat swirled all around me.

"Stay close to me," Laylen whispered, and we stepped through the doorway and out onto a balcony.

I had no problem with staying close to him—I was already clinging to him like a scared little child.

Below the balcony, a room opened up packed with tables, chairs, and lots and lots of people. Black Angel's "Young Men Dead" was blasting through the speakers. The lights were low, and the air was heavy with smoke.

We started to make our way down the stairs, the metal railing pressing cold against my skin as I held on to it. Looking down at the room, I didn't seem to notice anything out of the ordinary, like I'd expected to. People were just sitting at tables, drinking, talking, and smoking. But as we got closer, I realized that most of the crystal glasses were filled with a deep red liquid, which I assumed was blood.

I tried hard not to stare at anyone as we walked across the room—I swear I did. But as we passed by the tables, it felt like everyone's eyes locked on me. That's when I noticed some of these "people" had fangs pointing sharply from their mouths.

Laylen wrapped his arm around me and pulled me closer to him, which brought me some comfort, but not much. We went up to the bar that was in the heart of the room, and Laylen tapped his hand on the glass countertop. "What's up, stranger?" he said to a woman, who was wiping down the countertops.

The woman looked at us and her brown eyes lit up. "Well, hello, stranger, to you too." She had a slight southern accent, and her dark hair ran down her back in dreads. She was dressed like a biker chick; in steeled toed boots, leather pants, and a rhinestone-decorated tank top. A vine tattoo cuffed each of her wrists.

She leaned over the counter and gave Laylen a small kiss on the cheek. "It's been awhile. What ya been up to?"

"Nothing much really. Just the usual trouble," he said, teasing her with a smile. The woman glanced at me, and then Laylen looked at me. "Oh, Gemma, this is Taven."

"Hi," I said, trying not to sound as anxious as I felt.

She stared at me with an intrigued look. "Nice to meet ya, sweetie." She raised her eyebrows at Laylen. "Finally picked yourself up a human, huh?"

I felt Laylen tense up beside me. "Yeah, something like that."

Taven smiled, giving me a glimpse of her fangs. I tried not to flinch.

"So, I need to see Vladislav," Laylen told Taven. "Is there any way you could buzz me in?"

She gave him a curious look. "Depends on what ya need him for."

Laylen let his arm fall off my back, and rested both of his arms on the counter as he leaned in toward Taven, keeping his voice low. "I need to speak to him about The Underworld."

Taven's expression fell. "You're not in any trouble, are ya?

He shook his head. "No. It's nothing like that. I just have a question to ask him."

"Okay." She relaxed. "Hold on just a second and I'll check to make sure y'all can go in."

Laylen moved his arms away from the counter while Taven picked up a phone. She muttered a few words into the receiver and then hung up.

"Alright," she said, turning back to Laylen and me. "Go on ahead and go in."

"Thanks," Laylen said with a nod.

As we turned to walk away, I noticed Taven give a very distinct look at my eyes, and I tensed up. Back in Colorado, when Alex and I had gone into town, he'd been worried that my eye color would give me away. He'd also mentioned that word might have spread about me carrying the star's energy, and that my violet eyes would make it easy for someone to identify me. What if word had gotten around? What if these vampires we were going to meet knew what I was?

Crap.

I glanced around anxiously, wondering if I should say something to Laylen. If I did, though, I might get overheard. I mean, for all I knew vampires could have super hearing powers.

"What's up?" Laylen whispered in my ear as we ducked underneath the stairwell. "You seem nervous. Is it just this place? Or is it something else?"

I swallowed hard. "No, I'm fine," I lied, figuring it wasn't worth the risk of bringing it up on the chance I might get overheard. "Can we just hurry? It's getting really cold."

He nodded. "But try to relax, okay? They'll pick up that you're nervous."

Great. "Okay."

We started down a long, narrow hallway with walls the same blood-red color as the door. Halfway down the hall, we passed by two very big men dressed in black suits that looked like bodyguards, neither of which acknowledged our presence. We kept walking, the music from the bar fading and fading the further down we went.

When we reached the end of the hall, there was a door made of metal so shiny I could see my reflection in it.

"Okay, try to stay as calm as possible, no matter what happens," Laylen told me, before knocking on the door.

Try to stay calm no matter what? What exactly was I about to walk into? Something bad, I could feel it in my bones. But I guess all I could hope for now was that, in the end, I would find out my mom was alive. And that there was a way to free her.

60

Laylen waited a moment before knocking on the door again. I heard several clicking latches being unturned, and then the door cracked open.

"What do you want?" someone snarled through the crack.

"I'm here to talk to Vladislav," Laylen said, and the door shut.

I shot Laylen a puzzled look and he put his finger to his lips, signaling at me to keep quiet. A second later the door opened, and smoke rushed out so quickly I had to choke back a cough. A man stood on the other side of the door, his hair all greasy, and his skin as pale as snow.

His fangs pointed out like knives. "Please, come in."

I almost shut my eyes as we entered the room in a pathetic attempt to try and hide their violet color. But then my brain turned on, and I realized how stupid and suspicious I'd look walking around with my eyes closed.

A long rectangular table stretched down the center of the room, which was surrounded by leather chairs, each one of the chairs holding a man that had fangs sticking out of their mouths. They were playing a game of poker and smoking cigars. Standing behind some of the men were women, bound up in old fashion corset dresses. The women looked fangless, and I wondered if they could be human.

My heart thumped so loudly in my chest that I swear everyone could probably hear it. The only thing I really

61

had going for me was that it wasn't as cold in here, but the stench of cigar smoke was killing me.

Laylen approached the table with confidence, dragging a very unconfident me along with him. Right as we reached the table, though, a fight broke out between two men. Both of them jumped to their feet, baring their fangs at one another.

"You're cheating," a bald man with a stubby body growled. "I know you are."

"You better not be accusing me of anything." The other man bit back and a lizard-like tongue slipped out of his mouth.

My jaw dropped to the floor, and I started to turn for the door, but Laylen caught me by the arm and shook his head, warning me to stay calm.

"Easy, boys." A man sitting at the head of the table rose to his feet. He had dark hair, black eyes, and pale skin. The room went silent and the men who'd been arguing slid back down in their chairs. "We have guests," he said and looked at Laylen and me.

Then everyone was staring at us, and I suddenly wished I could shrink myself away.

The dark-haired man ambled over toward Laylen and me, his hands tucked into the pockets of his black pants. The sleeves of his black button-down shirt were pushed up just enough for me to see the mark of immortality sketching his forearm. "So, Laylen," he said, stopping in front of us. "What brings you here on this fine night?" His black eyes flicked over at me, assessing me. "And with such lovely company."

Unsure of what to do, I kept my expression blank, hoping that Intimidating Vampire Man wouldn't be able to pick up that I was scared out my wits.

He gave me an inquisitive look, before moving his attention back to Laylen. "I've never seen you with a human before. What's the occasion?"

"I just decided it was time," Laylen replied coolly.

"Is it?" the vampire said thoughtfully. He gave me another intrigued look and said, "Allow me to introduce myself. My name is Vladislav." He stuck out his hand, and even though I really, really didn't want to, I took hold of his hand to shake it. But instead, he wrapped his ice-cold fingers around my hand and moved it up to his lips, placing a kiss just below my knuckles. Then, to make things even freakier, he took a slow deep inhale, breathing in my scent before letting my hand go.

Despite the grossness of the fact that he'd just smelled me, I managed to force a smile.

"So, I need a favor," Laylen said to Vladislav.

"A favor?" Vladislav said, his black eyes still fastened on me. "And what would that favor be?"

Laylen looked around at the group of vampires sitting around the table. They were no longer playing poker, but watching us. "A...would it be okay if we spoke in private?"

63

Vladislav considered this and then, without taking his eyes off of me, he called over his shoulder, "Boys. Could you excuse us for a moment? It seems we must discuss something privately."

Without arguing, the vampire men got up, leaving their cards behind on the table, and they headed past us and out the door, ushering the women with them. A few of their gazes landed on me as they walked by, and the severity of the situation I was in hit me like a punch to the stomach, nearly knocking me to the floor. I should have never come here. Laylen had let me choose whether I wanted to come or not, because he thought I should be able to make my own decisions. And he was right—I should be able to. But maybe I should start making better ones, because I had this gut wrenching feeling that something bad was about to occur.

After everyone had left the room, taking some of the smoke with them, Vladislav gestured at Laylen and me to take a seat at the table. So we did, and then he sat down in a chair across from us.

"So, Laylen, what could possibly be so important that you would need to discuss it with me in private?" Vladislav asked.

"I need to know if there's any way to find out if someone's still alive in The Underworld," Laylen said, getting straight to the point. "And whether there's a way to get them out of there if they are."

Vladislav raised his dark eyebrows at us, asking, "And may I ask who this person is that you want to know about?"

"Her name is Jocelyn Lucas," Laylen told him.

The mention of my mother's name seemed to be making my oxygen supply shrink.

"Jocelyn Lucas," Vladislav pondered. "It wouldn't be the Keeper Jocelyn Lucas, would it?"

Laylen nodded. "That would be her," he replied.

"Hmmm...I have heard of her." A wicked look flashed across Vladislav's face, and I had the feeling that getting the information from him was going to end up being quite a challenge.

"So do you know if she's still alive?" Laylen causally asked.

Vladislav's eyes darkened. "I do know if she's alive or not. However..." He trailed off, looking right at me as he licked his lips. "This woman, Jocelyn, I'm guessing is very important to you?"

Vladislav was still looking at me, but Laylen answered him. "Yeah, she is."

Then, very abruptly, I could feel it in the air. A condition—something that was going to have to be done in order to find out about my mom.

Vladislav's dark eyes were smoldering black, and his voice purred. "So, tell me, what would you be willing to give up to find out if she is alive or not?"

Don't freak out, Gemma. Don't freak out. Which wouldn't have been as difficult if Vladislav would just stop staring at me as if he was...well, like he was hungry.

"I don't know," Laylen answered, biting at his lip ring as he thought about what Vladislav had asked. Then he flashed me a quick what-do-you-think look. All I did was shrug, because I had no idea what to do. I wanted to know, but I was worried what the cost would end up being. And what if Vladislav was lying and we ended up giving him something and getting nothing in return?

"What exactly do you want?" Laylen asked evenly, and I was so glad he was our spokesperson, because I'm about ninety-nine percent sure my voice would have shaken as bad as my hands were right now.

Vladislav reached toward the middle of the table, toward an old cigar box. He lifted the lid off of the box and removed a cigar. "I want one thing in exchange for telling you what you want to know." He dragged the cigar along the bottom of his nose, breathing in the scent.

"And what is it?" Laylen asked.

Vladislav struck a match on the table and lit the cigar. He took a puff, blew out the smoke, and then smiled, his fangs glinting dangerously in the light. "If only things were that easy. They never are, though. Are they?"

Laylen twisted at his lip ring, and I held my breath as I waited for him to respond to Vladislav. "Alright, tell us what you know and we'll give you what you want."

My heart faltered and my legs began to tremble. Why did it feel like Laylen was making a deal with the devil?

Vladislav took another puff off his cigar, before resting it in an ashtray, the smoke still rising off the end of it. "I've heard of a Jocelyn Lucas, the one and only Keeper who has ever been sent to The Underworld, and the longest person to survive down there. She has quite the reputation."

Whoa. My blood howled in my ears. She was alive. My mother was alive. The prickle showed up, releasing an abundance of eagerness so great it made me go all lightheaded.

"However," Vladislav said, and I swear my heart stopped. "To get her out of The Underworld would be nearly impossible. Not just because getting anyone out of there is nearly impossible—especially without them drowning—but also because I've heard that her long survival rate comes from the fact that she is a slave for the Queen, which makes her very valuable."

Slave for the Queen of The Underworld. That sounded awful. My breathing had suddenly become erratic and it caught Vladislav's attention.

"Tell me, girl." He licked his lips. "What's your name?"

I swallowed hard. "Gemma."

He eyed me over, staring at my eyes for longer than necessary, which made me even more nervous. "And how do *you* know Jocelyn?"

My instincts told me to deny, deny, deny. "I don't know her," I lied.

He looked unconvinced. "You don't, do you?" He stood to his feet, putting his arms behind his back. "You know, Gemma," he said, pacing in front of us as if he was some kind of grand lecturer, "I do not like it when people lie to me."

I opened my mouth to say that I wasn't lying, but Laylen shot me a look that told me to keep my mouth shut.

"I find it hard to believe that Laylen would show up here with a human, for the very first time," Vladislav continued, "and you not play a part in why he's asking about a Keeper who's been trapped in The Underworld for more than a decade."

Laylen started to speak, but Vladislav held up his hand. "Silence. Do not interrupt me." He stopped pacing and faced us, his dark gaze shooting a chill up my spine. "Now, I'll ask you one last time." He leaned toward us, pressing his hands onto the table. "How do you know Jocelyn?"

I was scared to death, but for some reason my brain was screaming at me to keep quiet; that if I said that Jocelyn was my mother, that perhaps it could be traced to me being the one with the star's energy in me.

I kept my voice as even as I could. "I really don't know her, I swear."

Vladislav fixed me with a baleful look and said, "Well then. If you're saying you're telling the truth, then you must be."

I started to relax a little, but then as suddenly as a lightning bolt flashes, Vladislav was charging at me. Before I could even finish my blink, he'd flipped over the table, grabbed a hold of me, and pinned me against him.

Laylen jumped to his feet, starting to run toward us. Vladislav backed away from him, towing me along with him.

"Come any closer," Vladislav hissed, exposing his fangs, the tips brushing against the skin of my neck, "and I'll drain every ounce of blood she has in her."

Laylen froze, and I pretty much stopped breathing.

"Wise choice," Vladislav said, his ice-cold hands gripping me so tightly I was sure I was going to have bruises from it....if I made it out of here alive, that is. "I think it's time I collect on what I want from you."

"But you haven't even told us how to get her out of The Underworld," I cried.

Laylen's bright blue eyes went so wide they practically bulged out of his head, and I realized I should not have opened my mouth.

"Yes, that is true." He pressed me tighter into him — too tight — and I winced from the pressure. Moving his mouth to my ear, he purred, "However, if you didn't know her, then why would it matter whether I told you anything?"

Great. Me and my stupid mouth. I was starting to understand why Alex always seemed to be telling me to keep my mouth shut.

Vladislav let out a deep growl, and then his fangs sunk into my neck. They sunk in deeper and deeper, and I gasped as I was blinded by images flickering through my mind like a flashing picture show. Vampires. Teeth. Stars. Alex. I felt faint. Lightheaded. Dizzy and weak, yet at the same time relaxed. The prickle was poking my neck wildly. My vision went blurry. And then, all of a sudden, I felt content with Vladislav biting my neck.

It was okay....

Okay...

There was a sharp snap, followed by a loud thud, and my neck was released from Vladislav's fangs and his grip. I blinked down at Vladislav, lying lifelessly on the red-carpeted floor, a broken chair leg sticking out of his chest.

"What happened?" My voice floated out of me as I turned to Laylen.

"We have to go." He took a hold of my hand and the world swayed as he pulled me toward the door.

My fuzzy brain only allowed me to pick up on a few words Laylen was saying to me: careful, normal, don't panic. He wiped my neck where Vladislav had bit me with the bottom of his t-shirt, before creaking the door open. He peered up and down the hall, and then we stepped out.

Someone was calling me.

The lights were bright. The music loud.

I saw red.
And then I fell.

Chapter 6

It was so cold. As cold as death. Was I dead?

My eyes fluttered opened. I was lying down on a floor, the wood flooring cold against my cheek. I slowly sat up and gazed at my surroundings. Where was I? A cabin. Not the cabin in Colorado. No, this was a different cabin; a much smaller one, with no furniture, no fireplace, nothing.

I got to my feet and made my way over to the window and tried not to flip out when I noticed it had bars on it. *Trapped.*

"What in the world?" I muttered to myself.

A bang came from behind me and I whirled around, coming face to face with myself. Not the younger version of myself, but the actual eighteen-year-old Gemma.

So I was in a future vision, at least I think I was. This brought no sense of comfort to me, especially since I had no idea where this place was, and also because...well, because in the vision my violet eyes looked drained of all emotion.

I watched myself lie down on the floor and curl up into a tiny ball. Then, I just lay there, silent and unblinking. *Numb.*

What was going on? Had my emotions been erased? Was this actually where I was going to end up?

A surge of fear pulsated through me, and I took off running for one of the two doors the small room had and threw it open. It was a bathroom. I turned around, ran for the other door, and with a lot of effort shoved it open.

My heart stopped.

Miles and miles of snow-covered mountains, trees poking out of them like little tepees. And the log cabin I stood in was smack dab in the middle of it all, secluded from all civilization, for as far as I could see.

I turned around and looked at myself curled up on the hardwood floor. How had I ended up like this? And what was wrong with me? I had an idea, but before I could look around and try to figure out more, an icy gust of wind swept up, and I was blown back, falling into the darkness.

When I opened my eyes, it took my brain a second to process that I was lying on warm asphalt, with a very dim lamppost shining down on me. And that Laylen was kneeling next to me.

"Are you okay?" he asked worriedly.

I gradually sat up, my neck burning with my every movement. "Ahh" I winced, reaching for my neck—then winced again from the pain my touch brought on.

"Easy," Laylen said, his voice soothing. "It's going to hurt for a little bit."

"What's going to hurt?" I asked, and then I remembered I'd been bitten by a vampire. I began to panic.

Laylen must have seen the panic in my eyes, because he said, "You'll be okay, Gemma. The fogginess will wear off in awhile. The actual bite, though, will take a few days to heal."

I started to get to my feet, but the world started spinning. I almost collapsed back to the ground, but Laylen caught me by the arm.

"You're going to have to take it easy," he told me, holding me steady. "You've lost a lot of blood."

Well, that explained the wooziness. "I think I might be sick."

"That'll wear off in a little while too."

I lightly touched my neck, the skin burning beneath my fingers. "How did we get out of that place?" I asked because my memory was missing some pieces of what just occurred. In fact, the only thing I could remember clearly was the vision I'd just gone into, and how my eyes in the vision had looked so empty. I wondered if it meant it would actually happen to me—if I would end up at the cabin that way. The thought was scary.

"Well, by the time we made it out into the bar area, you'd fainted," Laylen said. "Luckily I caught you before you hit the floor."

Yeah, I guess that could be considered lucky. But everything else…hmm, not so much.

74

"So you, what?" I asked. "Just carried me out and ran? How did we not get caught?"

"We were lucky we didn't." He started to walk, guiding me along with him. "But I think we need to get back to the house before someone realizes I killed Vladislav."

Good idea.

We headed across an empty parking lot, making sure to stay in the shadows.

"How much trouble are you going to be in for staking Vladislav?" I asked, gripping onto Laylen's arms as I was rushed by a spout of dizziness.

He shrugged, but I felt him speed up. "We need to get back to the house and out of sight for awhile. Eventually it'll be forgotten, but I probably won't be able to show my face in the vampire world again."

"Is that a good thing or a bad thing?" I asked him, carefully maneuvering over a pot hole.

He shrugged. "I don't know. It wasn't like I completely enjoyed being around other vampires. But they were the only ones who didn't judge me for being a vampire."

His voice was sad and it made my heart hurt for him. "So what do you do then?" I asked "Just wait it out until the vampires do what? Decide they're over it?"

We turned down an alleyway, tucking ourselves into the dark and out of sight.

"I'm going to have to lie low for awhile," he said, dodging us around a stack of wooden crates.

Lay low for a while. Wasn't that what we'd already been doing, to keep me away from Stephan and the Death Walkers? But now I guess vampires were going to have to be added to the "Who We Were Hiding From Now" list. Jeez, if it kept up every evil creature was going to be after us.

"So what about my mom?" I said to Laylen as we squeezed past a dumpster, the air smelling like rotten eggs mixed with old bananas. "Do you think Vladislav was telling the truth and that she's still alive?"

"Yeah, I do," he said, sounding absolutely certain.

We reached a tall chain link fence with no way around it. At least that was what I thought. But then Laylen reached down and pulled on the bottom of it until the metal links snapped and he was able to lift up the fence high enough for me to scoot underneath it. Then he ducked under himself and let the fence go with a clank.

"Vampires have this connection with each other that allows us to sense if the other one's lying," he told me as we stepped out onto a sidewalk and back underneath the lights of the lampposts. "I knew from the beginning that Vladislav was going to tell us the truth."

"You can tell if each other are lying?" Wow. It was like he had his own little lie detector built into him. Too bad it didn't work on beautiful, bright green-eyed Keepers. "Although Vladislav never did get around to saying how we can get my mom out of The Underworld."

76

"I have a hunch, though," he said as Adessa's red brick building came into view, "that there just might be someone else that we can talk to about getting her out of there. And maybe now that we know Jocelyn is alive, he might be more on board with rescuing her."

I tilted my head to the side, confused as I looked up at him. "Who?"

"Alex," he said.

The gravel speckling the parking lot crunched underneath our shoes, filling up the silence. I stared at Laylen like he had to be joking, but then he met my eyes, and I realized he was absolutely, one-hundred percent serious.

"You think Alex knows how to get my mom out of The Underworld," I said, making sure that's what we were talking about here. Because I had talked to Alex about my mother before and whether or not she could still be alive, and he had said there was a slim chance that she could be. Never did he ever mention that there was a way to get people out of The Underworld. Yeah, he might not have known my mom was alive—although I wouldn't put it past him if he did—but if he knew a way to rescue someone from The Underworld, he should have said so. But I guess this was *Alex*, so why was I so surprised?

"He *might* know something," Laylen stressed. "Since Stephan's his father and was the one who was in charge of sentencing people to The Underworld, he may have told Alex a way to get down there without being yanked down through the lake."

77

"So you don't know for sure if he does." I frowned, disappointed. "You're just guessing."

He nodded. "But I think for now he's probably our best bet—because I think I just eliminated all of my other options."

"If we can get the truth out of him," I muttered.

Laylen nodded in agreement. Honestly, though, I wondered if telling Alex what we had found out tonight would do more bad than good. I mean, for one thing that would require us to explain to him how we received the information, which in turn would result in a full-on freak out on Alex's part. And most of his freak out would probably be directed at Laylen. I knew Laylen could deal with it and everything, but it didn't mean he should have to. He already helped me out enough, so why make him pay more?

Besides, I wasn't sure if Alex could be trusted still. His story of what had happened back at the cabin seemed off. For all I knew what really could have happened was that the memory erasing rock couldn't erase my memory and so Stephan had put Alex in charge to keep an eye on me until he found an alternative way to extract my memory.

As I went back and forth with what I thought we should do with the "telling Alex" dilemma, a set of head-lights flashed across the parking lot, and Laylen quickly hid us behind a black Mazda. A car pulled into the parking lot and parked. Then two people climbed out of the car; a short, round man, and a thin, tall woman wearing neon pink high heels that clicked loudly against the ground as the two of them walked toward a tan brick building that was right next to Adessa's house.

"Are they vampires?" I whispered to Laylen.

He shook his head slowly. "I don't think so..."

We waited until the people had disappeared around the corner of the building before stepping out from behind the Mazda. We made the rest of the walk hurriedly. The rest of our conversation consisted of creating a plan for what we should tell everyone happened to my neck, because I was sure they were going to ask. Laylen insisted that we should just blame the bite on him, since Alex was probably going to accuse him of it anyway. I thought this was a ridiculous idea, and told him we didn't need to tell Alex anything, and that I would just wear a turtle neck or something. But then I realized that wearing a turtle neck in the scorching hot desert would look a little bit suspicious

So that problem just hung in the air.

It was when we reached Adessa's that we both realized we had another problem. One that needed to be dealt with really fast.

During our little jumping-out-of-the-building thing, it never had occurred to either one of us that getting back up might be a little tricky. So we just stood there, staring up at the window we'd jumped out of, trying to come up with some kind of solution.

"Maybe there's a fire escape somewhere?" I suggested.

79

He shook his head. "I don't think there is."

In the distance, dogs were howling like crazy, and I saw Laylen tense up as he glanced around apprehensively. When the dogs stopped howling, he shook his head and let out a frustrated sigh. Then he kicked a plastic bottle that was on the ground and it whipped up in the air and thumped against the side of the brick building.

"Dammit," he cursed noisily, and now I was the one glancing around apprehensively.

"Laylen," I whispered. "You need to be a little quieter or someone's going to hear us."

He ran his fingers through his blond hair, and I sensed that a meltdown was about to take place. "Who cares? I'm already screwed anyway."

"Why are you screwed? Because you staked Vladislav? I thought you said you just had to lay low for awhile and it would pass over," I said.

He looked at me gravely. "Gemma, I didn't just stake Vladislav. I staked Vladislav, one of the oldest vampires."

"So is that worse than staking a young vampire?" I asked.

He stared at me, not answering, and I suddenly grasped that he was in more trouble than he first let on.

"Laylen, you shouldn't have let me go with you," I told him, guilt choking up inside me.

"It was your choice, Gemma," he said. "You should be able to choose what you want to do."

"Well, I think I picked the wrong one." I swallowed hard. "I'm really sor…" I stopped as a spark of electricity coiled up my spine. "Ah, crap."

"What's the matter?" Laylen asked, his eyebrows dipping down.

Before I could tell him what was up, or try to find a place for us to hide, Laylen's gaze darted over my shoulder, and I knew without even looking that we were so busted.

"So, funny thing," Alex's voice came up from right behind me. "I was up in my room, and I just happened to look out the window. And boy was I surprised to find you two standing down here, in the middle of the night, for God knows what reason."

I caught Laylen's eye, and I tried to communicate to him telepathically what we should do. Of course, I didn't have telepathic abilities and neither did Laylen, so guess how well that went.

I shook my head, and decided to face the inevitable. I took a deep breath and, covering the bite on my neck with my hand, I turned to face Alex. I wasn't too worried about what he was going to say to me. He could chew me out all he wanted;—I was used to it. I just felt guilty because I knew Alex was going to put most of it on Laylen.

Alex's eyes were all over me as if he could sense something was wrong. "What's the matter with your neck?"

The lighting was scarce, so I was hoping that it was dark enough that he couldn't see the blood dried up on my skin. "I have a kink in it."

He gave me a yeah-right look. "You have a kink in it?"

I shrugged. "It happens."

He shook his head, irritated. "So why are you two standing out here?"

I had no idea what to tell him and the way he was staring at me was making my brain all hazy.

"How about we go inside, and then we'll tell you?" Laylen said restlessly.

Alex glanced back and forth between Laylen and me, looking a little lost. "Okay. Let's go inside then."

So apparently Alex had woken up Adessa when he'd seen Laylen and me standing outside in the dark. He had to wake her up or he wouldn't have been able to walk out the front door without getting blasted by Adessa's charms.

I still had my hand on my neck, trying to keep my bite mark hidden, as we stepped into the living room. But as the light hit me, I realized that there was blood all over Laylen's black thermal shirt that I still had on, and there was no way to cover it up.

"What the hell is all over your shirt?" Alex asked as soon as he caught sight of me in the light. He came up and took a closer look at the thermal shirt I had on. "Is that blood?" Before I could answer, he picked up the hem of the shirt. "And why do you have Laylen's shirt on?"

I yanked the hem of the shirt out of his grasp. "I have his shirt on because it was cold outside."

He gave me a disbelieving look. "It's like seventy degrees out there, Gemma."

"Well, I get cold easily," I said as casually as I could, which strangely enough sounded casual.

He raised an eyebrow at me. "So where'd the blood come from?"

"It came from—" Before I could finish coming up with a lie, he reached over and lifted my hand away from my neck.

He let out a sequence of too-inappropriate-to-repeat words and then lunged for Laylen. Laylen, taken off-guard, stumbled back as Alex slammed into him, and both of them went crashing into the wall, causing the wall to crack.

Laylen quickly regained his footing, and he shoved Alex hard. But Alex barely budged.

"You bit her," Alex said, coming at Laylen again. "Are you freaking crazy?"

"That's not what happen—" I said, but was cut off as Laylen rammed into Alex, making them both fly backward and onto the apothecary table, which instantly buckled beneath their weight. It didn't even faze either one of them as they rolled around on the tiled floor, crashing into the shelves and sofas, while they threw punches at each other.

I'd just decided that I might need to go get some help—because let's face it, I am not strong enough to stop a fight between a Keeper and a vampire—when Aislin and Adessa appeared in the doorway. Adessa was wearing a long navy blue robe decorated with bright pink flowers, and Aislin was dressed in a plaid pajama set.

"What in the world is going on?" Aislin screeched, her bright green eyes wide.

Laylen and Alex didn't even so much as acknowledge she was there, still throwing swings at one another.

"Gemma, what happened?" Ailsin asked, looking horrified.

"Um…we were—"

"*Subsisto,*" Adessa said, her hand out in front of her.

Laylen and Alex flew away from each other, Alex landing by Aislin's feet and Laylen smacking onto the floor not too far from me.

"What the heck are you two doing?" Ailsin asked Alex as she tried to help him to his feet.

Alex shook her hand off, breathing heavily as he got to his feet. His bottom lip was spilt and he had a cut above his right eyebrow. "He bit her," he said, storming toward Laylen again.

Aislin grabbed Alex by the back of his shirt and, with a lot of effort on her part, held him back. "Who bit—what?"

Irritation shone in Alex's bright green eyes. "Laylen," he said with an attitude. "Bit Gemma."

Aislin's eyes widened even more as she took in the sight of my blood-stained shirt and the two holes in my neck. "Oh my God."

"Laylen didn't bite me," I told her. "Another vampire did." I looked down at Laylen, who had a small bruise on his cheek, and waited for him to jump in and help me explain.

But all he did was stand to his feet, dust himself off, and pop his neck. Then he strolled toward the doorway, doing that thing that guys do when they take a quick step towards the other one to "psych" them out.

"Laylen," Aislin said, shocked. "What's the matter with you?"

"Nothing's the matter with me," he replied, kind of being a jerk.

Aislin looked hurt as she let go of Alex's shirt.

Laylen left the room, and I figured I'd explain what we'd been up to while he cooled off. Of course, I had absolutely no idea how I was going to go about doing this.

Aislin chased after Laylen, and Adessa took one look at Alex and me and left, as if she could sense something bad was about to go down and wanted to avoid being around it when it did.

Smart woman.

I stared at the doorway for awhile, if for no other reason than to avoid Alex's gaze that I could feel burning into me. Sparks of static were dancing all over my skin, and I wished I could tell them to stop because they were very distracting.

"So, are you going to explain to me what in the heck you and Laylen were doing outside in the middle of the night?" Alex asked. "And where the bite mark came from?"

"I guess that depends on whether you're going to freak out when I tell you." I told him, still not looking at him.

"You expect me not to freak out when you've got blood all over your shirt and two holes in your neck?" he said incredulously.

I touched the tips of my fingers to the bite on my neck, and then looked at him. "I'm not going to tell you what happened unless you promise you'll stay calm." Then as an added bonus I tacked on, "Besides, you owe me."

He started to walk toward me. "Oh yeah? How do you figure?"

"Because of what happened back at the cabin," I said, backing away from him because I knew the closer he got to me, the more unclear my mind would be. And I needed my mind to be clear. "When you let your father try to take my mind away."

He looked pissed and suddenly he was moving toward me at a rapid speed. I backed away until I bumped into the wall. He kept coming at me, slamming to a halt only inches away from me, the tips of his DC sneakers brushing with the tips of mine. He was so close that I could feel the warmth of his breath dusting across my cheeks.

He put his hands on the wall, trapping me between his arms. "I already told you I wasn't going to let him do it," he breathed, leaning in. "I knew the necklace would protect you."

My heart thrummed insanely in my chest, the electricity buzzing passionately from the intensity of his eyes.

What was I supposed to be doing again?

And then I felt the metal of the locket pressing against my neck, and remembered. Vladislav. My mother. The Underworld.

"Okay...I believe you." Which wasn't the truth at all, but I was working on something here. "But you have to promise to stay calm while I tell you what happened."

He shook his head. "I'm not going to promise anything."

"Then I'm not going to tell you anything." I went to duck under his arm, but he slid it down further so that I would have to limbo really low to get out.

"Fine, I'll try to stay as calm as I can as long as you'll stop throwing in my face what happened back at the cabin." He waited for me to answer, but when I said nothing he added, "Deal?"

I weighed up my options and came to the conclusion that the best way to get information about The Underworld was to make the deal. Now, whether I'd hold true to the deal or not depended on what happened here. "Fine, it's a deal."

We sat down on the purple velvet sofa—the one still remaining upright—and I began searching my mind for an idea of where to begin, and what details I should give him. But before I could figure any of this out, he spoke.

"So who bit you?" he asked.

Figures he'd start there. "A vampire," I said, kicking a broken piece of the apothecary table with the tip of my shoe.

"And what's this vampire's name?" he asked impatiently.

"Vladislav."

"Vladislav!" he exclaimed, slamming his hand down onto the arm of the sofa. "You've got to be kidding me."

"So...I take it you know who I'm talking about?"

"Of course I know who he is." He sank back in the chair, the muscles on his arms flexing tensely as he crossed them. "I also know how big of a problem it's going to be if he figured out who you are."

"Does it even matter if he did?" I asked. "I mean, aren't we pretty sure that the stars power isn't going to stop the portal from opening anyway? So what does it matter if someone knows I have it in me?"

"We don't know for sure what the star's power is for," he said, staring straight ahead at the dark blue wall, looking as though he was pondering something deeply. "So until we do, we need to be careful about anyone finding out about you. Besides, the more people who know about you, the easier it'll be for my father and the Death Walkers to find you."

I raised my eyebrows at him, questioning his words. "You don't know what the star's power is for?"

He sat there with his arms folded, staring at me so powerfully that my skin felt like it was on *fire*. "No. I don't. I already told you I didn't."

I wasn't sure if I believed him, but decided to stick a tack in it for now and move on to my next problem. "We went to see Vladislav for a really good reason."

"Oh, I'm sure you did." Alex let out a laugh. "What, did Laylen tell you that Vladislav would have all the answers to your problems?"

"No, it wasn't even Laylen's idea," I said defensively. "I asked him if he knew whether we could find out if my mom was still alive, and he suggested that Vladislav might know something. And you know what? He did."

"And where in *that* brilliant plan did Vladislav biting you come into play?" Alex asked snidely. "Or was that just an added bonus?"

I shook my head. "Why would you even say that?"

There was this awkward silence that built between us as I realized where Alex was going with that. Vampire bites stimulate people's desires. Although, I wasn't sure that was what it had done to me. All I had seen were a bunch of images. And, yes, okay, some of those images — some of the ones that included Alex — did kind of make my

89

body buzz a little, but there was also the vision that came after the images, and that was anything but stimulating.

"So, anyway," I said, attempting to change the subject away from my desires. "Vladislav told me my mother was still alive in The Underworld."

Alex shook his head. "Gemma, that's not possible."

"Even you said that there might be a small chance that she could still be alive," I pointed out.

He looked confused. "When did I say that?"

"Back at Adessa's, after I'd been pulled into my first vision, and we didn't know it was my mother I'd seen forced into the lake."

"I don't remember ever saying anything like that," he muttered, his eyebrows furrowed as he stared down at the floor. "And if I did, I'm sure I just said it to try and get you to calm down."

"So why would Vladislav tell us she was alive if she wasn't?" I said. "There's no reason for him to lie."

"Of course there is." He looked at me like I was a total nut job. "That's what vampires do—they lie."

"How do you know that for sure?" I asked hotly. "I mean, how do you know that all vampires lie? Laylen doesn't lie." *You do.*

"I just do," he said, but his voice had lost some of its confidence.

"Vladislav didn't lie, Alex." I rested back in the chair, keeping my eyes on him. "Laylen said that vampires can pick up on when other vampires are lying, and he said Vladislav wasn't lying."

Alex ran his fingers through his messy brown hair, and then he turned and faced me, a serious expression on his face. "Look, Gemma. You're too trusting with Laylen. You need to be careful."

I gave him an are-you-serious look. "*You* think I should be careful when it comes to trusting Laylen." Was he joking?

"Vampires are not good," Alex said sternly. "They're evil."

"Laylen's not," I snapped. "And besides, Vladislav knew that my mother was a Keeper before we ever told him. That has to mean he's heard of her."

"So what if he has heard of her?" he said. "That doesn't mean he was telling the truth about her being alive. He might have just been messing with your head."

"Alex." Without even thinking, I grabbed hold of his arm, electricity tickling my fingertips. "It could mean that there might be a chance that my *mom*, who I haven't seen since I was four, and who just might have some answers to what Stephan is planning to do with the star's energy, could still be alive. And not just alive, but she could be trapped down in The Underworld, *and* has been trapped down there for fourteen years now, working as the Queen's slave."

Something I said made his expression change. "Why do you think she's the Queen's slave?"

91

"That's the reason why Vladislav said she was still alive," I told him, my fingers still wrapped around his arm, his bare skin pressed against my own, causing lots and lots of static to flow through me.

"The Queen's slave," he said, shaking his head. "I can't believe it."

"Why?" I asked. "Is it...bad?"

He shook his head. "No...well, it's better than being the Water Faerie's torture victim...but the Queen usually doesn't use humans for slaves."

"But that's the reason she's still alive, right?" I asked.

Silence.

"Even if she is alive," he said, looking at me gravely, "she probably wouldn't be the same Jocelyn—being there for that long, it most likely will have changed her."

I swallowed hard, my voice barely audible as I said, "Okay...I understand."

"Do you?" He raised an eyebrow at me. "Because just imagine being stuck in a place like that—a place of death, where fear and torture is common—for over fourteen years." He lowered his voice. "Even if Vladislav was telling the truth—even if she's still alive—she's probably not your mother anymore."

"She's probably not my mother anymore," I repeated in outrage as I let go of his arm. "She'll always be my mother, no matter what."

He shook his head. ""Gemma, you don't understand. The torture that goes on...the way the Water Faeries instill fear in people...her mind is probably gone."

I touched my locket with my hand, thinking of how my mother had given it to me when I was little, even though I couldn't remember her doing so. "It doesn't matter what she's like now, because I don't have anything to compare her to before."

There was pity in his bright green eyes. "Gemma, still—"

I cut him off. "Do you know a way to get her out of there or not?"

"I don't," he said simply.

I held his gaze. "Is that the truth?"

He paused and I felt my heart skip a beat. *He knows something.* Oh yes he did. I could feel it. I could see it on his face and how he avoided looking at me.

"Please just tell me the truth," I practically begged.

He sighed, leaning back against the arm of the chair. "Even if I did...know something...I wouldn't actually do it. It's way too dangerous."

"So what if it's dangerous?" I said. "Everything's dangerous—I'm dangerous, and yet you're still here helping me." *I hope.* "She's my mom, Alex. And besides, she might know something. Your dad didn't just send her there for no reason."

"Even if she does know something, and she is actually mentally there enough to tell us what she knows, it doesn't mean I think it's a good idea to go there. We can get our answers somewhere else."

I told myself to keep my cool—*breathe in, breathe out*—but it was hard when it came to Alex. Especially when it came to getting answers from him. It was like a freaking mind game of who could outwit who. "Where else can we get answers?"

He didn't answer me, and I started to wonder if he wasn't going to answer me because he really didn't have an answer to give me. And honestly, at that moment, I questioned whether he knew anything at all. Maybe he was just as lost as everyone else, and perhaps deep down inside he wanted to save my mother, if for no other reason so that maybe he could figure all of this out. Of course, even if this were true, it didn't mean he was going to help me out.

I got to my feet, giving up on him. I had other people I could go to.

He jumped to his feet as I tried to scoot by him. "Where are you going?"

"To find Laylen—see if he and I can figure out a way to save my mom." I started for the doorway.

He caught me by the arm and pulled me back down on the sofa. "Hang on just a sec, before you go freaking out."

I wiggled my arm free. "I wasn't freaking out. I just don't want to hear what you have to say unless it's going to help me get my mom out of that awful place."

He massaged the sides of his temples with his fingers and let out a stressed breath. "If we were to do this—if we were to go to The Underworld and try to save your mother, you'd have to promise me that you'd do everything I told you to do." He looked up at me. "If I tell you something's too dangerous for you, you'd have to listen."

I considered this. I know I might sound like a brat here, but the idea of doing *everything* he told me to do was making my insides burn. I'd done that too much already. And besides, what if he was playing me? "I don't know...."

He shrugged. "Then no deal."

No deal. His words echoed in my head, and I felt torn. In the end, though, I think I knew that I would make the deal. I just hoped that his side of the deal was genuine— that Alex would finally come through for me. "Okay, it's a deal. Now, how do we do it?"

He sighed, got to his feet, and looked down at me with a very unhappy expression. "The first thing we do is bring Nicholas here."

Chapter 7

"Bring Nicholas here?" I frowned at him. "Like the fae-rie/Foreseer/likes-to-invade-my-personal-space Nicholas?"

He nodded, trying hard not to smile as he slipped his hands into the pockets of his jeans. "That would be the one."

I sat there for a second, processing this. "But why do we need him?"

"Because we need a Foreseer."

I pointed at myself. "You have one right here." *Hello.*

He pressed back a grin as if I'd just told him a joke or something. "I understand that, but it's not just the power of a Foreseer that we need. We also need a special kind of crystal ball called an *Ira.*"

"Okay, but...does Nicholas have to be the one to give us this *Ira?*"

"I think he'll be our best bet." When I kept frowning he continued, "None of this is going to be easy, Gemma. Nothing ever is. You should know that by now."

"I do know that," I said, thinking about my mom, me, my soul, and my emotions. None of them were easy. "I know that way too well."

We stared at each other, having this weird moment of understanding, like our thoughts had momentarily connected. Sometimes I really wished our thoughts could connect; that way I'd be able to read his mind and know if he was telling the truth.

"So...what do we have to do then?" I asked, breaking our weird connection moment. "I mean, how do we get Nicholas here? Or do we have to go get him?" God, I hoped we didn't have to go get him because I really didn't want to go back to the City of Crystal again.

"No, we can't go get him." He sighed. "We have to bring him here."

"Okay...well...Are you sure there isn't another way to get this *Ira* crystal ball?" I asked. "Maybe Adessa has one."

"It's not the kind of a crystal ball she'd have," Alex explained. "It's one of a kind—the one Foreseers use to travel to and from places that no one is allowed to travel to."

"Of course it is," I said, feeling frustrated. "Because if it wasn't, then it would make things easy. And I think we both already agreed that nothing is ever easy."

He gave me a small smile. "Yeah. I think we did."

"So what do we do then—to get this *Ira* traveling crystal ball thingy?"

He shifted his weight uneasily. "We get Nicholas here and see if we can persuade him to give it to us."

I thought about the half-faerie, and how being around him had creeped me out. And asking him for a favor…Nicholas was so the last person I ever wanted to *persuade* for a favor. Well, besides Stephan.

"Are you sure there's not someone else we can go and get it from?" I asked again just to make sure.

He shook his head. "Only another Foreseer—they're the only ones who know of its existence."

"Well, then how do *you* know it exists?" I wondered.

He didn't look at me. He was staring off into space as he answered, "My father told me about it once."

"Oh," was all I could think of to say.

Next to my feet lay a clock that had been knocked on the floor during Laylen and Alex's fight. The glass had been shattered and it was letting off an unsteady tick tock, which was the only sound filling in the silence. Tick tock. Tick tock. Just like a ticking time bomb. It was like a warning that we were running out of time. We needed to find answers, before Stephan found us—or should I say found me. The world was depending on it.

"Okay, so we get Nicholas, and then what? We just ask him to give us the Ira crystal ball?" I asked, doubting that it would be that easy.

"Something like that." Alex spoke through gritted teeth.

"Are you okay?" I asked, picking up on some uneasiness flowing off of him.

"Why wouldn't I be?"

I shrugged. "I don't know…you tell me."

He didn't answer as he picked up the broken clock and flipped it over to the back, fiddling with the knob. Tick tock. Tick tock. The ticking and tocking was slowing down to a gurgle.

"So we get the Ira crystal ball, and we use it to go to The Underworld?" I asked, making sure that was the plan.

Still no answer as he twisted the knob on the soon-to-be-dead clock.

I stood up. "Alex…if I use this Ira crystal ball, what does that mean for the promise you made to Dyvinius?"

Tick…tock…tick…The clock stopped.

Time's up.

Alex set the clock down on the floor. "That's not for you to worry about."

"Just tell me what happens if I use the crystal." I asked, taking a step back as he walked by me.

"I already told you, that was my problem," he said, his voice tight. "I made the promise. Not you."

"But that doesn't—" I started.

"Look," he turned around to face me. "I'll figure something out, okay? Do you want to get your mother out or not?"

I nodded. "I do, but I—"

"Okay, then let's go summon Nicholas."

Before we set out to bring Nicholas here, we first went to go find Laylen and Aislin and let them in on our little plan. I felt kind of proud of myself that I'd gotten Alex to

99

cooperate, but I also had a pang in my gut when I thought about how he was going to have to fulfill the promise he'd made to Dyvinius. Although I wasn't sure what that promise was exactly, I figured it had to be bad. The dark look that had passed over Dyvinius's eyes when he gotten Alex to make the promise had proved that it was bad.

As we searched the downstairs for Laylen and Aislin, I casually mentioned to Alex that maybe he should apologize to Laylen for accusing him of biting me, because I figured it would make things easier if the two of them weren't fighting. He ignored my casual suggestion, though, so I decided I would drop it....For now, anyway.

We found Laylen and Aislin in one of the bedrooms upstairs. Aislin was sitting cross-legged on the bed, still wearing her plaid pajamas. Laylen was sitting in a corner chair, and I could tell he was still all worked up over the fight. But I also got the impression that Alex and I might have interrupted a very serious conversation going on between the two of them, like we might have shattered a private moment they had been having.

Alex gave both of them a quick rundown of our plan. After he had finished, Aislin sat on the bed, a shocked look frozen on her face. Laylen secretly gave me an I-told-you-so look because he had guessed that Alex would know how to get into to The Underworld.

Something occurred to me as I stood there staring at the maroon walls of the bedroom, with my hand pressed to my bitten neck. Had it really been necessary to go speak to Vladislav? I mean, if Alex knew a way to get to The Underworld, maybe he knew another way to find out if she was alive. Of course, I'd had to use what Vladislav had told us about my mother being the Queen's slave for Alex to admit he knew a way. But still...maybe our little trip could have been avoided.

Well, I guess we had really messed up on that one. And now Laylen might end up getting hunted down by a bunch of revengeful vampires.

"Jocelyn's still alive...in The Underworld..." Aislin said. "For all these years?"

"Well, according to *Vladislav* she is," Alex replied, shooting Laylen a glare.

"He wasn't lying," Laylen assured him, standing up from his chair. "I could feel that he wasn't."

"I already said we'd go try to rescue her," Alex said sharply. "I don't need you to try and convince me."

"I wasn't trying to convince you," Laylen said. "I was just pointing out the fact that despite what you believe, vampires do tell the truth sometimes."

"That might be true," Alex replied. "But your little trip out there also backed up my theory that vampires can't control their need to bite."

"Well, I can control my need." Laylen took a threatening step toward Alex.

"Yeah, but for how long?" Alex asked, taking a step toward Laylen. "How long do you think you'll be able to keep it under control before you lose it?"

"Can you two just stop arguing?" I cried out, startling myself and everyone else in the room. All their eyes were on me. "The longer we stand around here arguing, the longer my mom has to be down there suffering. And the more time we waste not trying to figure out what the heck Stephan is trying to do with me and the star."

They were all speechless for a minute, which almost always happened when I made a big speech like that.

"But how do we get Nicholas here?" Aislin asked, fidgeting with one of her diamond earrings. "Isn't going to the City of Crystal the only way to find him? And to do that don't we need another special kind of crystal ball that is hard to come by? I mean, the only other alternative I can think of is to go to the Kingdom of Fey and see if he's there. But he doesn't spend much time there. At least I don't think he does."

"Besides," Laylen added, "whether we end up finding a way to enter the City of Crystal, or if we decide to go to the Kingdom of Fey, both places are not very accepting of unwelcomed visitors."

"Kingdom of Fey?" I asked.

"It's where the Fey live," Aislin explained. "And since Nicholas is part Fey, he goes there sometimes. But I don't think he's very fond of it because...well, because the fey can be..."

"Everything's a joke to them," Alex interrupted. "Which means there's a lot of running around in circles. And it doesn't matter, because I'm not planning on going

102

to either one of those places." Alex caught my eye. "Gemma's going to bring him here."

"What?" I gaped at him. "*I'm* going to bring him here? How am I...oh..." I stopped as it dawned on me what he was referring to. I was going to use a good, old, normal crystal ball, which in turn would allow the Foreseers to know that I was using a crystal ball again, something I'd been forbidden to do until I'd been trained, and something Alex had promised Dyvinius I wouldn't use until I had. So if I used the power of the crystal, Nicholas would show up here to collect on Alex's promise.

"But if I bring him here that way then you'll have to—" I started to say.

Alex shook his head at me, trying to get me to stop talking.

"Have to what?" Aislin asked curiously.

I gave Alex a funny look, wondering why I couldn't say anything to Ailsin and Laylen about the promise he'd made to Dyvinius.

"Then he'll be super annoying, just like he always is," Alex said quickly, taking me by the hand, which threw me completely off guard. "Look, I have to talk to Gemma for a minute about what's going to happen when Nicholas gets here, so excuse us for just a second."

Before anyone could respond to this, Alex was pulling me toward the door. Laylen and Ailsin exchanged a perplexed look, which I'm sure matched the look on my own face.

"What's wrong with you?" I pulled my hand from his grip after we'd made it out of the room. "Why can't I say anything about the promise you made to Dyvinius?"

"Because..." he glanced back at Ailsin and Laylen, and then shut the door. "Ailsin will freak out if she finds out about it."

"Why? How bad is it?"

"I told you, that's for me to worry about." He backed away toward the stairs. "We need to get that bite cleaned up before we bring Nicholas here. The less he knows about what's going on, the better." And with that, he headed down the stairs.

I sighed, trotting down the stairs after him. "But what happens when he gets here?" I asked, following Alex into the kitchen. "Are we just supposed to ask him for the Ira crystal ball and hope that'll he'll give it to us?"

Alex started opening up the top cupboards that surrounded the cooking area of the kitchen. "No. You're probably going to have to do that."

"Why would I have to?" I asked, wondering what he was looking for.

"Because…" He bent down and opened the cupboard below the sink. "I probably won't be here."

"Huh….Why won't you Alex, what the heck is going to happen to you when I use the crystal ball?"

He reached inside the cupboard and pulled out a first aid kit. "I told you—"

I cut him off. "Just tell me, *please*."

He looked at me, and I looked back at him, the electricity coursing all around.

"I'm just going to be gone for a little while," he finally said with a shrug. "It's nothing major."

"But you'll come back, right?" I asked, suddenly worried I'd never see him again. Hmm...That was weird.

He paused, considering what I'd asked him. "Eventually, yeah."

Chapter 8

As Alex patched the bite on my neck, his words lingered in my head. *Eventually.* Eventually he'd be back, but when? Did he even know?

I was sitting on the kitchen table, with my feet up on one of the chairs, as Alex stood in front of me, patting my neck with a cotton ball.

"What exactly do you mean by eventually?" I asked him, flinching from the pain. "'Just how long are you talking about? And why will you be gone? Can't you just break the promise?" I mean, he was good at breaking promises to me, so why not to Dyvinius?

He gave me a funny look. "You know, you ask more questions than anyone I've ever known."

I rolled my eyes. "Well, if you'd just tell me things then I wouldn't have to ask the questions."

He shook his head, trying not to smile. "Well, I'm not sure when I'll be back—there's no time frame for what I'll be doing. And I won't break the promise because I can't. It's binding because I made it in the City of Crystal. It's how things work—promises are unbreakable when made there."

"Well, can you at least tell me what you have to do while you'll be there?" I asked as he pulled out a square piece of gauze.

"It's better if I didn't." He peeled off the wrapper from the gauze. "Trust me, you're better off not knowing."

It was bad—I could tell. "Well, if it's that bad then why are you doing it?"

He took the roll of tape out, looking very uncomfortable. "Because…as of right now it's the only way I can think of to get some answers." He ripped two pieces of tape off and tossed the roll back into the first aid kit. "And also because…" He struggled with his words as he taped the gauze to my neck. "Because I'm hoping if I do, then maybe you'll start…trusting me more. And perhaps…" He closed the first aid kit, picked it up, and headed back toward the cupboard where he'd gotten it from. "You'll forgive me."

He said it so quietly I wasn't sure if he'd actually said it. Before I could get around to asking him to please repeat himself, Laylen entered the kitchen.

"So I'm assuming you need a normal Foreseer's crystal ball to get this Ira crystal ball," he said to Alex as he slid onto the table beside me.

Alex shut the cupboard and nodded. "Yeah, does Adessa have one?"

Laylen nodded, and we followed him out of the room to go get one. I couldn't help but look at Alex, thinking about what I thought he said—that I'd forgive him. The more I thought about it, though, the more I was convinced I'd misunderstood him.

After we got a regular old vision-seeing kind of crystal ball from Adessa, we went into the now clean living room. Evidently Adessa had used magic to clean and mend up Laylen's and Alex's mess. The shelves were back up on the dark blue walls, the knickknacks standing on them. The apothecary table was no longer broken and the black candles were topping it once again. And the crack in the wall had miraculously been fixed.

It was really early in the morning, and Adessa had decided she needed to do some inventory in her store. Alex had suggested to Aislin that she should go help Adessa. I think he did it so that Aislin would be distracted from the fact that when Nicholas showed up, he would be taken away to the City of Crystal. I couldn't believe he wasn't going to tell her, but there was no use trying to argue with him. Whatever the promise was, he wanted to keep it a secret from her.

While we had been getting things set up, Alex had informed me that he still wasn't sure if this was going to work. All he knew was that Foreseers did have a Ira crystal ball, which allowed them to travel to and from places that people normally couldn't travel to—like, say The Underworld—but he wasn't sure how it would work exactly. All we could hope for was that we'd be able to get Nicholas to tell us. For some reason, I had a feeling that this was going to be tricky. Faeries were tricky after all, so getting information from one seemed liked it would be tricky.

The violet ribbons swirled and danced inside the crystal ball, which was balanced in its stand on top of the apothecary table in front of us. Laylen sat on one side of me, while Alex sat on the other side of me. I'd put myself in the middle of them intentionally, figuring it'd be best to separate them just in case they decided to get mad at one another again.

I felt a little afraid looking down at the glinting crystal ball. I worried where I would end up when I went in, and if I would even be able to get myself out. But we were all taking risks here, and I guess this was mine.

All I could do was cross my fingers, and hope that I would return to Adessa's and find a more than cooperative Nicholas awaiting to tell me in detail what needed to be done to get my mother out of that horrendous place known as The Underworld.

But I had a feeling it wasn't going to be nearly that easy.

"Okay, so now what?" Laylen asked. "Gemma's just supposed to go into a vision and faerie boy will show up here and hand over this Ira crystal ball and then, BAM, we'll just be able to travel to The Underworld without having to get dragged down through the lake by a Water Faerie?"

"Something like that," Alex mumbled quietly as he stared at the crystal ball. He looked at me. "Whenever you're ready, go ahead."

I eyed the crystal ball warily. "Okay...." Well, here goes nothing. I reached for the crystal ball, but Alex caught my hand before my fingers grazed the glass.

"You need to make sure you go somewhere safe," he insisted, holding onto my hand. "Just think of something simple that might have happened in your past. You have to be careful you don't alter anything. Or get yourself stuck. You do remember how Nicholas got you out of the vision when you went in with him, right?"

"Yeah." I nodded. "He just blinked and we were out."

He frowned. "But he didn't have you try."

I sighed. "Look, I'll be okay. I've gone in and out of visions on my own before. Some without using a crystal ball."

"What?" Laylen said, at the exact same time Alex shot me a pointed look.

"You can go into a vision without a crystal ball?" Laylen asked, his bright blue eyes wide in amazement.

"Alright, let's get this done and over with," Alex said before I could answer. It was funny, but I realized that Alex was doing the same thing with Laylen as he did so often with me—dodging the truth and answering questions.

110

Alex let go of my hand, and I took a deep breath and reached for the crystal. Then I was surrounded by nothing but light.

Chapter 9

I'm not sure what went wrong. But something was definitely wrong. All I could see was light, everywhere. Bright and blinding, stinging at my eyes. For a split second, I thought somehow I'd sent myself to the sun or something.

But it wasn't hot or anything. In fact, it kind of made me feel sparkly, almost like whenever Alex touched me. It wasn't making me panic or anything. In fact, I felt peaceful and calm.

I started to move through the light. "Where am I?" I whispered.

"You're in your future," someone said from behind me.

I spun around and squinted through the light. My nostrils were instantly hit by the smell of lilacs, rain, and forest. And I knew, even though I couldn't see him, that there was a faerie standing out there in the light.

"Nicholas," I called out. "Where are you?"

He didn't answer, but I could feel him next to me, warmth radiating from his body.

What is this place?" I asked, turning around in circles, searching for him.

"I already told you, it's your future," his voice purred in my ear.

I jumped to the side, startled by how close he was to me. "My future? How do you know it's my future?"

"Because I do."

"But how..." I glanced around, trying to see something—anything—but was blinded in return. "How can this be my future? There's nothing here."

"Is that what you see?" Nicholas's voice encircled me. "Nothing?"

I'd always been cautious around Nicholas. When I had gone into the vision with him, I had been careful not to let him know what I saw. But now...There was something off about this particular vision. I could feel it. I just felt...

I just felt too peaceful.

A feeling which I'd never felt before. Yet there was no prickle to help me acknowledge it. I just knew what it was.

"I see light," I told him, my voice soft. "It's everywhere."

"Are you sure that's all you see?" he whispered in my ear.

This time I didn't flinch away. "Yes."

"Well then."

"Well then what?"

There was a pause. "Then I guess that means your future's dead."

Dead. *Dead.* Before I could dig into the details of why he had said this—or if he meant that I would be dead soon—I felt his hand touch my arm.

"Let's go back," he said. "I have some business to take care of with Alex."

Which was exactly what this was all about—taking care of business. But Nicholas was never supposed to show up in my vision. And I was never supposed to go into a vision so...heavy and severe. I was supposed to keep it simple. But if what Nicholas said was true, then I failed miserably.

For now, though, as hard as it was going to be, I was going to have to push this vision out of my mind so I could take Nicholas and myself back to Adessa's.

So I did, shutting my eyes tightly, wishing I could forget what I had seen—or what I didn't see, maybe I should say—but also wanting to keep the peaceful feeling with me.

"Alright," I said. "Let's go back."

When I reopened my eyes, there was no bright light. The only light was coming from the chandelier on the ceiling. Dark blue walls surround me, and black and white checkerboard tile made up the floor beneath my feet. I was sitting in the velvet purple sofa with Alex on one side of me and Laylen on the other. The crystal ball was no longer in my sight because Nicholas was standing in front of me, blocking it from my view.

His sandy blonde hair swept over his forehead, his golden eyes were locked on me, and his hand still rested on my arm. The navy blue t-shirt he was wearing made the Foreseer's mark on his wrist visible.

"What the—" Alex shouted, leaping to his feet as he took in the sight of Nicholas and me. He swatted Nicholas's hand off of my arm. "Why did you...How..."

"He showed up in the vision," I explained quickly. "Instead of here."

"But that's not allowed," Alex said, his bright green eyes burning with rage. "Foreseers are not allowed to go into another Foreseer's vision without permission."

"Maybe I did have permission," Nicholas said with a sly smile. "How do you know for sure that I didn't?" He looked at me, and I could feel trouble boiling. "Besides, I think it was a good thing I showed up there, so I could explain to Gemma what she was seeing."

Alex gave me a so-what's-going-on look, in which I responded with an eye roll and a don't-worry-about-it shake of my head. I didn't think this was the appropriate time to bring up that Nicholas had just told me my future was dead. Besides, just because he said it didn't mean it was true.

"So is there a reason why you let her use the crystal ball again?" Nicholas asked, dropping down on the sofa across from us and kicking his feet up on the apothecary table. "Or did she just decide to do it all on her own and let you suffer for it?" He paused, his golden eyes glinting wickedly. "Personally, I'd love to think it was the latter."

"Well, it wasn't the latter," Alex said, irritated. "It was for a good reason."

"And what reason would that be?" Nicholas asked with a sparkle of amusement in his eyes.

Alex hesitated and sat back down on the sofa beside me. "The reason she did it is because I needed to talk to you about...about a way to get into...The Underworld by using the Ira crystal ball."

I looked at Nicholas, but his expression was blank, giving me no idea what he was thinking

"You think an Ira will take you to The Underworld?" He let out a laugh. "I've never heard of a more ridiculous thing."

"I know it can be done." Alex's face reddened with anger. "So cough it up—where can we get one?"

Nicholas pressed his lips together, holding back a grin. "Like I said, I have no idea what you're talking about—I've never heard of such a thing before."

Laylen and Alex exchanged this strange look that I couldn't interpret. Then they both jumped to their feet and charged at Nicholas, Laylen taking out the apothecary table with him. They each grabbed one of Nicholas's arms, tipping over the sofa as they dragged him over the back of it. Then they shoved him against the wall so violently that it made me wince.

What in the world? Had they planned this while I was gone? What happened to their wanting to beat the crap out of each other thing?

I got to my feet and made my way over to them.

"Now, like I said," Alex practically growled at him. "We know an Ira can take us to The Underworld, so just tell us where we can get one and how to use it."

"I don't kn—" Nicholas started to say, but Alex pushed on him harder. "Okay. Okay. I might know where to get one."

"And you'll tell us where." Alex's tone was firm.

Nicholas glanced at everyone and then this look passed over his face and all I could think was, *Great, what does he want?*

"I think if I do, I should at least get something out of it." His eyes landed on me, and I took a step back. "Something I want."

I took another step back as the three guys all looked at me.

Alex shook his head. "No. No way. You're not having anything that comes from her."

"Then I won't help," he said simply.

Alex waited a second, and then shoved Nicholas against the wall again. "Think of something else."

Neither one of them looked as if they were going to back down, and when Laylen glanced at me, I decided it was time to take matters into my own hands. I'd already

117

been bitten by a vampire, so why not see what faerie boy wanted to add to my Stipulation list.

"What do you want?" I asked, walking toward him.

Alex shook his head. "Don't."

I ignored him. "What do you want?"

A devious smile rose on Nicholas's face. "A kiss."

Ugh. "Really? That's all you want, and then you'll just hand over the Ira and tell us how to use it so we can get into The Underworld?" I was having a hard time believing that a kiss from me—Freaky Girl With Violet Eyes Who Couldn't Feel—was going to seal the deal. But Nicholas was a weirdo, so...

He nodded, his smile so impish I wanted to slap it right off of his face. And then that's when I felt it—the prickle, releasing a new kind of confidence I never felt before. In fact, I felt kind of strong.

"Okay then," I said. "I'll do it."

Alex looked at me with anger blazing in his eyes. "No."

"You're paying your dues for this," I said, taking a deep breath. "This is mine."

"You act like it's such a bad thing," Nicholas said with a smirk. "But deep down I think you know it really isn't."

I shot him a glare and then, with a wave of my hand, told Alex, "Let him go."

Alex did not take his eyes off of me as he gave Nicholas one more hard shove against the wall before letting

118

him go. Laylen let go of him as well and Nicholas rubbed his arm where Alex had been holding him.

"God, you Keepers think violence is the key to everything," Nicholas remarked.

"And you faeries think tricking people into doing things is the key to everything," Alex bit back.

"You're right," Nicholas said, his golden eyes locking onto me. "We do."

I scowled at him. "Let's just get this over with."

He stepped toward me, never taking his eyes off of me, and it took a lot of effort on my part not to back away from him. Laylen walked toward the doorway, looking really uncomfortable with the situation. And that was okay. The fewer people watching this painful scene, the better. Because kissing a half-faerie—the only other guy I've kissed besides Alex—in front of Laylen and Alex was absolutely mortifying. I wished they would just leave the room, but instead Laylen leaned back against the trim of the doorway, folded his arms across his chest, and stared out into the foyer. And Alex...well, he went over and punched a hole into the wall.

I shook my head and took a deep breath as Nicholas leaned in.

I wasn't sure what to expect from the kiss. Honestly, I expected a little more than what happened. I mean, it wasn't like Nicholas was hard on the eyes or anything, just a little weird and annoying. But as his lips brushed against mine, all I felt was...nothing. I felt absolutely nothing. In

119

fact, it made me feel empty, like it was all wrong, and I needed to fix it somehow.

Weird.

I let Nicholas finish his one-sided kiss and then he pulled away, licking his lips.

"Okay," I said, jumping right down to business. "Now get us the crystal and show us how to use it."

Nicholas considered this with a sly look on his face. "The thing is, there's a slight problem with your plan. Yeah, the Ira can take you into The Underworld without having to go through the whole process of being dragged down into the lake by the Water Fey. However, it also takes a very strong Foreseer to channel enough energy to use the Ira crystal. And I'm not that powerful yet."

"So where can we find a Foreseer who has enough power?" I asked, trying to stay calm, something which Alex wasn't trying to do—I could tell by the look on his face.

"You can't," Nicholas said. "At least, probably not one that will actually help you do it." He paused. "See, the thing with Foreseers is that not a whole lot of people like us because we can practically see anything—good or bad. We can go to places where most can't go, like The Underworld. And so when we do show up in The Underworld unannounced, it pisses the Queen off. And no one likes being around a pissed off Queen, especially a Queen who likes to torture people so her Water Faeries can feed off of the fear. So most Foreseers are unwilling to help another Foreseer go there."

I felt like I was being choked. "Are you sure there's absolutely no one that will?"

He shook his head. "Nope. There's not."

Okay, now I was pissed. He just tricked me into believing there was a way just so I would kiss him. Stupid faerie. "You know what? I think I'll let Alex and Laylen take over from where they left off before the kiss."

"Great," Alex said, looking a little too happy about it. He along with Laylen started to corner Nicholas again.

"Okay, okay," Nicholas said, surrendering with his hands out in front of him. "There might be a way…but it will take some time."

"How much time?" Alex asked, still moving for him.

"A few weeks; maybe a few months," Nicholas said with his back up against the wall. "It really all depends on Gemma."

"On me." I pointed at myself. "Why would it depend on me?"

"Well, I think if there were two Foreseers, then we might have enough power to use an Ira to go into The Underworld."

Alex and I exchanged a look, and then Alex said to Nicholas, "How sure are you that it'll work?"

"If she trains enough and builds up her power, then it should work," Nicholas said, looking—for once—like he was telling the truth.

Alex glanced at Laylen and Laylen shrugged. "It's your call."

Alex looked back at Nicholas. "You'll train her *here*." It wasn't a question.

He nodded. "I'll bring the Ira ball back with me after I've dropped you off at the City of Crystal to make good on the promise you broke to Dyvinius—something I can't get you out of, even if I wanted to. Which I don't."

"Fine," Alex agreed. "Take me to the City of Crystal to pay my debt. And while I'm gone, you'll get Gemma ready to use the *Ira*."

"Alright," Nicholas said, and slipped from his pocket the ruby-filled crystal ball that would take Alex and him to the City of Crystal. "Let's go then." He balanced the ball in the palm of his hand and held it out in front of Alex.

"Just one second before we take off," Alex said to Nicholas. Then he turned to me, giving me this strangest look ever.

"What?" I asked, confused.

Still looking at me weirdly, he leaned in toward me.

I wasn't sure what he was going to do at first—kiss me? Yeah, that thought flashed through my head until I realized that he was heading for my ear, not my lips.

"Make sure to be careful around Nicholas." His breath was electric against my ear, and I had to try very hard not to gasp. "Faeries are tricky. He'll twist things around and try to confuse you if you're not careful."

So you're a faerie, too, I thought, but aloud I said, "Okay, I will."

"And whatever you do, don't take the necklace off," Alex added, before stepping away from me. He went back over to Nicholas, who was waiting impatiently with the ruby-filled crystal ball in his hand. "And, Nicholas," Alex said, his hand extended toward the ball but not touching it yet.

What?" Nicholas's tone was mildly tolerant.

"I want you to remember one thing," Alex said, his voice sharper than I'd ever heard. "Try anything, and I mean anything like what you just pulled with Gemma while I'm gone and you'll have to deal with two very powerful witches and a vampire who are more than willing to protect her."

"Whatever," Nicholas said, but looked a little worried.

Alex didn't say anything else. He placed his hand on the crystal ball, and in a blink-of-a-second later he was gone.

Chapter 10

Why did Alex make me feel this way? Why was he the only guy who could steal my breath away? Make my knees weak—yet at the same time drive me absolutely insane?

After Alex and Nicholas took off to the City of Crystal, I was left with this horrid feeling of loneliness in the pit of my stomach; loneliness that always seemed to show up whenever Alex left me. I felt cursed by this feeling that tied me to a guy who had lied, been rude, and tried to control me. But for now, I guess I was bound to it, until I could figure out what was causing this electric bond between us. Something that I was hoping my mother might know about.

As Laylen and I sat on the purple velvet sofa, waiting for Nicholas to return, I decided to tell him what I'd seen in the vision—see if he knew anything about a vision filled with bright light.

But after I'd finished explaining to him what I'd seen, Laylen looked about as puzzled as I felt.

"I have no idea what that could mean," Laylen said, sweeping his blue tipped bangs out of his eyes. "A bright light—that's all you saw?"

I nodded. "And then Nicholas showed up and when I told him what I was seeing, he said my future was dead."

Laylen's face twisted with confusion. "I have no idea, Gemma. I really don't. But...I really wouldn't worry about it too much. I mean, there's a chance that Nicholas could have been messing with your head."

I nodded, but I still felt uneasy. I tried to think of something else, but all my brain wanted to do was think about Alex. Stupid brain. And it wouldn't stop, it just kept going and going until...I remembered.

Alex.

Alex and me.

My memories were flashing back to me. Not all of them, but some. Alex and me picking flowers in a field; watching other Keepers practice sword fighting; playing, having fun, smiling.

"Gemma, what's wrong?" Laylen's voice was only a glitch in my head.

My voice was soft, barely audible. "I can remember some stuff...about my childhood...about Alex and I being friends."

"You remember? Like actually remember?"

I nodded. "They're real memories. And I can feel how I felt when I was there."

"Hurry, try to remember other things too," Laylen said encouragingly. "See if you can remember what happened before they took your emotions away—if anything was said that might tell us what Stephan is really planning to do with the star."

"Okay." I closed my eyes, concentrating on my thoughts that were floating back to me. The feelings I'd felt during them, the prickle making the connection. But no memories contained Stephan. Just Alex. Alex and me. Alex...

My eyes shot open, and for a moment, I just stood there, unable to react because...well, because it had happened again. I'd made myself go into a vision. God, what did I look like to Laylen? Was I just sitting there with my eyes closed? Or had I fallen out of the chair and onto the floor?

I shook my head. This was getting out of hand. If I didn't figure out how to control this power of mine, one day I was going to slip into a vision at the worst time possible. Like, say, when I was driving or something.

I shook my head. That was a scary thought.

Deciding I should focus on the vision, I pushed that thought aside. I was standing in a forest thick with trees, where I caught a glimpse of the tip of a grey stone castle peeking through spaces between the trees. I knew I had to be the forest that surrounded the lake—the lake that was the entrance to The Underworld.

It was bright outside, the sky a clear blue. As I started to move through the trees, heading for the castle, I wondered what I was supposed to see. Perhaps something with Stephan? Although, I sure hoped it wasn't the vision of my mother being forced into The Underworld. I had seen that more times than I ever wanted to.

But as a cool breeze swept through my hair and kissed at my cheeks, the impulse to head to the castle drifted away, and I found myself suddenly heading in the opposite direction, deeper into the forest.

I walked for what seemed like forever, my legs practically moving on their own, maneuvering me effortlessly past bushes, trees, and tipped over tree trunks. I swear it was like I knew where I was going without really knowing. If that made any sense.

As I'd just started to wonder just how far my legs were planning to take me, I came to a stop in front of a steep hill. I stared up at it skeptically, taking in its loose dirt and the steep incline. How the heck was I supposed to climb up it?

But I wasn't supposed to climb up it. That's what my thoughts were telling me. So instead, I moved to the side, walking at the bottom of the hill, searching for…well, I wasn't sure. But I hoped I'd know when I saw it.

After awhile, I began to get frustrated at the fact that this vision seemed pointless. I mean, why hadn't I seen anyone? And why did it feel like I had to put together a puzzle in order to understand the meaning of the vision? This had never happened before—usually I just watched the vision. So why was it different now?

127

Before I could conjure up an answer for these questions, I spotted something. A bush, budding with violet flowers at the foot of the hill. Violet flowers...hmm, it was ringing a bell.

I walked up to the bush and picked one of the violet flowers. The smell was intoxicating and caused my memories to spin in my head, little images of the countless times that I'd picked these flowers when I was a child. It also brought up a memory of this bush and that there was something behind it.

Yes, behind it.

I squatted down and examined behind the bush, letting my fingers dig through the damp soil as I inched my way up the steep side of the hill and around to the back of the bush.

My jaw dropped. A small hole had been dug into the hill. It was hidden by the violet bush so well that I wouldn't have seen it if I hadn't been looking for it. I grabbed a hold of the branches of the bush, the thorns cutting at the palms of my hands as I hoisted myself up to where I could see down into the dark hole. There was a ladder that led to...well I couldn't tell—I could only see a dirt floor. But there was a light on, glowing faintly from somewhere inside.

I took a deep breath and lowered my feet down to the top step of the ladder. Another deep breath and I started to climb down, my hands sweating against the cool metal. When my feet reached the floor, I immediately spun around. I wasn't going to lie, but I half expected a Death Walker to pop out and grab me. But no. What was there was probably more surprising than finding a Death Walker.

I was standing in a hollowed out room, the floors and walls made of dirt. There was an old wooden table pressed up against the back wall where a candle burned, the orange glow of the flame lighting up the tiny dirt room. Next to the table was a blue metal trunk, and right in front of trunk was me. Well, the younger me anyway, sitting on the dirt floor. Small, and around four years old, my violet eyes giving away that it was indeed me. Sitting across from me was a little boy with dark brown hair and bright green eyes.

Alex. I knew that now—my memories were able to make the connection.

"So, what do you think's going to happen?" Little Gemma asked. "After they take me away?"

Little Alex shook his head. "I don't know."

"Do you think we'll ever see each other again?" Little Gemma asked, her violet eyes wide with fear.

He nodded. "I promise we will, no matter what they say."

She looked terrified, tears bubbling up at the corner of her eyes, and I could actually feel her fear, worry, and sadness inside me, as if we'd connected. "Do you think Marco and Sophia will be nice to me?"

"How could they not?" Little Alex said. "No one could ever be mean to you."

Okay, well, that was the biggest bunch of crap I'd ever heard. But I think he actually meant it.

If only he knew.

As I stood there watching this peaceful scene between the younger Alex and me, I couldn't help but think how grown up we were acting for being so young. And look at us now, arguing all the time, lying to one another. It made this moment—although peaceful—almost painful to watch, because I knew that right after this happened everything would change. This Alex and Gemma would be no more.

"I have an idea," Alex said, pulling a small, silver pocket knife out of his pocket "How about you and I become blood brothers?"

Little Gemma scowled at him. "I'm not a boy."

Alex laughed. "Okay, how about blood friends?"

The tears in her eyes escaped down her cheeks. "What do I have to do to become one?"

"I'll make a little cut on my hand and on yours, and then we press them together and make a promise, okay?"

She looked wary. "Will it hurt?"

"Only for a minute."

She wiped the tears away from her cheeks and looked at Alex with confidence. "Okay, let's do it."

She gave her hand to Alex and he carefully made a small cut in the palm of her hand. She winced ever so slightly, but didn't put up a fuss. I glanced down at my hand, looking closer at the palm of it, and sure enough, right in the center there was a trace of a very thin, small white scar. Strange...I'd never noticed it before.

Alex made a small cut in his palm and then he raised his hand out in front of him. "Okay, put yours up to mine."

She did, and they pressed their palms together.

"*Forem*," Alex said. "Now you say it."

She took a deep breath. "*Forem.*"

Alex dropped his hand and so did she. "There, that's all it takes."

"But what does *forem* mean," Little Gemma asked.

"It means—"

Someone yelled from above. It was too muffled to understand exactly what the person yelled, but the deepness of the voice told me it belonged to a man.

The children's eyes went round, and Alex jumped to his feet. "We have to go," he said, holding out his hand to help Little Gemma to her feet.

"Do you think your dad will be mad at us," Little Gemma asked, panicking. "for disappearing?"

"I don't know." Alex sounded scared. "Let's just hurry up, okay?"

Little Gemma, all big eyed and sad, nodded. Then she glanced around at the little hideout, taking one last look as if she knew she'd never return. "Okay."

They climbed up the ladder, and I followed up after them. I stepped out from the behind the violet bush just in time to see Stephan waving his finger violently as he scolded Alex and me for wandering off. Then he marched them back through the trees, toward the castle. I didn't follow. I didn't want to see what happened next. I couldn't watch my soul get ripped away. I couldn't watch the little girl with the sad violet eyes be no more. So I sat down on the ground and shut my eyes, waiting to be yanked away.

Chapter 11

Something was wrong. Something was very, very wrong. I was stuck. Yes, stuck. Stuck inside the vision. Not only did this have me worried, but it also made me furious because I wanted to get back to Nicholas and the Ira crystal ball so I could start training to save my mom.

But nope. Instead, I was tromping through the forest, leaves and twigs and grass crunching loudly beneath my angry steps as I charged for the castle. I could see the grey stone tower of it sticking up from above the trees, like an arrow pointing to the sky, and I kept my eyes on it as I shoved my way through the bushes, finally stepping out of the forest with an ungraceful stumble.

The sky had shifted a deathly grey and the wind had begun to howl, causing the waves of the lake to roar up against the shore and leaves to whip through the air. Thunder boomed in the distance, and I could almost feel the terror waiting for me inside the castle.

With a loud breath I started up the hill, trying hard not to look at the lake, but it seemed to be calling me, taunting me with its whisper. I glanced over at it, and through the dark, murky water, I could make out faint white figures. Water Faeries. For a split second—and I mean, a split micro of a second—I actually contemplated going into the water, wondering if I did so, if the Water Faeries would take hold of me and drag me down to The Underworld where my mother was trapped.

But the idea that I would even consider this freaked me out just enough to jerk me back to reality, and I ran.

By the time I reached the front door of the castle, the air had gone ice-cold, and the clouds had started to rain down. I shivered in my wet clothes as I shoved the door open. Inside, the light was dusky, and the air wasn't much warmer. Extending out on each side of me was a hallway, and in front of me was a marble stairway curving up to the second floor. Three options to choose from— three places I could go. But how was I supposed to choose when I didn't even know what I was looking for?

With a shaky breath, I proceeded down the hallway to my right, my feet thudding against the rocky floor as I weaved my way further down it, feeling as though my feet were no longer in my control, as if my brain subconsciously knew where it was heading. I passed by doors, not bothering to check what was behind them, continuing to walk until the hallway hit a dead end. There was a set of heavy doors, and that was it. I knew without a doubt that this was where I was supposed to go.

With a trembling hand, I reached for the handle, but jerked back when thunder boomed from outside and scared the living daylights out of me. I took a breath, trying to calm my nerves, clicked the handle down and pushed open the door.

I'd seen this room before; instantly I was aware of that. There was a fireplace squaring the front wall, and a Persian rug spread across the stone floor. A single chair sat at the back of the room. This was the chair I hid behind in one of my visions; the one where I heard Demetrius and Stephan discussing how they had gotten rid of my mother and how they took care of me. There was no one in the room now, but I felt I needed to be here, because there was something I needed to see. But what?

Just as I thought it, a cold breeze whipped through my body and I gasped as I realized Stephan had walked right through me. My eyes widened. Holy crap. No one had ever walked through me in a vision. Yeah, I knew I was transparent to them and that I couldn't touch them, but actually walking through me...and Stephan of all people...it gave me the chills.

Stephan strolled up to fireplace; the bright orange glow of the flames reflected in his dark eyes. I walked toward him slowly, my legs shaking more and more the closer I got.

I didn't know what I was doing exactly, but I found myself staring at him—the man who'd taken away my life. His dark, soulless eyes, the scar on his left cheek, rough and jagged as if he'd been cut with a dull knife. When his gaze moved away from the fire and landed on me, I let out a gasp and quickly backed away.

His gaze did not move away from me. It locked on me like a target, making me tremble from head to toe. *He can't see you*, I told myself. But then I remembered how, during the first time I had accidently slipped into a vision—the one that had taken me to this very room—Stephan had acted like he could sense I was there. I started to freak. What if he knew I was here?

The door creaked open behind me, and I jumped to the side as Sophia and a man with light hair and brown eyes walked into the room. It was strange seeing Sophia fourteen years younger. She practically looked the same, though, except with fewer wrinkles. Her auburn hair was still done perfectly, and she was sporting the same 1950's TV sitcom look, wearing a cream colored dress with high-heeled shoes that matched.

"Where's the girl?" Stephan asked the man whose name I didn't know.

"She's coming," the man replied, bowing his head as if Stephan was some kind of king or something. "Marco is bringing her."

So this was it. This was what I was supposed to see— my last day as a normal little girl. Well, normal except for the whole carrying-a-star's-power-in-me thing.

This was absurd. I didn't want to see this.

I turned to leave, but the door opened again and Marco and Little Gemma walked in. My violet eyes were huge and I wondered, from the terrified expression on my face, if when this had all taken place I'd sensed something terrible was about to happen to me.

"Here she is," Marco said, handing me over to Stephan.

Stephan stared down at me with what only could be described as the most sinister look I've ever seen. "Hello, Gemma. Are you ready to go?"

Little Gemma shook her head. "No."

"Well, too bad." Stephan raised his eyes away from me and looked at Sophia. "Let's get this taken care of."

Seeing Marco and Sophia standing there, being a part of all of this, had me shaking with anger. Yeah, I already knew they played a part in this, but seeing it...It was sending me into a fit of rage.

Stephan told Little Gemma to go sit down in the chair, and with great reluctance she obeyed. I wondered if I ever thought about running. I wondered if I had any idea of what was about to happen to me.

Sophia stood in front of me as she hesitantly reached for my head. Little Gemma recoiled, pressing herself back into the chair. She knew something bad was about to happen. I could tell—I could feel it in my own bones.

To my surprise, Sophia pulled back her hand. "Are you sure this has to be done?" she asked Stephan. "She's just a little girl—Jocelyn's little girl."

"I understand that. But even before she disappeared, Jocelyn agreed that this must be done." Stephan's voice seemed to have a hypnotic effect on Sophia, like he had

137

lulled her into a calming state of mind. "We have to do this to save the world. If Gemma keeps..." His eyes wandered over to Little Gemma, who was listening intently. "Yes, we have to do this. Now get it done."

Looking extremely upset, Sophia turned back to me, and put her hands on my head. "Just relax, Gemma. It will be over in a moment."

Marco put his hand on Sophia's shoulder, comforting her. And I—and I mean the real Foreseer-traveling-me—stood gaping in horror at this scene. They didn't know. Marco and Sophia hadn't known what Stephan was really planning to do. They thought they had been doing the world good. All those horrible, torturous years of living with them, their cold and distant behavior, had all been because of Stephan's lies. I never thought I could hate someone so much. But, oh yeah, I did. The rage of prickles on my neck was letting me know that.

"Just a second," Stephan said suddenly. He moved toward Little Gemma and grabbed hold of a thin chain hanging around her neck—my locket.

"Hey," Little Gemma protested as Stephan yanked it off of her neck, snapping the chain. "My mom gave that to me."

Stephan gave her a look that I'm sure had to have sent a shiver down her spine, because it sent one down my own. "You'll get it back just as soon as Sophia is done."

Liar.

Putting her hands back on my head, Sophia muttered something under her breath, and her hands started to glow a bright gold. I gasped at the same time Little Gemma gasped, and I actually saw...I actually saw the life slip from her violet eyes, like a light switch had been flipped off.

Sophia pulled her hands away, the golden light fading from her hands. "There, it's done." She turned to Stephan. "Now what do we do?"

"Now you and Marco will take her to Afton, just like we talked about," Stephan said, seeming pleased. Umm...How could they not be suspicious of him? "And you'll make sure she stays this way. Understood?"

Sophia nodded. "Okay then."

As they all gathered to leave, I watched Little Gemma move robotically as Sophia guided her out of the room. I did not follow because I didn't want to follow. I wanted to go back and forget this ever happened. But deep down I knew only one of these things was possible.

I closed my eyes and willed myself to leave this place. And before I knew it, I was being yanked back.

Chapter 12

My eyes shot open and the first thing I saw was a dark blue ceiling. Then Laylen's worried face appeared above me.

What just...happened?" He spoke slowly as if he was too terrified to speak.

I started to sit up, but he put his hand on my shoulder, pinning me down. "Don't sit up until we figure out why you passed out."

"I didn't pass out," I told him. "I went into a vision."

Laylen's eyes widened just like I knew they would. "That's what happens when you go into vision without a crystal—you just black out."

I nodded, and then came the voice.

The most annoying voice ever.

"So you went into a vision?" Nicholas asked. "Without a crystal?"

"Ah, crap." I didn't even bother to say it in my head. I lifted Laylen's hand off of my shoulder and sat up, dizzy and getting a total head rush. I blinked a few times while I waited for the room to stop spinning. "Did I hit my head?" I asked Laylen. "When I blacked out?"

Laylen shook his head. "No, I caught you before you did. You scared the crap out of me though. One minute you were talking, and then next you were falling out of the chair."

"Nice," I muttered.

"Nice for you," Laylen teased. "But do you know how difficult it is to catch falling dead weight?"

I shook my head and got to my feet.

"So you can go into visions without a crystal ball?" Nicholas asked with intrigue.

Nicholas knowing about this was probably not a good thing. "No, I used a crystal ball," I lied.

"No you didn't—I'd have known if you had," he said with a smirk. "But nice try."

I rolled my eyes. "Whatever."

"So," Nicholas said, marveling at me as though I was the most fascinating thing he had ever laid eyes on. "You can go into a vision without the help of a crystal...fascinating."

Even though Alex wasn't here, I could picture him giving me a twenty minute lecture about my stupid mistake of letting Nicholas know about my uncommon Foreseer ability.

"I guess," I said, acting like it wasn't a big deal, when really it was since a Foreseer traveling into visions minus the crystal is a very unheard of—if not completely unheard—thing.

"How long have you known you could do it?" Nicholas asked with way too much interest.

I shrugged. "Not too long."

Nicholas's golden-eyed gaze practically burned into me, not in a bad way, but in a good way. Or should I say a bad/good way, because the guy had already shown way too much interest in me, and with the way he was staring at me, I had a feeling that his interest way going to increase. A lot.

"Do you know how rare that is?" Nicholas awed at me.

I gave a shrug. "I guess. I mean, Alex said there might be one other guy that could do it."

Nicholas's eyes devoured me. "That other guy is Dyvinius's younger brother, who's been a Foreseer for a really long time, and comes from a line of many, many powerful Foreseers. He isn't some girl who just got her Foreseer's mark only a couple of days ago. Do you know how unlikely it is for anyone to be able to do that? You would have to be..." He trailed off.

"Have to be what?" I asked, dying to hear what came at the end of that. What if Nicholas knew something about my little gift?

"Very powerful," he finished.

Well, crap. Powerful I was. Or at least I had a lot of power flowing around inside me. But Nicholas was not supposed to know this.

Play it cool, Gemma. "Yeah, well, if I am, then that's news to me."

"Really?" he said, and I could tell he wasn't buying it.

"Yeah, really," was all I could think of to say.

"So, weren't you supposed to be bringing back that Ira crystal ball with you?" Laylen interrupted, in an effort to sidetrack Nicholas.

"Yeah," Nicholas said, his eyes still fixed on me as he patted the pocket of his jeans. "I have it."

"Well, shouldn't you get to work then?" Laylen was trying really hard to direct Nicholas's attention away from me and my power, but Nicholas wasn't having any part of it. "I mean, I'm sure it's going to take awhile to train Gemma, or whatever it is you're supposed to be doing."

"Maybe..." The way Nicholas was looking at me made me want to crawl under the table and hide. "Maybe not."

"Regardless of how long it'll take, I think we should get started now," I told Nicholas. The sooner the better, at least for my mom's sake.

"Fine," he said. "Let's get started."

I was quickly catching on that Nicholas had the attention span of a child. We sat down on the living room floor, all séance-style, sitting cross-legged, facing one another, a regular, violet ribbon crystal ball placed between us as he taught me how to become a "better Foreseer" and control my seeing ability. But it was going to take forever because

143

he kept asking me questions. Questions that I wasn't sure how to answer.

"Why do you need to go to The Underworld?" he asked, before we'd really gotten anywhere with my training.

"Um..." I hesitated, not sure what to do. Lie. Probably not, since he was going to end up finding out when he went down to The Underworld with me. "To get my mother."

He nodded. "I met her once. Didn't she disappear quite a few years ago?"

"Fourteen years ago," I said absentmindedly, my hands hovering over the crystal ball.

"And that's where she ended up?" Nicholas asked interestedly. "In The Underworld?"

"Yeah." I stared down at the violet ribbons swirling inside the crystal. "That's where she ended up."

"How?"

Crap. "I...a...I don't know."

I worried he would ask more questions, but instead he picked up the Ira that was sitting on the floor to the side of us, the moss colored glass sparkling beautifully when it hit the light.

"Well, this should get us there," Nicholas said, twisting the Ira in his hands. "Just as long as we can get you to control your Foreseer power a little bit better, which shouldn't be too difficult considering you can enter visions without a crystal ball."

144

I didn't say anything.

Nicholas tossed the crystal ball in the air like it was a baseball. "So who's your father?"

Good question. "I'm not sure exactly."

He raised his eyebrows quizzically. "You're not sure? How's that possible?"

"When your mother refuses to tell anyone before she gets trapped in The Underworld," I replied, with a small amount of bitterness because I wished she'd have told someone. I mean, why did it have to be a secret? Who was he?

"So for all you know," Nicholas tossed the crystal ball in the air again, and it spun so quickly that when the light kissed it, it looked like a mere reflection. "Your father could have been some powerful Foreseer." He caught the crystal ball in his hands and let out a dramatic breath. "Your father could be Dyvinius."

I pulled a face. "Eww. Gross. He's like sixty."

Nicholas shrugged, his eyes glinting mischievously. "You never know. Some girls have a thing for older guys. I mean, how much older is Alex than you?"

I glared at him. "First of all, I don't have a thing for Alex. And second of all, he's only two years older than me. I don't think that qualifies him as an 'older guy.'"

"You know your second reason kind of contradicts your first. If you didn't like him then why would it matter whether two years was a lot or not?"

"I don't like Alex," I assured him, but my inner conscience laughed at me.

"Whatever you say." Nicholas balanced the crystal ball on the black and white checkerboard floor. "But I think you're lying. And I think two years could be a lot if you think about it."

"How do you figure?"

"Well, for starters he's not even considered a teen anymore."

I rolled my eyes at the silliness of his reason. "Well, how old are you?"

"The same age as you," he replied, being evasive.

Faeries are tricky. "And how old would that be?" I asked, playing his game.

He smiled slyly, as if he knew what I was up to. "Eighteen, of course."

Of course. "Can we just get back to you teaching me, please?"

He stared at me for a moment with a slightly irritated expression. "Sure, that is unless you want to try our kiss again." When I shook my head, he rolled the regular crystal ball—my "training ball," as he'd explained to me earlier—toward me. I scooted back a little, concerned that if it touched me I would instantly be pulled in.

"So, until we can get you going into and out of visions that you're intentionally trying to go into, there's really no point in us trying to travel into The Underworld because it's one of the most difficult places to get to," Nicholas explained, finally getting to the point. "One false move and we could end up in the bottom of the lake, where we'd either drown or get taken to The Underworld by the Water Faeries which means we'd be prisoners there—we have to go in a specific way or we're in trouble. Got it?"

I nodded. "So how does it work, exactly? I mean we enter The Underworld through that ball." I nodded at the moss colored *Ira* crystal ball. "Then what? I mean how do we get the Queen to let my mom go? And how do we get her to let us go? Wouldn't we just end up prisoners as well?"

Nicholas shook his head. "No. The Queen can't keep us there—it's the law that comes with using the Ira—part of the reason the Queen hates it so much. We can show up whenever we want and leave whenever we please. Of course, no one really wants to show up there."

Law. I remembered Alex mentioning these laws once—about him having to let Nicholas take me to the City of Crystal.

I frowned. "This all sounds kind of difficult."

"It will be," he said, not giving me any amount of comfort. "It'll take a lot of power and control to pull it off, and I have no idea how you're going to get the Queen to let your mother go."

Whoa, neither did I. Why hadn't I thought of this problem before? I guess I would have to talk to Laylen about it and hope he knew a way. "Okay, so to practice for this extremely difficult task we're going to try and do, we

147

have to do what exactly? Practice going into visions through a regular crystal ball? I thought Dyvinius said going into visions could shift the world or something like that."

"If we don't see the vision correctly, it could," he said. "But we'll have to make sure we do."

This entire thing sounded so risky, and I wondered if I was being selfish for taking such a risk to save my mom. It could end up costing the world a lot if I messed up. But my mom might have answers that could save the world from whatever Stephan was planning. So it was kind of a lose-lose situation.

I stared down at the crystal ball, the violet ribbons twisting and turning in the sparkling water. "So what do I do first?"

He tapped his fingers on his lips. "First, I think we should take a break and get something to eat."

I stared at him, unblinking. "Take a break and get something to eat? We haven't even done anything yet."

He considered this with an amused look. "Yes, but I think it's important that we eat something before we go, so we're not weak from our hunger."

I felt like banging my head on the wall. "Tell me what you want to eat, and I'll go get it."

"What I want...hmmm." His golden eyes twinkled. "What I want is to go out with you and eat somewhere."

"I can't go anywhere," I said.

He gave me a curious look. "Why not?"

148

Well, for starters because I couldn't leave the house. And not just because I knew Alex would freak out if I did. No. There were way more risks I would be taking if I went out into public than just pissing off Alex. For one thing, after what happened with the vampires last night, I had a feeling that if I ran into any of them and they recognized me—which, let's face it, they would (hello, my eyes are violet)—then I'd be in some serious trouble. I also had to worry about running into a Death Walker or Stephan. And those were not risks I was willing to take just so I could leave the house to get something to east with faerie boy.

"Because I just can't, okay?" I got to my feet, dusting off the back of my legs. "If you're really hungry, I can go into the kitchen and get you something."

"What I want is to go out with you." His tone was light, but his eyes were determined.

"Look," I said, losing patience. "I really want to get this done because the longer it takes you to train me, the longer my mom's stuck in that godforsaken place."

For a brief second, and I mean a very brief second, I thought I saw the mischievous sparkle leave his eyes, like he actually understood my pain. But it happened so swiftly, I wasn't even sure it happened.

"Fine." He leaned back on his elbows, looking at me mischievously again. "We can eat here. Besides it's better that we eat here anyway. That way we get more alone time. Just you and me and this quiet, empty room."

149

I shook my head and, without saying another word, I left the room to go get him something to eat.

In the kitchen, I found Laylen standing at the counter, chopping onions on a chopping board. When he caught sight of me, he stopped mid chop. "Wow. You look really annoyed."

I went over beside him and dropped my head on the counter. "Nicholas is driving me crazy. He just keeps asking questions, and then when we finally get to the part where we should start practicing, he says he's hungry, and we should go out and get something to eat."

Laylen gave a soft laugh and started chopping onions again. "Yeah, that sounds like Nicholas. He's always been a little..."

I lifted my head up. "Annoying?"

Laylen laughed again. "I was going to say difficult, but yeah, annoying works. When he was younger, he went through this phase where he would answer every question with a question."

"That sounds fun," I said sarcastically.

Laylen shrugged, cutting the onion again. "He can't really help it—it's a faerie thing. They have this way about them where they can trick you into doing things—or saying things that you shouldn't. That's why you should be very careful around him."

"Yeah, Alex warned me about that." I fanned the front of my nose as Laylen dumped the chopped onions into a skillet and the smell over-took me. "And he told me not to take my necklace off."

Laylen scooted the onions around in the pan with a spatula. "This is probably the only time where I'm going to have to agree with Alex. You should be careful around him." He lowered his voice. "You can't let Nicholas know about the star."

I nodded. "I won't."

The pan sizzled and it reminded me I was supposed to be getting Nicholas something to eat. "So...what do faeries eat?"

Laylen busted up laughing.

I gave him a mystified look. "What's so funny?"

It took him a second to gather himself. "Sorry. But it's just so funny." He laughed again. "What do faeries eat?"

"Hey, I don't know much about this stuff," I said, half joking and half defensive. "I mean, for all I know they could eat leaves or something."

He cocked an eyebrow at me. "Leaves?"

I shrugged. "They live in forests, don't they?" At least in most of the faerie themed books I had read they did.

Still laughing, he wiped a few stray tears from his eyes. "Leaves."

"Oh, shut up." I gave him a playful shove. He continued to laugh, so I changed the subject. "How did Aislin take it when you told her about Alex having to go to the City of Crystal?"

That stopped his laughing. "I haven't told her yet." I opened my mouth to say that he probably should—that it would be worse the longer he kept it from her—but before I could say anything, he said, "I'll tell her. I promise, just as soon as she's done helping Adessa with her store. I think it'll be better if I tell her when no one else is around."

"Okay, well, I guess I'll get back to my *training*." I turned to leave.

"Don't forget your leaves," Laylen called out with a chuckle.

I ended up making Nicholas and myself a sandwich. We didn't really speak to each other while we sat on the floor and ate, and I had a feeling something was bothering him, but didn't feel comfortable enough to ask. Besides, even if I did, he probably wouldn't tell me. At least tell me the truth, anyway.

When we were finished eating and had slid our plates out of the way, Nicholas put the crystal ball back between us.

"So, the first thing that's going to happen is I'm going to go into a vision with you," Nicholas explained, spinning the crystal ball like a top. I wondered how he could touch it and not be pulled in. "What we want is for you to eventually be able to go into a controlled vision by yourself, gracefully and without any bumps."

What did he mean by gracefully—without any trips or injuries? "Okay, so how do we get me to be able to do that?"

"With practice." He shrugged. "Seeing visions is like riding a bike. The more you practice, the better you get."

But I didn't know how to ride a bike. At least I don't think I did. No resurfacing memories had contained me riding a bike. "Okay, well how much practice is it going to take for me to be able to be graceful and bump free?"

His mouth curved up into a smile. "Well, if I had my way, it would take a very, very long time. But in all actuality, with you being as powerful as you are, it shouldn't take that long."

Thank God. "So where do we begin?"

He held out his hand. "First, give me your hand so we can go in together." With reluctance, I took his hand, his skin clammy and cold against mine. "Now we need a simple vision to go into. I think it would probably be best if you just thought of a memory. Maybe something from your childhood."

That was not simple by any means. "Does it have to be from my childhood?"

He shook his head. "As long as it's simple, it doesn't really matter."

"Okay…." I searched for something simple to picture, but all I could see was the madness that filled up my life throughout the years.

153

"Gemma, place your hand on the crystal ball," Nicholas instructed.

My heart raced as I tried to think of a memory—any memory—that was simple.

"Gemma," Nicholas repeated. *"Put your hand on the crystal."*

I was still searching as I reached out and placed my hand on top of the crystal ball. A brief glimpse of me and my mother sitting in a field flashed through my mind, and I thought I had it.

Then I was yanked in, falling down the tunnel, toward the light, Nicholas still holding my hand. When I reached the bottom—and very ungracefully I might add—I realized I hadn't had the memory like I'd thought. In fact, if there was a complete opposite of where I was supposed to be taking us, this would be it.

The vision I was standing in was not of my past, but of the future. And not my future, but the world's future. How did I know this? Because I was standing on the main street of Vegas, beside the massive pirate ship I remembered seeing during my first drive into the busy city. But the busy city was no longer a busy city. It was dead quiet. Not a single soul was in sight. Even more disturbing was the layer of ice that covered everything. Just as if a million Death Walkers had marched through here and breathed their Chill of Death on everything in sight.

Just like they would if the portal opened up.

Chapter 13

I stood there silently in the empty streets that had once been packed with buzzing cars and people. The air was as cold as death. My breath puffed out in a cloud. I was shivering and shaking, but I wasn't sure if that was from the cold or from my nerves. My stomach felt like it had been punched, the wind knocked out of me. Shock was seeping in, and I'm pretty sure I would have stood there in silence forever if Nicholas hadn't brought me back to reality.

"Gemma." His voice was soft—cautious—as if he could sense something was up.

I glanced down at his hand still holding mine, and then I looked up at him. "What?"

"Are you okay?" he asked. "You've been standing there staring at whatever it is you're seeing for over five minutes now."

I swallowed hard. "I...um..." I didn't know what to say to him.

"What is it?" Nicholas glanced around, even though he couldn't see anything. It is a rule of seeing visions: only the seer can see the vision. To Nicholas everything looked blank and empty.

Lucky him.

I wanted to erase what I was looking at from my mind. Wipe it away forever.

Even though it was day, the sky was gray, and blanketed by a frosty sheet of ice. A gust of wind swept up, chilling the back of my legs. I turned around, staring at the frozen, vacant streets. There were no cars. No people. Nothing. It was as if everyone had known what was coming and had tried to take cover somewhere.

"Gemma?" Nicholas said. I'd almost forgotten he was there. "What's going on?"

I shook my head, trying to pull myself together. Nicholas could not know what I was seeing, that was for sure. "It's nothing."

He raised his eyebrows at me. "If it's nothing, then why do you look like you just saw someone die?"

I swallowed the lump in my throat, taking my hand out of his. "No. It's nothing like that. It's just that...," *Think, Gemma, think.* "It's just that there's nothing here. We're just in the middle of the desert, so I don't get it."

"Well, I told you to think of something simple, didn't I? So I guess it worked."

I gave a shrug. "I guess, but I thought—"

A loud shriek shattered the air and cut me off. The sound echoed through the empty streets, vibrating the ice like an earthquake. Every limb in my body seized up as I became aware of what that shriek belonged to. And as the fog crept out from a nearby building, swirling its way toward me, I started to panic, even though I knew I couldn't be seen by them.

"I-I think we should go," I stuttered.

Nicholas frowned at me. "Gemma, where did you take us?"

"I-I already told you," I stammered, my eyes locked on the fog crawling toward my feet, "we're in the middle of the desert."

"No, we're not," he said, following my gaze. "What do you see?"

"Nothing," I said as a cluster of Death Walkers emerged from the glass doors of a nearby building. *Stay calm. Stay calm.* "Can we just go back to the house? *Please.*"

Nicholas watched me, the weight of his sandy eyes nearly burning into my skin. "You know whatever's out there can't harm you, right?"

I looked at the Death Walkers, the glow of their yellow eyes reflecting across the ice like fireflies, their black cloaks trailing along behind them with a *swoosh*. "Yeah, I know, but I..."

"You what?"

The Death Walkers were so close now that I could make out their faces—the rotting flesh, the bits of and pieces of bone showing through their skin like a corpse. The sight almost made me gag.

I blinked my eyes a few times, trying to blink us away, but it didn't work. "Nicholas, *please*," I begged. "Take us back."

Nicholas tapped his finger on his lip, glancing in the direction of the Death Walkers. "I don't think so. Whatever's scaring you, I think you should face it. It'll be good practice for when we go to The Underworld."

I glared at him, my heart thumping in my chest, which seemed to match the thumping of the Death Walkers' march. The closer they got, the more the fog twisted around us, spinning in circles, clouding my vision in a menacing way. Closer, closer, closer they marched. I held my breath as they went by me, one by one, glaciating the air with their chill. My breath rose out in a puff, as my teeth chattered. I held as still as a statue, my muscles tensing up when one of the Death Walker's shoulders went through mine.

"Gemma," Nicholas said, oblivious to what was going on. "What are you doing?"

"Be quiet." I breathed through my teeth, and then tried not to freak out when one of the Death Walker's glowing eyes landed right on me.

I held my breath until they all had passed and disappeared around the corner of the street. I didn't relax though. I wouldn't relax until we got the heck out of here.

I let out my breath, about to ask if we could go, but I stopped when I caught sight of someone else emerging from the building. Stephan. And beside him was Demetrius. Without even thinking, I jumped toward Nicholas, bumping my shoulder into his.

He grabbed his shoulder. "What are you—"

"Shhh," I hissed.

Standing out in the middle of the icy street, I felt vulnerable with Stephan and Demetrius walking toward me. Demetrius's Death-Walker-like cloak swished behind him, and Stephan, dressed all in black, held something shiny and silver in his hand...The Sword of Immortality.

"I wish you wouldn't carry that around," Demetrius said to Stephan. "It makes me nervous."

"It makes me nervous when I'm not carrying it around," Stephan replied. "It's the one thing that could end all of this." He gestured around at the frozen, desolate street.

"Yes, but who is left to get a hold of it?" Demetrius asked with a laugh. "The ice killed everyone off who was still left around."

"There are a few Keepers around who might try." Stephan held up the sword, twisting it in his hand as he examined it, the jagged blade hitting the light sharply. "Do you remember when Octavian made this after the vision was first seen?"

Demetrius laughed. "He was so convinced that if he created it, I would never be able to pull off what he'd seen. Too bad for him, he didn't see you."

"Well, that was the doing of my parents." Stephan touched the jagged scar on his left cheek. "Thinking if they cut off the mark, it would change things—change who I was. But they couldn't change the blood that runs through my veins, could they?"

159

The scar on Stephan's cheek was a mark that had been cut off by his parents? I cringed at the idea, and then cringed again at the idea of what kind of mark would make a parent cut their child's face just to get rid of it.

Stephan and Demetrius were close to Nicholas and me now, their footsteps hitting the ice with a dull thud.

"The Mark of Malefiscus is a gift," Demetrius told Stephan. "My parents seemed to understand this."

"Yes, but your parents weren't Keepers," Stephan replied bitterly. "Mine were. And to have a child who bore the Mark of Malefiscus was a disgrace in their eyes."

"Malefiscus's mark is not a disgrace," Demetrius said to Stephan as they walked by us, and I had to turn so that I could keep my eyes on them. "It's a gift. We have been chosen since birth—since before birth—to free him and everyone else who was bound by his sentencing."

"And now we have," Stephan said thoughtfully as he lightly traced his finger down his scar.

"Yes, and now we have," Demetrius agreed.

"Gemma," Nicholas said so abruptly that he scared the crap out of me and I screamed.

I flung my hand over my mouth, breathing heavily. And that's when it happened. Stephan stopped, his head tilting to the side as he glanced over his shoulder.

"Nicholas," I whispered. "You need to get us out of here. Right now."

Nicholas gave me a look, and I could tell immediately that it was going to be a pain in the butt to get him to cooperate. "I don't know about that," he said, "I think before I do, you should explain to me what's got you freaked out."

I looked at Stephan, who seemed to be looking right at me. Fear pulsated through my body. "I will, okay, just as soon as we get back."

Nicholas dithered, and I wanted to smack him right across his pretty-boy faerie face. "I don't know. I kind of like being out here alone with you."

"Nicholas," I shouted. "Get us out of here. Now!" Glancing over at Stephan, I saw he was walking toward us, swiftly moving across the ice.

"What are you doing?" Demetrius called out. Stephan didn't reply, still heading at us, as if he knew we were there. But how could he? It wasn't how visions worked.

I grabbed Nicholas by the arm, my eyes pleading. "There is someone in this vision that I'm pretty sure can either see or sense that we're here. And if he can, then it's very, very bad."

I thought he'd argue with me and say that no one in visions could see the vision seer, but instead, to my surprise, he grabbed my hand, looking rather anxious. "Okay, let's go."

I cast one last glance at Stephan, who was now charging at us full speed with the Sword of Immortality clutched in his hand. He was so close that I could see the darkness in his eyes and the roughness of his scar.

161

Chapter 14

"Holy...crap!" I was standing back in Adessa's living room, but the fear of what had just happened still lingered in my body and had me gasping for air.

"Who was it?" Nicholas asked quickly and with very little patience. "Who was in the vision?" He still had hold of my hand and I tried to pull it out of his grip, but he tightened, refusing to let go. "Gemma." His tone was a warning as he put a hand on each of my shoulders and looked me directly in the eyes. "Tell me who it was that could sense our presence. It's important."

"Why?" I asked. "Why would anyone be able to sense we were there?"

"Because..." He paused, eyeing me over. "Because it means the vision has already been seen or told to the person who is in the vision."

For some reason this did not surprise me. I knew Stephan had been told visions of the future and the world at its end. It was what had started the whole star thing. A simple vision of the end of the world and how one star's energy could save it. Although, that particular story was probably not accurate, but at one point I thought it was.

"So…How does that make it so they can sense me?"

"Because they've been told by another Foreseer that a Foreseer will be present at that moment. It wasn't like he could see you or anything, just that he could sense you were there."

"So is it bad?" I asked, my shoulders sliding out from under his hands as I took a step back. "That he knew I was there?"

Nicholas shook his head in puzzlement. "What is it with you? There must be something extraordinary about you." He shook his head again, watching me with intense eyes. "First you can go into visions without a crystal ball and now you're going into other people's visions…It's amazing."

I tried to play cool. "It's not that amazing."

"Yes, it is."

I searched my mind for a way to move off this subject since my being "extraordinary" or whatever had to do with the star, which I was supposed to be keeping a secret from Nicholas.

"I've got to go ask Laylen something," I announced and started for the doorway.

He caught me by the arm and the smell of lilacs and rain blasted my nostrils. "You didn't tell me who it was."

"Who what was?" I played dumb.

"The person who could sense you in the vision."

"I...um, don't know who he was. He was just some guy." Man, sometimes I could be a real mastermind at lying.

Not.

Nicholas gave me a doubting look. "You don't know who he was?"

I shook my head, and then tugged my arm away from him. "I have to talk to Laylen," I said, then bolted out of the room.

Nicholas didn't follow me, which I thought was kind of weird. I mean, I had left suspiciously, but for some reason he stayed in the living room. This was a good thing, though, because I needed to talk to Laylen about what had happened. And not just about Stephan sensing me. No, I was more interested in the mark Demetrius and Stephan were talking about. And the name...Malefiscus...I think that's what they had said.

I found Laylen alone in his bedroom, lying on the bed, reading a book. He had his head down; his eyes glued to the pages.

"Hey," I said, sounding breathless because I had run all the way up the stairs.

He looked up from his book. "Hey, what's...." His bright blue eyes went huge when he caught sight of me. "What happened? You look upset."

165

I nodded. "Something bad happened when we went into a vision. And Nicholas is getting suspicious that there might be something wrong with me."

"You think he knows about the star's power?" Laylen said, setting his book down, and then climbing off of the bed.

I shook my head. "I don't think he knows what exactly it is, just that there's something...different about me." I almost choked on the word "different."

"Okay, well as long as he doesn't know exactly what it is, then I think we're okay." Laylen paused. "Although, I'm not really sure it's so great that he knows about your special Foreseer thing."

I nodded in agreement, but then shook my head, remembering I had bigger problems to discuss than Nicholas. "There's something else I need to tell you about. It's what I just saw in the vision."

Laylen walked over and stood in front of me. "Which is what?"

I shivered as I remembered the sight of what the Death Walkers' cold had done to a once bright and sunshine-filled city. "The end of the world."

It got so quiet, I swear, I could hear our hearts beating. Or at least mine, anyway. I wasn't sure if Laylen had a beating heart or not.

"The end of the world," Laylen said, aghast.

"Covered in ice," I added with another shiver.

166

His blue eyes went wider than they already were. "Then the portal opens up."

I nervously glanced out into the hall, and then shut the door. "At least from what I saw it does."

Laylen went over and sank down on the bed. "So that's it then. The portal opens and the world ends."

I sat down on the bed beside him. "I guess...unless we change it...somehow."

"How, though?" Laylen's eyes were still wide, staring off into nothingness. "How are we supposed to stop something that's already been seen? It's not supposed to work that way."

"It's not?" I questioned. "Because I've been told for the last few days that my whole life has been centered on trying to do just that."

"Yeah, but are we even sure about that anymore? I mean, no one knows for sure why Stephan really wants the star's power? Or maybe," Laylen turned to me, "he doesn't want it at all. Maybe he's trying to get rid of it."

I tapped my fingers on my knee, thinking. "If he didn't want it, though, wouldn't he have just killed me or something to get rid of it, instead of sending me away to live with Marco and Sophia? Why keep me alive? And put all that effort into keeping me unemotional? What'd be the point?"

"The point." He twisted his lip ring from side to side as he contemplated this. "Who knows what the point is. This is Stephan we're talking about."

167

I thought about the vision, and Demetrius and Stephan's conversation. "Who's Malefiscus?"

Laylen's jaw just about hit the floor. "Where did you hear that name?"

"In the vision," I said. The horrified look on Laylen's face caused goose bumps to sprout on my skin even though it was nowhere near cold. "Demetrius and Stephan were talking and they—"

"Wait a minute," Laylen cut me off. "*They* were there—both of them were there?"

I nodded. "Yeah. I was in Vegas, only it didn't look like Vegas anymore. There was ice covering everything and there was no one in sight. Well, no one except a few Death Walkers and Stephan and Demetrius. They were talking to each other and Demetrius said something about Stephan's scar once being the Mark of Malefiscus, but his parents cut it off when..." The look on Laylen's face made me trail off. "What's wrong?"

Laylen looked utterly shocked. "So what you're saying is that the scar on Stephan's face used to be the Mark of Malefiscus?"

"Yeah, but what's the mark for?" I asked. "I mean, who gets it?"

The fear in Laylen's eyes had me worried. Well, more worried than I already was after seeing the world frozen at its end. "It's the mark of evil."

168

Why did that revelation not surprise me? "So Stephan has the mark of evil. No wonder he's probably trying to make the world end."

Laylen shook his head. "No, Gemma. The Mark of Malefiscus isn't just the mark of evil. It stands for so much more. Malefiscus is also a man." He shifted uncomfortably on the bed, and then leaned in so we were huddled together, and dropped his voice. "There's this story that's told among the Keepers, kind of like a bedtime story."

"A bedtime story," I repeated, dumbfounded. "The Keepers tell bedtime stories about a man who's evil?"

"An evil man the Keepers destroyed," he explained. "But anyway, the story goes that Altamium, the very first Keeper to ever be born, fathered two sons—twin sons, Hektor and Nikon. Apparently, right before they were born, a Foreseer told a vision about these sons. He said that one of the sons would grow up to be a great warrior, and the other would grow up to be jealous of the other one. And that jealousy would become so great that it would turn into hatred. Eventually, that hatred would bare a mark no one had ever seen before. The mark of evil. Or the Mark of Malefiscus, as Nikon would later name it after he changed his name to Malefiscus, which means evil in Latin."

"So the vision came true?"

"Yes, the vision came true." Laylen took a deep breath, loud enough that I could hear the shakiness it held.

169

"And if what you saw is true, then it means Stephan bears the Mark of Malefiscus, which isn't good at all."

"Yeah, that is bad, but I think we already knew he was evil without the mark, didn't we?"

"No, it's a lot worse than him just being evil." Laylen leaned in even closer to me, his weight sinking the bed in, causing his leg to bump into mine. "After Nikon—or Malefiscus—got the mark, he began causing havoc all over the place. He joined forces with the Death Walkers, who up until then had been living in hiding for hundreds and hundreds of years." Laylen shook his head. "And things continued to get worse. The number of Death Walkers seemed to be multiplying and taking to the streets. It would have probably ended up being the ice age all over again if it wasn't for Hektor."

"Malefiscus's brother?" I asked, checking to make sure that I was keeping up.

Laylen nodded. "Hektor eventually defeated Malefiscus, but couldn't bring himself to kill him, so the Keepers sentenced him to a place...I'm not really sure where it was. In fact, I think no one knows, which was part of the point...so no one can find him and set him free again."

"*Can't* find him? But what would it matter if anyone found him—he'd be dead by now, right?"

Laylen leaned in more, his knee pressing against mine. "Right before Malefiscus was sentenced, he found a way to become immortal, at least that's what people say."

"How did he make himself immortal?" I asked, fully involved in his story.

Laylen slowly shook his head. "As far as anyone knows, becoming immortal isn't possible unless someone becomes like a Black Angel or a Death Walker or a...vampire."

I glanced down at Laylen's forearm, where the black symbols of his mark of immortality were tattooed. "Did he actually get the mark of immortality?"

"I don't know...I'm not sure if my parents left out parts of the story to sugar-coat it for me, or if there are parts that even they didn't know about." A look of deep thought passed over Laylen's face.

"Well, if Stephan has the same mark as Malefiscus, then what does that mean?"

"It means Stephan has to be a descendant of him, at least he most likely has to be. There are very rare cases where someone gets a mark without being a descendant from someone with the same mark." He paused, glancing down at the mark on his arm. "Well, except for the mark of immortality that is."

We sat there in silence, and I wondered if he was thinking about his mark of immortality. I was thinking about a million different things that ranged from my end-of-the-world vision, to the Mark of Malefiscus, to my Foreseer's mark and how I didn't seem to be a descendant of a Foreseer. Well, at least that I knew of. Since I didn't know who my father was, it was still possible that I might be.

171

"So Stephan could be a descendant from the most evil man that has ever walked the earth?" I asked with a shiver.

"If he is," Laylen said, the heaviness of the situation ringing in his voice. "That would explain why he is controlling the Death Walkers. Those who have the Mark of Malefiscus have control over them. And…"

"And what?" I pressed.

"And it would give him a reason to open the portal." Laylen's eyes pressed the gravity of the situation. "And why he'd want to try to end the world," Laylen added. "It's in his blood."

Silence dripped by. The house was quiet and I wondered what Aislin and Adessa and Nicholas were doing, and in a way I wished I were them and didn't know about all of this.

"Do you think my mom knows Stephan had the mark?" I asked quietly.

"I think your mom may know even more than that." Laylen's bright blue eyes never left me.

Something else was bothering me. "Laylen, do you think it's possible that Stephan… that he…," I let out a breath. "That Stephan wants to use the star's power for something bad? That maybe that's why he's been keeping me around all this time. Do you think he might be using it to open the portal?"

Something about the way Laylen was looking at me made my heart stop.

"I don't know," he said, quickly looking away from me.

"Laylen, please just tell me if you know something," I begged. "You always tell me stuff. Don't be like Alex."

He turned his head back toward me. "The thought has crossed my mind that maybe...that maybe that's *exactly* what he's doing."

I felt like I'd been kicked in the stomach. Even though I had thought it myself, it was a lot harder to deal with hearing him say it aloud. That I could be carrying something around inside me that could end the world. That my very existence could be bad. "How long have you thought this?"

"Since Aislin and I showed up at the Hartfield cabin back in Colorado—when Stephan showed up with the Death Walkers, but yet he didn't try to kill you. He wants you alive for some reason. And that reason I'm sure isn't a good one."

I nodded. *Keep it together. Keep it together.* "Okay...okay." I was trying very hard not to fall apart. But at the same time, how could I not fall apart?

"Are you okay?" Laylen asked, concerned.

I had to force myself to speak and was startled by the hollow tone my voice had taken on—something I hadn't heard it do in awhile. "Yeah, I'm fine."

He looked like he wanted to say more, but I decided to stop him, because honestly, I didn't want to talk about how I was feeling at the moment. Or about the fact that the

173

prickle was poking at the back of my neck, releasing an abundance of worry and panic at a level I had never felt before.

"I think I better get back to Nicholas and my training." I stood up from the bed.

"Gemma." Laylen got to his feet. "Are you sure you're okay?"

"Yeah." My voice sounded numb. "I just need to get back, if for nothing else, so I can get into The Underworld to save my mom. Then maybe we'll get actual answers, instead of just a bunch of guesses."

"Okay…" Laylen watched me as if I were a scared mental patient who was about to go off the deep end, and I left the room with a giant lump swelling in my throat.

Chapter 15

Nicholas was turning out not to be so bad to be around. Let me stress the not *so* bad part, because he still got under my skin more times than he didn't. This could have been because, after what Laylen had said to me about him thinking that I just might be carrying around something that would end the world, I really just didn't care anymore how Nicholas was. I mean, why waste time getting worked up over a guy who was a little bit friendly? Okay, well a lot friendly, but at least he was friendly. And yeah, he did smell strongly of flowers and rain and forest, which was kind of a strange smell to be coming off of a guy, but he was a faerie, and these little things seemed like they might just be faerie traits, and something he probably couldn't help.

At least that's what I was telling myself.

It'd been two days of excruciating training, falling into visions, blinking out of visions. Fortunately, I hadn't dropped down into anything world-ending, because I really didn't want to see that again. In fact, I hadn't dropped into anything important at all, which was okay with me.

I needed a break from seeing things I didn't want to see, like the world frozen over by ice, my soul getting removed, and me curled up in a little ball with my eyes looking very empty.

It was too much.

After my crazy little episode I had during the world-ending vision, Nicholas had decided to take control over where we went for now, and all these places had ended up being fairly dull places so far. What Nicholas didn't know—but desperately wanted to know—was what I had seen when I dropped into the end-of-the-world vision. He pressed me to tell him for over an hour before finally giving up.

And now here Nicholas and I were, sitting on the black and white tile floor of Adessa's living room, with the shimmering, violet ribbon crystal ball balanced between us.

"So where's the next place we're going?" I asked Nicholas.

He was wearing a bright green shirt, and a pair of dark blue jeans. Each night, after everyone went to bed, he'd leave, and when he would return in the morning he would be all cleaned up and ready to go.

"Hmmm…." He tapped his finger on his lips, which he almost always did when I asked him a question. "That's a good question."

"And it's a question only you can answer," I pointed out, crossing my legs.

176

"Maybe...or maybe not," he wavered. "I think maybe it is time for you to try and pick the place again."

I shuddered as I remembered the end-of-the-world vision I had thrown us into the last time I'd tried to control going into one on my own.

Nicholas must have sensed something was wrong with me because he said, "If you don't practice going into and out of visions on your own then you're going to be no use when it comes to trying to go into The Underworld. Besides, practicing might help you when you drift off into one of your visions without a crystal ball."

Okay, time to change the subject. "Okay." I took a deep breath and extended my hand out to Nicholas, my other hand hovering over the crystal ball. "Then I'll try again."

"Do you have an idea where you're going to take us?" Nicholas asked, taking hold of my hand and unnecessarily intertwining our fingers.

"Yeah, I have an idea." I shut my eyes and brushed my fingers across the cold glass of the crystal ball.

Yeah, it might have been a stupid idea, but I figured it was the best way to get an answer to my current problem. I mean, how bad could it end up being? I had already seen the world at its end, and there weren't many things that were worse than seeing that.

But as inexperienced as I was, I knew I was taking a risk, especially since Nicholas had warned me before that when we actually tried to enter The Underworld through the Ira, many things could go wrong.

I needed to know, though, how I was going to do it—how I was going to get my mother out of The Underworld. Because I had no idea, and neither did Laylen. When I had asked him how I was supposed to get my mom out of there, Laylen had looked as perplexed as I felt. And asking Alex was not an option, at least not until he got back, and his release date hadn't been determined yet.

It was important that I knew what kind of bargaining tool we would use to get the Queen to let my mom go, and the only way I could think of to do this was to see what I would do. Of course, I wasn't sure if it was going to work or not. For all I knew, the vision would show me that I would fail—that I don't free my mom.

But I had to try.

I honestly wasn't sure whether I had pulled it off; as I had taken us through the crystal ball, all I kept thinking was: The Underworld, my mom's freedom, the Queen. But even after I landed with a great stumble and a bump of my elbow, I still wasn't sure I was in the right place.

"So where'd you take us?" Nicholas asked, rubbing his hands together excitedly. "Somewhere good I hope."

"Um..." I stared down the tunnel we were standing in, the walls dripping with musty water and moss tracing the cracks in the dirt floors. Was this The Underworld? "I think I..." I tried to think of something to tell him—and then I thought, you know what, who cares. We were here so I might as well tell him the truth. "I think we might be in The Underworld."

He was not happy. And I found out right then and there that faeries can get very angry very fast.

"You what?" He was struggling to contain himself.

"I think I took us to The Underworld," I repeated, feeling like I might need to duck down and take cover.

He opened his mouth and sputtered a bunch of incoherent words and then kicked the wall of the tunnel, causing bits and pieces of mud and dirt to crumble to the floor. He was pissed, and I totally got that, since he had told me a bunch of times to take us to a simple place. But then a shriek ricocheted through the air, and all of my attention went to solving where the noise had come from.

"What's wrong?" Nicholas followed my gaze, even though he couldn't see anything. "Is it a Water Faerie?"

I squinted through the blackness of the tunnel, trying to see what was at the end of it—something white, but I couldn't make out precisely what it was.

"I don't know..." I moved forward, straining my vision. "Something..."

"Something what?" Nicholas demanded with urgency.

"White and wavy and..." Oh no. I'd seen this thing before, in a dream when I had heard my mother call out my name. It was the thing that had sent a new level of fear charging through me. "Ghostly and boney."

179

Nicholas tugged on the back of my shirt and pulled me to the side of the tunnel, pressing us up against the wall. "It's a Water Faerie," he hissed.

"Yeah…but it can't see us," I pointed out.

He shook his head and whispered, "It'll be able to sense I'm here."

I stared at him, shocked. "How?"

"Water Faeries are fey, so it'll be able to sense I'm here because I'm part fey." His tone singed with anger. He pushed himself closer against the dirt wall. "And if it does…." He didn't finish, taking a shuddering breath.

I leaned toward him, keeping my voice low. "So what do you want me to do then?"

"Keep me away from it." He held out his hand for me to take. "I can't see it—you know that—so you'll have to guide me away from it. Once we get far enough away from it, take us back to Adessa's. But don't do it while the Water Faeries are close—it'll more likely be able to sense I'm here, and that'll make things even worse for me."

I looked up and down the tunnel, trying to decide which way to head. The only difference between the two ends was that one had a Water Faerie floating toward us and one didn't.

"Come on." I grabbed his hand and led him toward the unoccupied side of the tunnel, moving fast, the air swelling damper with each step we took. At one pointed I shot a quick glance over my shoulder and saw the Water Faerie a little ways behind us, gliding through the air, all pale and mirage-like, and close enough that I could see its eyes were hollowed out like a skeleton.

We ran faster.

Finally, after what seemed like an eternity, Nicholas and I were stepping out of the tunnel and out into a large, open cave. Rays of white light glittered from all over, hitting the rocky floors and walls like tiny laser beams. In the center of the cave stood a throne-shaped graphite rock, the back of it snaking up to the domed quartz ceiling.

"Where are we?" Nicholas asked, giving a quick glance over his shoulder even though he couldn't see anything. "And where's the Water Faerie? Is it gone? Can you get us out of here?"

Looking back over my own shoulder, I saw that the Water Faerie had vanished. "It's gone." I turned back around. "And we're in some sort of cave with a throne."

"It's the Queen's quarters." Panic laced his voice and he jerked on my arm. "We need to go. Now."

I didn't budge. "Just a second. I just need to see something first."

Nicholas kept pulling on my arm, but I refused to move, digging my feet into the dirt as I waited for something to happen. I could feel that something would; I just hoped it was the Queen entering, along with a future me and future Nicholas as we tried to strike up a deal to get my mother out of this creepy place.

"Gemma!" Nicholas hollered. "We have to get out of here!"

I looked at him, his expression petrified with fear, and a realization clicked. "If it's so bad that a Water Faerie can sense you're down here, then how are you supposed to come down here with me to save my mom? And if you want to leave so badly, why don't you just take us out of here yourself?"

"Because..." He let out a breath. "Look, I can't give you the details, but I can say that there are certain reasons—rules—that won't allow me down here. And I can't take us out of here, because I can't—my Foreseer power is no use down here."

I gaped at him. "So, if all that's true then how did you ever plan on helping me save my mom?" His silence told me what I needed to know. "You weren't ever planning on it, were you?"

More silence. I wanted to smack him.

"I can't believe this. These last few days have been nothing but a bunch of lies and games, haven't they?" I balled up my fist, infuriated. "This whole training thing was just a charade, wasn't it?"

He shrugged, being super obnoxious.

"Why would you do that?!" I cried.

He shrugged again, his scared expression now replaced by a deceitful smile. "To spend time with you, of course."

I opened my mouth, ready to scream a few choice words at him, but then snapped it shut when I saw her out

182

of the corner of my eye—a woman with long brown hair and bright blue irises. My mother.

She had entered the cave and walked up to the throne, where she started to dust it off with a white cloth, as if she were a cleaning maid. After she had finished, she stood there for a moment, staring at the throne. Even from where I stood, I could see the emptiness in her eyes; an emptiness that hadn't been there when I had seen her in the previous visions.

Another scream shook at the air, like the one I heard earlier, and moments later another woman came into the cave. She was dressed in white. Her eyes were two sunken holes, and her snow-white hair trailed down her back like a wedding veil. I knew she had to be the Queen by how she carried herself: with utter confidence, as if she owned the place. And also by the way my mom's eyes lit up with fear when she saw her.

Unlike the Water Faeries, the Queen didn't float, and she looked mostly normal except for that fact that her skin was nearly translucent and she didn't have any eyeballs.

My mom bowed as the Queen walked by her, and then backed away as if she was terrified out of her mind.

The Queen sat down on the throne and her voice echoed out, "Where are they?"

"I think Sarabella is bringing them in," my mom answered with a quivering voice.

The Queen watched the cave entryway with her eyeless eyes. "Does anyone know why they're here?"

183

My mother shook her head. "They haven't said any-thing yet."

Nicholas tapped me on the shoulder, and demanded for me to take us away, but I disregarded him, my eyes fixed on my mother and the Queen of The Underworld — the Queen known for torturing people to insanity.

Another scream rang, this time sounding much closer. But I didn't move, watching as a tall and thin figure, with the same snow-white hair and pale skin as the Queen, strode into the cave, accompanied by no other than yours truly and…Alex?

What? Why was Alex here with me? And better yet, how had we even gotten here if Nicholas supposedly wasn't able to help me?

Alex remained close to me as we followed the woman across the room and to the throne. I could see in my ex-pression that I must have been really struggling to keep my fear under control.

"Thank you, Sarabella," the Queen said to the woman after we all reached the throne.

Sarabella smiled, revealing that her mouth was noth-ing more than a toothless hole. "You're welcome," she breathed, and swept the tail of her white dress across the floor as she turned around and headed out of the cave.

The Queen tapped her fingers together the way evil villains do in movies, her bare eyes locked on Alex and me, her mouth set firmly in a straight line. "So, you two are the humans who dared enter my world without my permission." Alex started to speak, but the Queen held up her hand. "Silence. I do not want to hear your excuses. All that is important is there are going to be consequences for you coming here." She glanced us over, like she was contemplating our death in her head.

"You look familiar," the Queen remarked to Alex. "Have you been here before?"

Alex shook his head. "I haven't."

"Are you sure?" The Queen's empty gaze bore into Alex. "There's something about you that's so...familiar."

Alex shook his head again. "I swear I've never been here before."

The Queen continued to stare at Alex. "Tell me then, what it is that made you enter into my world?"

My mother, who'd been hiding behind the throne, stepped out and I saw the violet eyes of my vision self light up as I realized who she was.

"For her," Alex told the Queen, and gave a nod at my mother.

My mother looked like a robot, staring at us like she had no idea who we were.

"She's doesn't know who I am," I whispered underneath my breath.

"Who doesn't?" Nicholas asked from behind me.

I had been so caught up in watching the vision that I completely forgotten he was there, and the sound of his voice made me almost jump out of my skin.

"No one," I replied quickly, my eyes glued to my mother.

"That's impossible," the Queen roared. "No one ever leaves The Underworld, at least not alive. Something you probably should have considered before you entered here."

"We entered here in a way that you have no control over if we get to leave," Alex said in a somewhat arrogant tone.

"You better watch your tone, boy," the Queen warned, leaning forward in her throne. "I've cut off tongues of those who dared show such disrespect to me."

That remark frightened the vision Gemma—I could tell—but Alex acted unbothered, which wasn't surprising. Still, he didn't say anything, and the Queen gave a satisfied grin.

But then her grin faded. "So, which one of you is the Foreseer?"

"What do you mean?" Alex asked.

Her face hardened. "Don't play stupid with me, boy. The only way you could enter my world and still get out is by entering through the Ira, something that can only be done by a Foreseer. So, is it you? Or is it her?" The Queen looked at the vision Gemma, and I mean *really* looked at her, the Queen's empty-eyed gaze burning into her as if she were trying to read her mind. "Tell me, girl, what is your name?"

"I...um..." The vision Gemma glanced around nervously. "My name's..."

I shook my head at my stuttering vision self.

"And don't you dare lie to me." The Queen's voice held a secret warning.

"Gemma," the vision Gemma stammered.

"Gemma," the Queen said. "Would you please explain to me what your interest in this woman is?" She gestured her hand at my mother.

"She's..." The vision Gemma glanced at Alex for help.

"We just know her," Alex finished for me, shooting me a play-it-cool glance.

Wow. Did we not plan this at all? Because neither one of us was doing a very good job.

"If that's true—if you just know this woman—then why on earth should I let you take her?" She glanced at my mother. "Why would I let you take my best slave?"

Alex reached in his pocket and took out something that, when it caught in the rays of light, sparkled blue.

I stepped forward, trying to see what Alex had in his hand, wondering if it was the key to my mom's freedom, but before I could see what it was, Nicholas's fingers were suddenly pressing into the top of my arm, and then he shoved me against the wall.

I started to freak out, not because of Nicholas, but because I was worried I was going to miss what Alex was offering to the Queen.

"Let me go." I shoved my hands against Nicholas's chest. He stepped back, losing his balance for a split second, but then he came at me again.

He grabbed a hold of my shoulders and held me against the wall.

"Ow," I cried. "Let me go." I tried to push at him again, but he was too strong.

"Take us back, now." He spoke each syllable slowly, and a dark look shadowed over his face. His hands were pushing so hard against my shoulders that I was almost sure my bones were going to crack. He no longer looked like a tricky faerie, but a pissed off guy about to beat the crap out of me. Whether or not he would have actually hurt me, I wasn't sure. But the lethal look in his eyes was enough for me to blink us away.

Chapter 16

As soon as my mind processed that I was standing back in Adessa's living room with my feet planted firmly on the black and white tile floor, and that Nicholas no longer had a hold of me, I took off in a mad sprint for the doorway. But Nicholas grabbed on to the back of my shirt and yanked me backward, crashing me into him.

"Don't even think about running off," Nicholas breathed hotly. "You're not going anywhere until we get something straight."

I started to scream for help, but he slapped his hand down on my mouth. I raised my arm up as far as it would go and elbowed him in the ribs, but I think I did more damage to my elbow than I did to him.

"Nice try," Nicholas said. "But it's going to take a lot more effort than that."

A lot more effort as in a kick in the shin? It worked once for me, so why not give it a try? I brought my leg up, and kicked him in the shin with my foot, but I swear he'd gotten stronger since the last time I'd done it to him, because it barely fazed him.

"I don't know about you, but I could do this all day," he said in a tone that made my skin crawl. "In fact, I think I might take you back with me—keep a hold of you for awhile."

Take me back? Take me back where? I flipped out as the possibilities of where he was thinking of taking me poured through my head. I did the only thing I could think of to get away: I bit down on Nicholas's hand, sinking my teeth into his clammy skin. He let out a scream that vibrated at my eardrums, and then I felt his grip loosen, allowing me to squirm free.

"Laylen!" I shouted, sprinting for the doorway again.

Nicholas's footsteps thumped against the tile floor as he chased after me. I felt his fingers graze my back right as I took a step up the stairs. Then he was pulling me back to him.

"Help!" I screamed, flinging my weight forward.

And then a miracle happened. Laylen was suddenly there, prying Nicholas off of me, and I skittered away from them as Laylen gave Nicholas a hard shove onto the living room floor.

"If you ever touch her again," Laylen said, standing over Nicholas, "you won't be able to walk out of here."

At that moment I could have hugged Laylen, but I'm not sure it would have been very rewarding for him, since I've never really hugged any one and it would probably just end up as a very awkward moment.

"Are you okay?" Laylen's bright blue eyes examined me.

I nodded, rubbing my soon-to-be-bruised shoulder. "Yeah, I think so."

"Did he hurt you?" he asked.

I shook my head and dropped my hand from my shoulder. "No, I'm okay."

"Are you sure?"

"Yeah."

All of a sudden, Nicholas was on his feet. He swiped the Ira off of the apothecary table and ran across the room, to the far corner, putting as much distance as he could between himself and Laylen.

Laylen moved for him, but Nicholas winked at me, and then he was gone. And so was the one thing that could get me into The Underworld.

Chapter 17

"So he's been lying this whole time," Laylen said, stunned. "I can't believe it."

"I can," I told him. "The first time I ever met Nicholas, he pretended he was just a normal guy in the grocery store, not some faerie/Foreseer there to make me go to the City of Crystal with him."

After Nicholas had disappeared with the Ira, Laylen and I had sat down on the velvet purple sofa. The house was silent. After Laylen had finally told Aislin that Alex had gone away to the City of Crystal to fulfill a promise to Dyvinius, she got super stressed out. So Adessa had taken her out for the day, to get her mind off of things.

I explained to Laylen in detail what had happened between Nicholas and me, and what I saw in my Underworld vision. But what we were going to do about it, I didn't have a clue. And neither did Laylen.

"I still can't believe it," Laylen mumbled, shaking his head. "Why would he go through all that trouble to hang around here if he was never planning on taking you there—if he couldn't take you there?"

I shook my head, feeling more frustrated than I ever had—the prickle had confirmed this just a few minutes ago. "Who knows? But what I want to know is why I saw myself down in The Underworld...and with Alex. If I actually saw us there, doesn't that mean there's a good chance it will actually happen? We just have to find a way to do it."

Laylen contemplated this while fiddling with his lip ring that looped his bottom lip. "You said Alex was there..." He scratched his head. "Okay, well I think that might be where we need to start."

"With Alex?" I gave him a quizzical look. "But he's not here, and we don't know when he'll be back."

"Here's the thing, Gemma." Laylen leaned in toward me, his face holding such seriousness. "I think you're going to have to make a choice here on whether or not you think we should go get him, because for one thing, if you saw him in The Underworld with you, you're probably going to need him. Also, as pissed off as Nicholas probably is right now, Alex may be in some serious trouble."

"What kind of trouble?" I asked. "Alex never really explained what he was going to be doing there. Do you know, though?"

Laylen's Adam's apple bobbed up and down as he swallowed hard. "I think Alex didn't tell you because he thought it'd be better if you didn't know."

"It's bad though, right?" I shook my head. "Well, obviously it has to be bad, otherwise someone would have already told me what he was doing. Are they like hurting him or something?"

Laylen didn't answer, but his silence said it all.

Knowing that Alex was getting hurt...well, it was making me hurt. Literally. I could actually feel this ache in every part of my body. I think it was at this moment that I realized that Alex's and my electric connection might be even deeper than I'd originally thought.

I remembered the vision where I saw him and me as children, sitting on the floor of the little hide-out, with our hands pressed together, whispering secret words in Latin. Such a strange moment, considering how we were now. What had changed? Me losing my soul? Or was it something else—something more?

As I sat there next to Laylen, thinking about all of this, I suddenly became extremely aware that whether I wanted to save Alex or not, I had to. It really wasn't my decision to make. It was my connection with him that was going to make the decision, and the connection was telling me I had to go save him. It was a weird feeling.

"So how do we do it?" I took a shaky breath. "How do we get Alex out of the City of Crystal?"

"So then you want to do it?" Laylen asked. "You want to go get him?"

I nodded. "I think I have to. I mean, if I saw him in The Underworld with me, it probably means he has to be with me when I go there. Although I don't have the slightest clue how we're going to get there, since Nicholas took the Ira with him."

"Okay...Well, do you have any ideas about how to get us into the City of Crystal?" Laylen rubbed the back of his neck tensely. "Because it might take some time to find a Foreseer who will lend us their little ruby crystal ball that they use to travel to and from the city. Besides, we kind of need to do this on our own so no one knows we're there."

"I completely agree," I told him. "And I think I know a way."

Chapter 18

Those few days I'd spent with Nicholas ended up not being a total waste of my time. He'd covered a lot about Foreseers and the way that they use the crystal energy to go in and out of visions. He also explained to me that the crystal energy wasn't just for going into visions. It was also used every time Nicholas entered the City of Crystal. And apparently, *all* of the individual crystal balls ran off of the energy belonging to a massive crystal ball that stood in the center of the city. All the crystal balls were connected. Because of this, I had an idea that if I really tried, I just might be able to get us into the City of Crystal without a ruby-filled ball, thanks to my unique gift of being able to use crystal energy without actually having to have a crystal ball present.

But it was going to be tricky. I not only had to get us into the city, but I also had to get us into the city in present time, otherwise we wouldn't be able to communicate with anyone, or touch anything. This was the reason why Foreseers used the ruby-filled crystal ball to get in and out of the city, because it took them there in the present time.

196

Although I was a bit skeptical that I could actually pull it off, it was all I had at the moment. So I started practicing day and night. At first, I couldn't even figure out how to jumpstart whatever was sending me into visions. But then I caught on that it was connected to my emotions. Take for instance, when I was bitten by Vladislav. There had been a ton of emotion running through me then, which was why I think I ended up slipping into a vision. And when I'd drifted away while sitting on the couch with Laylen, I had been retrieving some of my lost memories, which, like Alex had pointed out once, were very deeply connected to my emotions.

So, after a lot of practice, I figured out that nine out of ten times experiencing an intense emotion equaled vision access. Of course, this put a lot of pressure on my new-found ability to experience emotion. And experiencing one on demand didn't always work out the way that I wanted.

It was with Laylen's help that I finally started to get the hang of things.

It was my fifth practice day, and Laylen and I were in the room he was staying in. I was sitting on the bed with my legs crossed, facing him as he sat in a chair he'd dragged over beside the bed.

"So, what do you want to feel today?" he asked me. "Happy, sad, scared, worried?"

"Not worried," I said quickly. "That one is not fun at all, and when we used that feeling last time, I ended up getting stuck in the vision for awhile, like the feeling wasn't strong enough to last or something."

"True," Laylen agreed. "Besides, the scared one, I think, was my favorite."

I shook my head. "No it wasn't—you almost gave me a heart attack."

He smiled, this beautiful, pleased smile. "Yeah, but it was fun."

I shook my head, thinking how in no way, shape, or form was Laylen jumping out from behind a closed door to scare me fun. "Well, let's not do that one, okay? Let's do something else—something easier on my heart."

He gave me an intrigued look. "How about we try happy? We haven't done that one yet."

My mouth instantly fell to a frown. "We haven't done that one yet, because I'm not sure I know how to feel happy yet. Well, I mean sometimes when I look at the stars I think I might feel happy...but I don't know. I think it might be a different kind of happiness than what you're talking about. Maybe not, though...I don't know."

He didn't look at me with sympathy like I'd expected him to do, but more with determination. "Well, then I think it's about time you knew for sure if you have."

Oh, Laylen. Sometimes he made my heart ache—in a good way. "I wish it was that easy, but...I mean, how—how do we do it—make me happy?"

"You can't force happiness; it just comes." He leaned back in his chair, his face twisted in deep thought. "I think

you and I both could use a little bit of fun; a little bit of re-
laxation."

I stared at him like he was insane. "How are we supposed to relax when we've got so many non-relaxing
things to deal with?"

"We take a break," he said as if it were that uncompli-
cated.

"You say it as if it's that simple, but it's not. I mean,
we can't go anywhere, since we have Stephan, the Death
Walkers, Demetrius, and a lot of vampires after us," I told
him, counting out the list on my fingers. "Besides, do you
know how to have fun? Because I don't."

He got a look on his face that could only be described
as a look someone got when they were about to do something they weren't supposed to. "I think I have an idea."

"*This* is what you think will make me have fun and be
happy?" I asked Laylen, staring up at the enormous rollercoaster, the tracks twisting and turning and flipping in
loops like a giant death trap. And the busy sidewalk we
were standing on made me even more uneasy. All it
would take was for one wrong person to walk by us and
we'd be screwed. But Laylen had sworn that we would be
fine, because almost everything that was after us more
than likely wouldn't come out during the daytime, and
that the bundles and bundles of people roaming around
would keep us inconspicuous.

However, I wasn't as optimistic. Being around people had never really been my thing. And when I had a crazy man with a scar, and his yellow-eyed, Chill of Death assailants after me, being around a huge group of people was definitely not my thing.

"This is what you think will make me feel happy?" I asked again, just to make sure I understood him right. "A rollercoaster?"

Laylen nodded, looking absolutely sure.

So we headed up.

I couldn't believe I was doing this. Riding a rollercoaster—never in a million years would I have ever thought I would be doing such a thing—and doing such a thing when we were being hunted.

But Laylen was persistent, guiding me along as we weaved up the aisle, until we reached the ticket area, where he purchased two tickets, and then the cashier sent us on our way to the loading area.

It was there that I realized that my jittery nerves weren't just because I was worried we might run into someone. I was also jittery about the idea of getting on a rollercoaster. So by the time I slid onto the leather seat in the far back cart, I was trembling.

"You'll be fine," Laylen assured me, pulling down the bars that would—hopefully—hold him in the cart when it whipped upside down.

200

I pulled down my bars and secured them tightly against my shoulders. I heard someone from the front let out a scream as the cart started to creak forward. I held as still as a statue, my hands gripping the bars tightly. The wheels clanked as the cart rose up the tracks; the brightness of the sun glared in my eyes. There was a pause where the cart just hovered at the top, and for a split second I thought we were stuck, but then it lurched forward and dropped. Then we were flying, wind blowing through my hair as the car went up and down, flipping loops and taking sharp turns. In the beginning I was terrified, but by the end I was laughing. And I mean really laughing. I wanted to hold onto this moment with every ounce of strength I had in me and never let it go.

By the time we stepped off of the cart and back onto the ground, I had tears rolling down my cheeks.

"Was I right or what?" Laylen asked, grinning from ear to ear.

I nodded, wiping my tears from my cheeks. It was the first time I'd ever had to wipe tears of happiness away. Who would have thought riding a rollercoaster would have brought them out?

"So you're happy?" Laylen asked, looking at me with hopeful eyes.

"Yeah…I think I am." I felt the back of my neck where the prickle was poking, and then I felt myself starting to fall. "I think I…I…" I was slipping away and before I crashed onto the floor, I grabbed a hold of Laylen's arm.

Chapter 19

My face smacked hard against the floor. And I mean hard.

I pushed myself up to my feet, rubbing my sure-to-have-a-goose-bump forehead. My jaw just about hit the floor when I noticed that my feet were planted firmly on top of a translucent crystal floor, a midnight river flowing beneath it, bits and pieces of gold twinkling in the water like stars. Dark red crystals hung from the glittery charcoal ceiling above, and to the side of me rubies waved across the snow-white crystal walls.

The City of Crystal.

I couldn't believe I'd pulled it off. I felt like such a bad ass.

I glanced to the side of me, praying that Laylen would be standing there, but he wasn't.

"Laylen," I called out quietly, my eyes searching the cave. The sound of a light breeze was the only thing that answered. "Laylen?" I started to walk toward a bridge that was paved with broken pieces of porcelain. "Are you here?

A soft bang came from behind me, and I spun around, afraid of what I would find, but my racing heart instantly settled when I saw Laylen.

I let out a breath of relief. "For a second, I thought I didn't bring you with me."

"For a second, I thought I died." He glanced around at the cave made of glass and crystal. "This place is...interesting."

"Yeah, it is," I agreed. "Wait...You haven't been here before?"

He shook his head, his fingers tracing the rubies curving along the crystal wall. "Not too many people have."

People? Neither of us were really considered people, were we? In fact, everyone I knew had a mark of some sort. "So, which way do you think will take us to Alex?" I asked him.

"Your guess is as good as mine." Laylen dropped his hand from the wall and turned to me. "You've been here before, though, so your guess is probably better."

"Well, you know what Alex is doing down here," I pointed out. "So if you'd tell me..."

He considered this, and then said, "He's doing something with this big crystal ball that channels energy to all the Foreseers' crystal balls. But, Gemma, I'm warning you that if we do find him, it's not going to be pretty."

"How so?" I asked. "I mean, what's he doing with this big crystal that's so bad?"

Laylen swept his bangs away from his face, looking uncomfortable. "Well...that big crystal collects its energy from...people. And the way the energy is collected...it's pretty bad from what I've been told."

I nodded, trying to ignore the sickening feeling building in my stomach. "Okay, I remember Nicholas mentioning a big crystal ball. I think he said it was in the heart of the City of Crystal, whatever that means."

Laylen glanced from left to right. "So which way?"

Wow. It felt so weird to be the one in charge, but I guess I'd give the position my best try.

"Well..." I looked to my right, at the bridge paved of porcelain, which I knew led to the Palace. Then I looked to my left, where all I could see was the crystal floor stretching down the cave. Having to pick between the two choices, I decided that it would be best to head away from the Palace because I figured we'd more likely get caught by someone if we went that way. "I say we go left."

"Left it is," Laylen said, and we started off to our left.

"So, do you think Nicholas was up to something, or do you think he was just hanging around?" I asked, keeping my voice low.

"He could have been just hanging around," Laylen said. "He seems to have a deep fascination with you."

"I don't know why, though." I shook my head. "No one's ever wanted to hang around me before."

Laylen gave me a strange look. "Why do you think that?"

I shrugged. "Because I never had any friends in school—well until Alex came along, but that was just him trying to figure out why I started to feel again. He wasn't hanging around me because he wanted to."

205

"Gemma." Laylen's voice was deep—pressing. "The only reason you never had any friends was because of how you *were*. But that's not how you really are, and you need to realize that. And trust me, Alex enjoys being around you more than he lets on."

"If that's true," I said, dragging my fingers along the wall as we walked, "then it's because of the electricity."

"Trust me, it's more than that." He pondered something for a good long while before continuing, "Alex puts on this huge front when it comes to how he feels about things, but if you've known him for as long as I have, then you'd know it's mostly an act."

I was just about to open my mouth and tell him that I still didn't believe that Alex liked being around me, but the sound of approaching footsteps made me stop.

Laylen and I froze, and we both shot a quick glance behind us. But there was nothing.

"Where's it coming from?" I whispered.

He shook his head, and scooted us over to the side of the path, where we stepped off of a ledge and down onto a glistening surface of blue glass that was as slippery as ice. He took my hand, and we hurried over to a massive crystal pillar that coiled down from the ceiling and connected to the ground. Right as we tucked ourselves behind the pillar, I caught a glimpse of a tall figure walking down the path.

"Someone's coming," I whispered to Laylen.

He gave me a nervous glance and then carefully peeked around the pillar. "What the..."

"Who is it?" I whispered.

"There's no one there," he told me, shaking his head.

I furrowed my eyebrows and then peeked around the pillar. I, however, was met by a pair of golden eyes that belonged to a very tricky faerie/Foreseer.

I jerked backward, but Nicholas caught me by the arm and reeled me into him. He moved away from the pillar, backing across the slippery glass at a speed I'd never be able to pull off.

"I knew you'd show up here," Nicholas breathed in my ear, still backing us away from the pillar—and from Laylen. "I knew you would come and try to save *him*."

I fought to get free, but my feet kept slipping out from under me.

Nicholas whirled me around, wrapped his arms around me, and pulled me forcefully against him. "Try anything funny and I'll have you out of here before you can even blink."

"Nicholas," Laylen called out as he chased after us. "Let her go."

"Come any closer," Nicholas warned, holding up the ruby-filled crystal ball that apparently he had in his hand the entire time, "and I'll have her out of her before you can reach us."

Laylen slid to a halt, but a look of rage on his face stayed.

"Wise choice," Nicholas said, his damp breath hitting my cheek.

"What do you want?" Laylen asked, his bright blue eyes targeted on Nicholas.

Nicholas traced a finger down my cheek, sending a shiver crawling down my spine. "I have what I want right here."

Yuck. I was so tired of ending up like this—trapped against Nicholas.

Laylen got this look on his face, like he was trying really hard to figure out how to free me from Nicholas before he took me away from the City of Crystal. I was panicking with the thought that Nicholas would end up winning. And if he did, then...well, I didn't even want to think about the possibilities of what would happen if he did.

Nicholas strengthened his hold on me, the ruby-filled ball glowing in his hand. He was breathing deep, his chest rising and falling, as he raised the crystal ball up in the air. There was a blur of color that swooshed toward us, and then came a loud crack followed by a soft thump.

I learned something new.

Vampires are fast. And I mean fast.

One second Laylen had been a ways away from us, and the next second he was right there.

It was amazing.

Another second and he'd knocked Nicholas out. Yep, actually knocked him out...I think.

"Is he...alive?" I asked, staring down at Nicholas's body sprawled across the icy blue glass.

"Yeah, he's good; just unconscious." Laylen bent down and looped his arms underneath Nicholas's arms. "We'll let him sleep it off, and hopefully we'll be long gone by the time he wakes up."

"And what if we're not?" I asked, scooting out of the way so Laylen could drag Nicholas behind the pillar.

"Guess we'll have to make sure we hurry."

"Hurry?" I looked around at the giant cave we were standing in. "But we still don't know where to go."

Laylen didn't say anything, only taking my arm to help me keep my balance as we walked back across the icy blue glass. By the time we'd stepped back up onto the translucent crystal floor, I was extremely worried. Nicholas could wake up at any moment, and he probably would be super pissed when he did. And we still needed to find Alex.

As I rattled my brain for a solution on how to do this, besides searching the entire city for him, something shocked me in the back. At first I thought I'd imagined it— that my brain was searching for an answer and had created the shock on its own. But then it happened again, and I knew.

"Alex is close," I sputtered out as I felt another spark, this time in my fingertips.

"What?" Laylen asked, looking confused.

"He's close...I can feel him."

209

Realization slowly rose in his expression. "The electricity?"

I nodded, and then we were running, following the path of electricity like an invisible trail of bread crumbs, which would hopefully lead us right to Alex. We kept running and running, going further into the cave, letting my electric sensors steer us as the sparks grew hotter and hotter, until they were going so wild I thought I was going to combust into flames. And when we reached a pair of silver doors, with the Foreseer's mark on the top of each one, I knew Alex had to be behind them.

"You think he's in there?" Laylen asked as I reached for the doorknob.

I nodded, slowly turning the handle, and pushed open the door. And what I saw made my stomach churn. People wrapped in chains that were binding them to a crystal ball the size of a football stadium. And all those people…well, they looked dead.

Chapter 20

I stood there, my hand still gripping the doorknob, my mouth agape. The people looked like corpses; their skin as pale as a ghost, their eyes sealed shut, their bodies strapped to the massive crystal ball that burned brightly like the sun. They were dead. They were all dead. Alex was dead. I couldn't breathe.

"Calm down, Gemma." Laylen's voice was soothing. "They're not dead."

I dropped my hand from the doorknob, unable to take my eyes off the crystal ball, the people, the chains. "Are you—are you sure?"

"Yeah, I'm sure. The crystal's collecting energy from them," he explained. "If they were dead, they wouldn't be useful."

Calm down. You won't be useful if you're freaking out. "Okay, so where's Alex?"

Laylen stepped cautiously into the room, and I followed. Luckily, there didn't seem to be anyone awake hanging around in there, like a Foreseer guard or something. The coast was all clear. So why did I still feel like I was going to throw up?

"Maybe we should split up," Laylen suggested. "You head right and I'll take the left?"

I nodded, and he headed off to the left side of the crystal ball. I headed to the right, searching the people's faces as I moved around the burning crystal. It was difficult to feel the electricity in here because the crystal seemed to be radiating off an intense amount of electric energy. But if I really concentrated, I could feel the difference between the crystal ball's electricity and Alex's.

With every chained up person I went by, I grew more nauseous. Yes, Laylen had warned me that what I would see would be bad, but I never pictured it like this...so sickening. What made it even worse was that it wasn't just the chains that were securing the people to the enormous crystal ball. There were also tubes coming out of their skin that extended up to the crystal ball, like how an IV attaches to its bag.

If this was how Foreseers collected their energy, I wasn't sure I wanted to be a Foreseer anymore. If you asked me, Foreseers weren't much better than Water Faeries. Whether they were feeding off humans' fear or their energy, they were still feeding off of them.

My sickening feeling nearly exploded out of me when I spotted Alex chained to the crystal ball, tubes jabbing out of him.

"Laylen!" I yelled as I ran up to Alex's lifeless body. "Over here."

For a moment I just stood there, staring at Alex in a state of shock. But then I snapped out of it and began pulling the tubes out of his skin, one by one. They were small tubes and didn't go in very deep, but each one left a tiny hole that dripped blood. "Laylen!" I yelled louder, looking for a way to get the chains off of Alex. "How the heck do I get these unlocked?"

Alex's eyes shot open, and I let out a gasp. He stared at me, his normally bright green eyes dulled over, and I wondered if he even recognized me. He looked so...weak. I had never seen Alex look so weak. It was strange.

"Are you okay?" I asked worriedly.

He opened his mouth to speak, but no sound came out.

"Laylen!" I yelled for a third time. Where was he? Had something happened to him? I started to freak.

"Coming," I heard him say. And then he was right next to me. "Hold onto him," he instructed, grabbing the chains.

I don't know why, but I hesitated. Not because I was afraid to touch Alex or anything. Well, okay, maybe a little, but it was also because he looked so breakable.

"Gemma," Laylen said with urgency, and I quickly wrapped my arms around Alex, ignoring the fact that a) he was shirtless and b) his skin, although cold and clammy, still spun a fiery amount of electricity that made my skin smolder.

I held onto Alex as Laylen snapped the chains like twigs. Alex fell onto me like a hundred and eighty pound weight, and I almost buckled to the floor. But thankfully, Laylen caught him before I did.

"Excellent catching skills," Laylen joked, flopping Alex's arm over his shoulder and balancing all of his weight on him.

"Hey, I never claimed to have them," I said. "Besides, I'm not a half-vampire, half-Keeper who is freakishly strong."

"Would you two stop messing around and get us out of here before we get caught." The frail voice came from Alex. His eyes were still closed and he was leaning on Laylen.

"Yeah, let's get out of here." I put one hand on Laylen and one hand on Alex, then shut my eyes, crossing my fingers I'd be able to get all three of us out of here and back to Adessa's, safely.

"Don't do anything from in here," Alex said. His voice sounded the slightest bit stronger. "There's too much power in here...you'll end up hurting yourself."

I glanced at the crystal ball blazing vibrantly, and at the people chained to it. "Maybe we should help them."

Alex's eyelids slowly lifted open. "No, we have to go. You never should have come here."

I couldn't seem to take my eyes off of the chained up people, feeling a pang of guilt building in my gut. I used their energy every time I touched a crystal ball. Maybe

214

even when I didn't. And now I was supposed to leave and use their energy again.

"Even if you let them go, there'd be no way for you to get them all out of here," Alex told me.

I swallowed hard and tore my eyes away from the people. "Okay, let's go."

Fortunately, Laylen was strong enough to hold Alex up as we headed out of the room and moved back down the cave, distancing ourselves from the massive crystal ball. Alex was really struggling to walk, his feet practically dragging across the translucent crystal floor.

"How far away do we need to go?" I asked Alex as we headed toward the spot where Laylen and I had entered the cave.

"Farther than this," he said, his eyelids fluttering as he forced them open.

So we went further and, for some stupid reason, it never dawned on us that we might run into a very awake Nicholas until we actually did. But Nicholas wasn't what was sending my pulse racing like a jackhammer. It was the three Death Walkers standing next to him, the hoods of their black cloaks caped over their heads; the glow of their yellow eyes reflecting across the translucent crystal floor.

"Crap!" I cried at the same time Laylen screeched to a halt.

"Okay, time to get us out of here," Laylen said as the three Death Walkers and Nicholas hurried toward us.

I grabbed a hold of Laylen and Alex, closed my eyes, and pictured Adessa's living room; the dark blue walls, the purple velvet couches, and the black and white checkerboard floor.

"Gemma." Laylen's voice was full of fear. "Please hurry."

I opened my eyes and saw that the Death Walkers were close. The air was slowly descending to a frosty chill, dotting my skin with goose bumps. I squeezed my eyes shut. *Concentrate.*

But nothing happened.

Focus.

Still nothing.

Fog laced the air as the temperature continued to plunge. I was in full panic mode, trying to force us to leave this awful place. But I just couldn't do it.

"Gemma." Alex's soft voice made me open my eyes.

His eyes were locked on mine; some of the brightness had returned to them. "Don't focus on them. In fact, pretend they're not even there."

I gave him an are-you-crazy look. Pretend that three ice-death machines weren't running straight at us?

Alex slid his arm off Laylen and placed a hand on each side of my face, so I couldn't turn my head. "Pretend they're not there."

As I stared into his eyes, my heart rate began to slow, and my nervousness and fear floated away. I felt a delicate spark, and then I felt myself being yanked.

I thought I'd done it. I thought I'd managed to get us out of there unharmed, but a set of sub-zero fingers seized hold of my arm, thrusting a crackle of cold through my body. I screamed, suspended somewhere between being in the City of Crystal and traveling back to Adessa's. My limbs acted as a tug-of-war rope, the Death Walker pulling me one way and my Foreseer ability trying to pull me the other. I wasn't even sure if I was still holding onto Laylen and Alex—my body was too numb from the cold to feel anything.

I let out another scream as the Death Walker jerked me toward it, and I could see its glowing-yellow eyes only inches away from me.

"No!" I yelled. "No!" It was not going to end up this way. I would get us out of here. I forced myself to breathe...relax...focus. I tried to ignore the monster that had a hold of me and mentally pictured Adessa's living room. There was a loud *snap*, and then a burst of images flipped through my mind: the Wyoming mountains...Adessa's...desert...snow...lake.

And then...nothing.

Chapter 21

The next thing I knew I was laying face first on the ground, my body sore from head-to-toe. I wondered if that *snap* I'd heard was my bones breaking from the Death Walker's death-grip pull. But as I pushed myself up, all my limbs seemed to be intact. The only thing wrong with me was that my arm was tinged a purplish-blue from where the Death Walker had grabbed me.

I knew right away I wasn't in the City of Crystal. It was too warm for Death Walkers to be nearby. So that was good, I guess. But I couldn't see my surroundings. Everything was all hazy, just like back when I first started going into visions and the people's faces would be blurred over. But this wasn't faces; it was everything. I had no clue where I was. Somewhere bright—and by the greenish shade the haze held, I wondered if I could be outside. I could also make out the faintest orange glow up above me that had to belong to the sun.

But why couldn't I see anything? And where were Alex and Laylen?

I shook my head and blinked my eyes, as if that might help. But it didn't.

"Hello," I shouted, starting to move through the haziness, feeling a little bit dizzy and queasy. "Alex! Laylen!"

Nothing.

"Dammit," I cursed. What was happening to me? First I'd gotten stuck in a vision, and now I was, what? Stuck in between one?

I kept walking, trying to stay calm, but it was hard to do because I couldn't tell where I was. In fact, everything was so out of whack, including my senses, that for all I knew I could have been flying.

I called out a few more times, but each time I got no response.

"Okay," I told myself, "calm down and focus." I took a deep breath and tried to focus on my surroundings. I let my eyes relax and tried not to think of anything else. Gradually, bit by bit, things started to shift into focus…the trees around me…the sky above me…the lake below me.

The lake!

A spilt second later I was submerged in the cold water. I kicked and paddled, trying to tear my way back to the surface, but not knowing how to swim was making it difficult. Water was seeping into my mouth. My oxygen was diminishing.

I was going to drown.

And then something remarkable occurred. I felt someone fold their arms around me and before I knew it I was breaking through the surface of the water. The sunlight, trees, and sky had never looked so lovely in my entire life.

Along with Laylen's bright blue eyes, which were watching me as he kept us both afloat.

"One of these days," he said breathlessly, "I'm going to have to teach you how to swim."

I didn't say anything because I was too busy hacking my guts out.

Laylen swam us to shore, and we both collapsed onto the muddy grass, where we laid on our backs and stared up at the bright blue sky, the sunlight stinging at my eyes. After I finished catching my breath, I rolled over and looked at the Keeper's grey stone castle soaring off in the distance. My gaze wandered over to Laylen, lying there on the ground, his damp hair glistening in the sunlight, beads of water glittering on his pale skin. If it hadn't been for him, I might be dead right now—he'd saved me from drowning.

"Where's Alex?" I asked him. "Did he make it here with us?"

"Yeah, he made it." Laylen squinted against the sunlight with his arm flopped across his forehead. "I left him back there," he pointed behind us, "when I saw you drowning in the lake. He's still a little weak." He gave a short pause. "Gemma, what happened back there? Why did we end up here? Were you thinking about taking us to The Underworld?"

"No," I said, a little offended he'd think that. "I was trying to take us back to Adessa's, but the Death Walker grabbed hold of my arm." I raised my arm up to show him the faint bluish-purple fingerprints that still marked my skin. "I kept trying to get us away, but then there was this *snap*...and I don't know, a bunch of different images started flashing through my mind. Then the next thing I knew I was here, but everything was all blurry, and I couldn't see I was on the lake until it was too late."

"You were lucky no one had just recently dumped any summoning ash in there," Laylen said, glancing at the lake.

"Summoning ash?" I asked. "What is that?"

"In order for the Water Faeries to come up to the surface, summoning ash has to be put into the water first," he explained.

I nodded as I remembered how I'd seen Stephan dumping some black ash into the lake before my mom was dragged away to The Underworld.

"Wait a minute," I said. "How can you see any of this? I thought only the vision seer was supposed to be able to see the surroundings?"

"I have no idea," Laylen said. "All I can think of is that maybe we're not in a vision, like when we traveled into the City of Crystal only we just traveled to somewhere else."

Strange. "So why do you think I screwed up getting us back to Adessa's?" I asked, picking at the grass. "Do you think it was because of the Death Walker?"

Before he could answer, a shadow cast over us.

Alex stood unsteadily in front of us. "That and probably because you've been using your Foreseer power too much."

I squinted up at him standing there, the sunlight gleaming behind him. There were shadows under his eyes, and he still didn't have a shirt on. Rounding his left rib cage was a circle traced by a set of fiery-gold flames—the Keeper's mark.

So that's where it was.

"I haven't been using it that much," I lied, trying hard not to stare at his shirtless chest. "I think it might have had something to do with the Death Walker getting a hold of me...which, why were they even there? And with Nicholas?"

Alex shook his head and sank down on the muddy grass. "Your guess is as good as mine. I honestly have no clue what the heck is going on." He gestured around us. "With any of this."

"Well, it might have something do to with the fact that Nicholas was tricking us when he said he could get me into The Underworld." I sat up and shielded my eyes from the sun with my hand. "He never even intended to help me get to The Underworld. In fact, according to him, he can't even go there."

Alex cocked an eyebrow at me. "What do you mean?"

I sighed and began explaining what had been going on for the last week while he was trapped in the City of Crystal, strapped to that awful crystal ball.

One good thing about Alex is that he's a somewhat calm person...well, at least when it comes to stressful situations. With me…hmm…not so much. Things that would freak out a normal person barely upset him. And as I told him about the visions I'd been going into, he stayed fairly calm. The only thing that got a rise out of him was when I told him about his father and the mark—the Mark of Malefiscus. However, it wasn't the rise I was expecting. I assumed he'd get pissed off and insist that there was no way that his father could have such a mark, but he didn't.

Instead, he stared out at the water, looking lost. He was quiet for so long that I began to worry he was going into a catatonic state.

I gave Laylen a what-should-I-do look.

He shrugged, like he had no idea.

"Alex," I said, keeping my voice low. "Are you okay?"

He didn't answer.

I tried again. "Alex?"

"So this blue sparkling thing you said I was giving to the Queen," he said suddenly. "Do you know what shape it was?"

"All I could see was that it sparkled," I told him. "Then Nicholas pulled me away and made me take us back to Adessa's."

Alex popped his knuckles, his jaw set tight. "Okay, well we need to find out what this blue shiny thing is before we even try to head down to The Underworld."

"And we need to get the Ira," I added.

The waves of the lake rolled up and back as we sat on the shore trying to figure out what to do.

"What would the Queen want that's blue and sparkly?" I thought aloud.

Unexpectedly, Alex jumped to his feet, a little too quickly, and he tipped forward. Laylen leapt up and caught him before he dove head first into the water. Alex swayed a little before regaining his balance, and Laylen let him go. It was weird, because before Alex had left, the two had been fighting.

"I think I might know what it is," Alex said, gazing over at the forest.

"You do?" I perked up and got to my feet.

"Yeah, and it's not too far from us." He nodded over at the trees. "It's over there."

I looked over at the tall green trees that encircled the lake. "It's in the forest?"

He nodded, stumbling as he took a step forward.

"Okay..." I was starting to grow concerned over Alex's balancing problem. "Are you sure you're okay?"

"Don't worry about me," he said, his tone sharp. "I'll be fine."

Well, if he was going to be rude about it, then fine. I wouldn't worry about it. Okay, fine, technically that wasn't true.

"Well, what is this thing?" I asked him as I wiped the mud off of the back of my legs. "And why do you think it's in the trees?"

"It's something that holds sentimental value to the Queen." He staggered off toward the forest like he was under the influence.

Laylen and I both exchanged a questioning look, and then we jogged after Alex.

"I still don't understand why something that's important to the Queen would be out in a forest," I said breathlessly to Alex.

"But yet it is," he said, and sped up. Apparently he'd gotten over his weakened state.

I sped up too, the fabric of my clothes scratching against my skin with my every movement. Also, since I had been wearing flip flops when I fell into the lake, they fell off of my feet, and now I was walking around barefoot. The leaves, twigs, and rocks rubbed sharply against the soles of my feet as I practically ran to keep up with Alex. But that was okay. Alex was barefoot too, and if he was tough enough to do it, then so was I. Besides, I'd felt worse pain in my life, both physically and emotionally.

Laylen trailed off a little ways behind us. He'd taken off his shirt while he walked and was ringing out the water. I didn't mean to stare at him for so long—I mean, it wasn't like I never saw a guy without his shirt off before. And really, I wasn't staring at him because he had his shirt off so much as what I saw on his shoulder. (Well, that was stretching it a little, but I was still partially staring at his shoulder.) Cupping his shoulder was the Keeper's mark— fiery-gold flames bordering a black circle. So there it was;

the mark that had branded him a Keeper. And right along his forearm was his other mark; the one that had branded him not good enough to be a Keeper anymore.

Laylen shook out his shirt and then noticed me gawking at him like a stalker. He gave me a funny look and I turned around, rolling my eyes at myself.

We walked through the forest for awhile, with Alex stopping every so often to glance around. He looked lost, and finally, with his forehead scrunched over, he muttered, "Where the heck is it?"

"Well, if you tell us what you're looking for, then maybe Laylen and I can help you," I pointed out as I shooed a bug away from my face.

"I don't know..." He was hesitant, which meant there was something he didn't want to say. "There's this little hideout I use to hang out at when I was little...there's a hill somewhere with a bush covered by violet flowers."

Well, there you go. I actually knew the solution to this problem. Go figure.

I turned in a circle, scanning through the trees and bushes, until I picked up on the direction I'd wandered in when I was in the vision and found the little hideout.

"It's over there." I pointed in the direction where I was ninety-nine percent sure the hideout was.

Alex gave me a funny look. "What is?"

"The hiding spot *we* used to go to when we were kids," I told him, adding emphasis on the "we" to make a point that I remembered.

"You remember that?" he asked, taken aback.

I watched him as I started to explain, wondering how he was going to react to the fact that I knew about our little promise we made when we were kids. "While Nicholas was taking you to the City of Crystal, I unintentionally went into a vision here."

He raised an eyebrow at me. "Anything important happen?"

I shook my head, trying not to think about how I had to watch my own soul get detached before I could leave the vision.

"Nothing important at all?"

Now I gave him a funny look. "What does *forem* mean?"

For a brief second, his bright green eyes widened in surprised, but then the look quickly disappeared and was replaced by Alex's lying poker face, as I was going to call the straight-faced look he got whenever he was going to tell me a lie.

"I have no idea what *forem* means," he said, acting all whatever.

My gaze drifted down to his hands and I looked for a very faint, very small scar.

He clenched his hands into fist and started off in the direction I had pointed toward.

I didn't follow him. Instead, I turned around and called out to Laylen, "Do you know what *forem* means?"

I heard Alex mumble curse words under his breath, but I ignored him.

"What?" Laylen came to a stop in front of me, his eyebrows dipping down.

"*Forem.* Do you know what it means?"

He gave me a puzzled look. "Yeah, it means—"

"Found it!" Alex yelled louder than was necessary.

Laylen and I headed off in the direction his voice came from and found him standing on the side of the hill, holding back the branches of the blooming violet bush. I climbed up the hill, my bare feet sliding in the rocks and mud, and Alex gave me his hand and helped me over the bush. I dropped my feet down into the hole and onto the first step of the ladder. Then I climbed down into my old childhood hideout.

Laylen, not even bothering to use the ladder, dropped in right behind me. It was pitch black, except for the soft sunlight trickling through the hole.

"Anyone have night vision?" I asked, and Laylen let out a laugh.

Alex pushed past us and vanished into the darkness. There was a lot of banging around, and then he struck a match. The pale orange glow orbed around the room as Alex hurried and lit a candle. Then he placed the candle down on top of a table, sat down on the floor, and began digging in the dirt.

"It's buried in the floor?" I asked, squatting down next to him.

He nodded, digging quicker until there was a fairly good size hole. Then he stopped and pulled out a small wooden box. On the top of the box, written in child-like handwriting, were the names Gemma and Alex.

"We had a secret box?" I asked him in awe as he pried the lid open.

He shrugged like it wasn't a big deal, but the glow of the candles showed a twinkle in his bright green eyes. He lifted the lid off, and all three of us leaned over the box, like we had just opened a trunk of buried treasure.

I had to wonder what was going to be inside a box that was made by two kids—two very strange kids, I might add. There was nothing too strange in it, though: a rock, a bracelet, a photo of me and my mom, which I immediately snatched up. In the photo, my mother and I stood out in a field dusted with violet flowers. The sun shined brightly in the background, and we were both smiling—happy.

I glanced at Laylen, remembering our silly little rollercoaster ride, and wondered if it was the same kind of happiness as what I felt when this photo was taken.

Alex removed everything from the box, and piled all of it onto the floor, except for one thing: a sapphire-blue teardrop diamond.

"Thank God," he said, clutching the diamond in his hand.

"That's it? That's what's going to get the Queen to agree to free my mom?" I slipped the photo of my mother and me into the back pocket of my shorts, which were almost dry now, and leaned toward Alex to get a better look at the blue diamond resting in the palm of his hand.

"Is that the *Cruciatus* diamond?" Laylen's eyes were huge as he stared down at the teardrop diamond.

"Yeah, it is," Alex replied, his voice wavering.

"Is it—does it do anything?" I asked nervously, worried that maybe my energy would set it off or something.

Alex closed his hand around the diamond. "The Queen used to use it to suck the fear out of people before one of the Keepers took it from her."

"But if no one can enter The Underworld, then how did they take it from her?" I asked.

"A long time ago things used to work differently," Alex explained drowsily. "The Queen used to be able to come up to the castle to discuss matters of business and to make truces with the Keepers. That's how the Keepers ended up sending people down there as a punishment. This," he held up the diamond between his fingers, "was once used during a bargain."

"Well, how did you end up with it?" I wondered.

He almost smiled. "You and I stole it."

"Stole it," I said, stunned. "Why would we do that?"

"For fun," he replied with a shrug. "We used to do a lot of things like that."

Interesting, I guess, and it was kind of nice that he was giving me a little insight into our past.

Alex closed his eyes, the blue diamond still clutched in his hand. He looked like he was sleeping.

"So what do we do now—just take the diamond with us when we go to The Underworld, and offer it to the Queen in exchange for my mother?" *Well, that's if we even get to The Underworld.* We still needed the Ira, which Nicholas had, and after what happened at the City of Crystal it appeared that Nicholas just might be working with Stephan.

Alex didn't answer, his eyes still shut.

"Alex," I said softly. "Are you okay?"

He still didn't answer me.

I looked at Laylen worriedly, and he shook Alex gently by the shoulder. "Hey, you okay man?" he asked.

But still Alex remained silent and motionless with the diamond resting loosely in the palm of his hand.

"Maybe the diamond's doing something to him," I said, reaching for Alex's hand that held the diamond. When I touched his skin, I noticed how dull the flow of electricity was, and I immediately panicked, worried he might be dying.

"Alex." My voice came out loud and panic-stricken. I grabbed his arm. "Wake up."

His eyelids lifted, and a rush of relief swept through me like a breath of fresh air on a warm summer day. I started to pull my hand back, but he caught hold of it and grasped onto my fingers.

I stared at his hand grasping mine. "What are you doing?"

"Shhh…" He shut his eyes again. "I just need a minute, okay?"

Like a light bulb clicking on, it suddenly occurred to me what he was doing. He was feeling weak and our little electric connection was…well, it was recharging him. I could feel it too, ascending and boosting my energy.

Laylen got to his feet and dusted the dirt off of his jeans. "I'm going to go check and make sure no one's coming. I'll be right back."

"You think someone would show up here?" I asked, glancing up at the hole.

He looked at Alex and then shrugged. "You never know."

I almost told him to stay. Something inside me felt afraid—a strange kind of afraid. One I couldn't quite explain and had never felt before.

Confused about my feelings, I sat there on the ground as Laylen climbed up the ladder and disappeared into the daylight. Alex was still holding onto my hand, the electricity growing hotter and hotter with each beat that went by. In all actuality, its heat was making me feel a little better too. I wasn't even aware I had closed my eyes until I heard Alex say my name. I cracked open my eyes and found him watching me with this intense look on his face.

I started to ask him what was wrong, but something in his eyes made me pause. I don't even know what the look was; maybe a mix between tired and...vulnerable. Or maybe it was just that he was really looking at me. And I mean *really* looking at me.

Then he was leaning in toward me, and I felt my body tense up. Half of my brain was begging for me to rip my hand out of his and run. But the other half was telling me to stay put. He had done so many bad things to me—terrible things—that maybe I should have run. But he also had gone to the City of Crystal, knowing he would be chained up to the energy sucking crystal ball, all so I could try to get my mother out of The Underworld. There were still small wounds in his skin where the tubes had been inserted. It wasn't pretty, and he had done it to help me.

So I didn't move away, watching, waiting, knowing I was going to let him kiss me.

"Gemma." His voice was soft and shaky. A moment later his lips brushed mine, and electricity spun through me.

But the kiss lasted only a split second, because right as our lips touched, someone shrieked from outside. Alex and I both pulled away, and both our gazes shot toward the ladder.

Alex's eyes scanned the room. "Where's Laylen?"

"He said he was going to go check to make sure no one was outside." My heart raced as I stood up. "Don't you remember?"

He shook his head and slowly got to his feet. "How long's he been gone?" he asked as he walked over to the ladder.

"I'm not sure...I lost track of time," I said stupidly. "Not too long I think."

Another shriek ripped through the air, and this time I knew what it belonged to.

A Death Walker.

Alex's eyes practically bulged out of his head. He ran over to the small little trunk in the corner and threw open the lid.

"What are you doing?" I asked, watching as he dug around in the trunk. "We need to do something—Laylen's out there."

"I am doing something." He took a small pocket knife out of the trunk and flicked open the blade.

"Why would you ever hide a knife in here?" I asked, gaping incredulously at the knife.

"Why wouldn't I?" he replied, brushing past me.

Well, look at him, all Mr. Prepared.

I followed him over to the ladder. "Yeah, but that tiny thing's not going to help us much if there's a Death Walker out there."

He stared up at the top of the ladder with his thinking face on. "You got a better idea?"

"I...no."

"Well then." He placed his hands on the ladder and then said, "Stay here."

"No," I told him firmly. "I won't. There's no reason for you to go up there alone. And besides, even if I stay down here, it doesn't mean I'm going to be safe."

He shook his head, and I suddenly felt the prickle. I wasn't sure what emotion was trying to surface, but a voice inside my head whispered, *Take the knife.* So I did, quickly snatching it out of his hand.

"I'm not staying here," I said, moving the knife behind my back. "You're still weak from being in the City of Crystal, and I can help."

He looked surprised by my sudden take charge attitude. But then he just looked pissed.

"Let's go." I tried to sound confident, but I was scared, and it showed through my voice.

Despite my lack of confidence, Alex climbed up the ladder, and I followed, wondering what would be waiting for us outside.

Chapter 22

After we climbed out of the hiding spot and slid down the hill, I gave the knife back to Alex because, let's face it, I was no Keeper.

Another shriek rang through the forest, and out in the open it sounded louder and more terrifying.

"If you're scared, then you can go back in there," Alex told me, his voice urging—begging—me to please go back.

I eyed him over. His skin was so pale. The little holes dotting his body looked like they had to hurt. He also had shadows under his eyes, and although he did look a bit better than when we'd first found him in the City of Crystal, he still wasn't his strong, normal self. And the voltage of electricity flowing off of him was still so muffled.

"No, I'm going with you," I told him. "You need my help. You're not strong enough yet."

"I'm fine," he snapped. "I don't need your help."

"Yeah, you do." My voice shook a little, but I stood firm. "I can *feel* that you're not okay."

He held my gaze powerfully, like he thought if he stared at me for long enough, I'd back down. And you know what? A week or so ago I might have, but today I wasn't. It was like I had this adrenaline pouring through me—this inner strength.

"Fine, come with me then." He pointed his finger at me. "But I swear to God, Gemma, if anything happens—"

"I know, I know. Run. Hide. Save myself."

His mouth quirked and an amused smile started to show, but then another shriek filled the air, and we ran into the trees.

Most people wouldn't run toward a shrieking monster that could quite possibly end up freezing you to your death. And normally we did run. But this was a different situation because Laylen could be in some serious trouble. The further we dipped into the forest without seeing Laylen, the more concerned I became. My gut was telling me something was wrong with Laylen, and that maybe this was a trap. And yes, the thought did cross my mind that Alex might be a part of it.

I almost turned back.

But then another shriek reverberated through the forest, and I thought of Laylen, and how the Death Walker might be trying to hurt him.

Then came the fog. It moved across the forest's damp ground like a snake, icing everything in its path.

Alex stopped as the fog reached our ankles, staring down at the ground, while holding his knife out in front of him. "Stay by me," he whispered, and I nodded.

238

The fog gradually seeped through my damp clothes and onto my skin, chilling my body to the shivers. I clenched my jaw tight to keep it from chattering.

I've had nightmares of being chased by Death Walkers in a forest that have come true. And here I was again, in a forest with Death Walkers, only I wasn't being chased.

Not yet anyway.

Alex scooted us behind the trunk of a very large oak tree and put a finger to his lips. We stood as still as people in paintings, and that's when I heard it. A voice. A very familiar voice that I was absolutely sure belonged to a half-faerie, half-Foreseer who might be working for the dark side.

"I can't believe this," Nicholas was saying. "I can't believe she managed to drag all of us into the present time."

I looked at Alex, and I knew he was thinking the same thing; that I'd brought Nicholas and the Death Walkers here with us. But if that were so then where had they been hiding?

"Well, it would have been a lot better if she hadn't dropped us in the middle of the lake," Nicholas said irritably.

Who the heck was he talking to? Himself?

Alex must have been thinking the same thing, because he took a cautious peek around the tree trunk. When he moved back, he looked completely mystified.

"Who is it?" I mouthed.

239

He shook his head and shrugged. Huh, so maybe faerie boy was talking to himself.

"I know, but where are they?" Nicholas asked, and the more he spoke, the more I wondered if he had lost his mind or something.

Another shriek rattled the air and shook at the trees, causing leaves to break off their branches and float to the ground.

"Would you stop doing that!" Nicholas exclaimed.

My eyes widened. Was he talking to the Death Walkers? No, that wasn't possible...was it?

"Well, stop smelling the blood then!" Nicholas's voice cut sharply through the forest.

Blood ?Blood! Oh, no, please, please don't let the blood he's referring to belong to Laylen.

"He tried to attack me first." Nicholas snapped. "It was self-defense. Besides, you would have frozen him to death anyway."

There was a pause where all I could hear was my heart thumping erratically.

"So what if he created Laylen?" Nicholas said, annoyed. "Creating another vampire isn't that hard."

Vampire. *Vampire.* Oh my God, they were talking about Laylen.

Without even thinking about what I was doing, I started to move around the tree, but Alex grabbed me by the arm and pulled me into him. He shook his head, and I glared at him, trying to wiggle my way free without making too much noise. He intensified his grip—apparently some of his strength returned to him—and met my gaze, his eyes begging me to stop.

It hurt. It actually physically hurt to stay behind that tree and know Laylen was injured, while Nicholas chatted away.

"I'm not messing around," Nicholas insisted. "I know what has to be done." Another pause. "I know, but it might be a little difficult to find her. She's very powerful and getting more powerful by the day. She can do things normal Foreseers can't." A shriek, and then, "Fine. Let's go back to the City of Crystal, and I'll see if I can get an exact location on her."

There was a *swoosh*, and then silence.

Alex peered around the corner of the tree trunk, before letting me go. And then we were sprinting though the lingering fog that was starting to tint my skin a bluish-purple. But at the moment I didn't care. All I cared about was that Laylen was laying on the ground, on top of the scattered leaves and twigs, with a stick stabbed into his chest, blood covering his shirt.

I'd never felt anything like it before. Panic, rage, fear— it all crushed through me.

Alex muttered something incoherently as he bent down to Laylen's lifeless body.

"He's not—he's not," I was on the verge of tears, "dead, is he?"

Alex examined the stick poking out of Laylen's chest. Being a huge science fiction freak, I'd read enough vampire books to know that a stake through the heart meant death for a vampire.

The stick was so close to his heart.

"He's not dead," Alex finally said, putting his hands on top of the stick. "Not yet anyway."

"Not yet anyway," I repeated, horrified. "Does that mean he's going to die?"

"Not if we can get him some..." Alex yanked out the stick, and I tried not to gasp at the sight of the very large hole in Laylen's chest or at the blood that was pouring out of it. Alex pressed his hand onto the wound, putting pressure on it.

"Get him some what?" I asked, fully freaking out. "Is there a cure?"

Alex avoided my eyes as he said, ""Yeah, blood."

"He has to bite someone?" I asked, remembering the first day I had met Laylen and he had told me he never brought out his fangs.

Alex hesitated, and I could see it in his eyes. "No, he needs another vampire's blood."

"Is that the only kind of blood that will work?" I asked.

He nodded, and even though I didn't believe him, I took a deep breath, placed a hand on Laylen's cold arm, and then shut my eyes, hoping I was strong enough to take us back, since what I could do with my extraordinary Foreseer ability was still a huge question mark.

"Take us to the Black Dungeon," Alex told me.

Keeping my eyes shut, I replied, "Why there?"

"Because there'll be vampires all over."

I nodded, thinking how Laylen wasn't supposed to go near vampires, but feared if he didn't, he would die. I pictured the alley, damp, scary, and covered with garbage. I envisioned the bright red door, and the flap at the top. I saw all three of us there.

I tried my hardest to focus on the details I'd seen when I was there, and when Alex took hold of my hand, I felt a surge of electricity, and the weakness I'd been feeling left me. I knew I'd get us there.

I had to.

Chapter 23

I didn't have to open my eyes to know I'd gotten us to the right place. The smell of garbage and musty air gave away our location.

I opened my eyes and saw Alex was kneeling on the ground beside me, still holding my hand, his other hand on Laylen's wound. It was the smoothest travel I'd ever pulled off and it couldn't have come at a better time.

"Okay, I'm going to go inside and get someone who'll help—hopefully someone who doesn't know Laylen was responsible for Vladislav's death." Alex took my hand and placed it on top of his hand that was covering the hole in Laylen's chest. "Put pressure on it, okay?"

I nodded, and he moved his hand away. Very quickly I replaced it with mine. The blood seeped warmly against my fingers, and Laylen's skin felt colder than it usually did.

"Hurry," I called out to Alex as he started for the bright red door. "Wait," I suddenly called out. "Can you go in looking like that?"

Alex stopped and gave a glance down at his shirtless chest. "Gemma, I don't think it's really going to matter whether I'm dressed appropriately or not."

"Yeah, but it's going to matter if that's showing." I pointed at the Keeper's mark tattooing the side of his ribcage.

"Crap,''" he said. Then without saying another word, he took off in the opposite direction.

"Alex," I hissed. "Where are you going?"

He didn't answer as he vanished around the corner.

I sat there, with my hand pressed to Laylen's bleeding chest, listening to dogs howl in the distance. The sky was beginning to shift from a bright blue to a pale pink as the sun ascended behind the shallow hills of the desert. Night was almost here, the air was getting colder, and I was freaking out. What if someone showed up—someone bad—and I couldn't protect Laylen? There were so many risks, and I was concerned that if Alex asked the wrong vampire—one that knew what Laylen had done to Vladislav—we would be in some serious trouble.

And maybe that's why I did what I did. But honestly, I wasn't sure what the exact reason was. But it really didn't matter. All that mattered was that I gave Laylen a soft shake to see if I could get him to open his eyes.

"Laylen," I whispered, keeping my hand pressed to his chest as I leaned over him. "Laylen, can you hear me?"

His eyes stayed closed.

"Laylen, if you can hear me, I need to know something."

Still nothing.

"I need to know if there's another way to save you without having to get a vampire involved." I took a shaky breath, tears stinging at my eyes. "Alex said there wasn't, but I don't believe him. Please wake up...please."

My heart was splitting in two. I watched to see if Laylen's chest was rising and falling, but it was too dark to tell.

"Laylen," I said, a little too loud, and Laylen's eyes shot open. I gasped as he sucked in a breath of air. "Oh my God." Tears streamed down my cheeks. "You're awake."

He nodded slowly, letting out a few coughs.

"Are you okay?" I asked, wiping my tears away.

He shook his head weakly. "I can't feel it anymore."

"Can't feel what?" I asked softly.

"The pain."

"From the wound?"

He shook his head. "From being alone."

I almost burst into sobs, but I held it back. I needed to be the strong one. "It'll be okay. Alex is going to get help."

"I don't think...." His eyes fell shut again.

"Laylen," I panicked. "Don't close your eyes."

He shook his head and said nothing.

"Laylen," I said. "Is there another way to cure you?"

I knew I might have been searching for something that didn't exist, but when I asked Alex the same question I swear he had been lying when he told me no. And in many of the vampire-themed books I read, *human* blood worked as a cure.

"Laylen." I kept my voice calm, but demanding. "Open your eyes. You have to open your eyes."

Slowly, his eyelids lifted open. His bright blue eyes were glazed over, and I wondered if he was even there.

"Can you hear me?" I asked.

He nodded lethargically.

His blood soaked my fingers—time was running out.

"Can you tell me if there's another way to save you?" I asked. "Besides vampire blood?"

He blinked a few times, his eyes coming into focus. "No, there's not."

"Are you sure?"

He hesitated.

"Laylen," I said in a gentle voice. "Does human blood work too?"

He didn't answer right away, but when he did, his voice was frail. "I can't...I can't do it."

"If it will save you..." I took a deep breath. "Please just do it, okay? Don't leave me here alone." Whoa. Where did that come from?

We stared at each other, and this moment passed between us—this moment of understanding. We both knew that our time was running out—that his time was running out. Alex still hadn't returned, and he still had to track down a vampire who wouldn't know what Laylen had done to Vladislav.

He let out a cough before nodding. "Alright, I'll do it."

"Okay," I repeated nervously. "Where do you want to...um..."

"On your wrist," he answered for me. "It's easier that way, at least from what I've been told."

Keeping my hand on his wound, I gave him my other hand. He took hold of it, his skin ice-cold, and through the looseness in his grip I could tell he was weak. Then, with a look of horror, he opened his mouth, letting out a whimper as his fangs descended. I held his gaze so he wouldn't think I was afraid of him. But I was afraid. Not so much afraid of getting bitten—well, maybe just a little. But I was more afraid of losing him.

As his sharp vampire fangs sunk into my wrist, a rush of adrenaline and a million other things whipped through me, just like when Vladislav had bitten me. But there were also different feelings there—things I'd never felt before.

I tried not to blink.

I tried not to look away.

I stayed with him.

Chapter 24

Minutes later, after the buzzing, humming, and so much other stuff had worn out of my body and my mind, Laylen and I both lay, yes, on the smelly ground of the alleyway and stared up at the stars.

He drank just enough of my blood for the wound in his chest to seal itself shut. Then he pulled away, putting his fangs back where they belonged. The only evidence that anything had happened was the two little bite marks spotting my wrist. Well, that and Laylen's guilt for biting me. I could tell that he felt guilty, which made me feel guilty for telling him to bite me. But that was okay. I would deal with my guilt as long as it meant he was alive.

The sky was a midnight black now, the glow of the Vegas lights shimmering across it in various colors. Car horns and roaring engines flooded the air.

"Why do you think Nicholas is helping Stephan?" I asked Laylen, staring at the crescent moon.

"I'm not sure," Laylen replied, his eyes glued to the sky. "I do know one thing, though. The next time I see him, he better run."

I cast a glance at him. The pale glimmer of the moon lit up the pain in his eyes. "Hopefully, we don't ever see him again."

"I highly doubt it'll be the last time we see the faerie," Laylen muttered, his jaw set tight.

He was probably right. Nicholas had an act for randomly popping up.

"But I just don't get it," I said. "It seems like he's been helping Stephan for awhile, yet he was there at Adessa's for all those days and never gave away our location? Why would he do that?"

"I think we'll never be able to understand why Nicholas does what he does," Laylen said. "What I think we need to do is focus on getting your mom back, just like we were planning. I just have this feeling she knows things that we don't."

I was abruptly reminded of something Nicholas had said back in the woods; that Stephan had created Laylen. Stephan had been the cause behind Laylen's vampirism. But why would Stephan need to create a vampire? Why not just go get one of the many premade ones that were wandering around? Did it have to do with the star?

I decided not to tell Laylen that Stephan was the cause behind him being a vampire. Don't freak out on me, though. I am going to tell him. I owed him the truth, no matter what—he always did the same for me. But I was going to let him get over biting me first, because he wasn't handling it very well. In fact, he hadn't made eye contact with me since he had done it.

"Are you okay?" I asked him. "I mean, with…biting me?"

He winced and then sat up, staring in front of him at the side of the brick building that had been decorated with florescent green spray paint. "I think I should be the one asking if you're okay."

I sat up way too quickly, giving myself a head rush. I pressed my hand to my head. "I'm fine. You don't have to worry about me. I told you to do it."

Finally, he looked at me. "Yeah, but you're the one who's going to be tied to me now. You can't erase the connection I just made with you. It'll be there forever."

"And that's okay." I pulled a few bits and pieces of rock and dirt out of my hair. "It wasn't okay with Vladislav, but with you it is." I didn't mean for it to come out how it sounded, considering the feeling we both knew I felt when he bit me.

There was this awkward moment, where we were both really uncomfortable. And because of that, I didn't notice Alex walking up, nor did I notice the sparks until he was right in front of us.

"You're alright." Alex now had on a shirt and a pair of shoes that looked a little tattered, like he'd bought them from a second hand store. "How—what happened?

Laylen and I jumped to our feet, like we were guilty of committing some heinous crime. Which we so weren't.

With as long as it took for Alex to get a shirt to cover up his Keeper mark, Laylen probably would have never made it.

"We weren't doing anything," I said quickly, making me seem guilty.

Alex furrowed his eyebrows at me. "I never said you were. I was just asking why Laylen's okay."

"Oh." I gave Laylen a what-should-we-do look. He shook his head and shrugged, like he had no idea what to tell Alex either. I tucked my arms behind me to hide the bite marks on my wrist. "Um…would you believe me if I said he just healed on his own?"

Laylen let out a tired sigh, distracting me so I didn't react quickly enough when Alex seized a hold of my arm and pulled it out from behind me. The two little bite marks marked my skin like a Scarlet G for guilty. Only I was not guilty of anything.

"What the hell?" he said, struggling to stay composed. He looked at Laylen heatedly. "You *bit* her?"

"*I* made him bite me," I said, pulling my arm away from him.

"I was going to get help." He was furious.

"He was dying," I said, simply but firmly. "And it was the only thing I could think of to do."

"I—How would you even know that would work?" he asked, working to keep himself contained.

I shrugged. "I had a hunch. Besides, you should have said it would work in the first place, instead of saying we had to go track down another vampire, which just wasted time. And it would have been more of a risk for Laylen if you brought back a vampire who knew about him killing Vladislav." My voice was ringing angrily, and I was breathing heavy. I was mad. A different kind of mad than I'd ever been. I was mad for someone else. I was mad at Alex for risking Laylen's life like that. And I was mad at Nicholas for almost taking Laylen's life. The prickle was going insane. I saw red, and suddenly I gave Alex a shove. It didn't really do anything to him; it just caused him to take an unsteady step back. But it shocked the heck out of everyone, including myself.

"Gemma," Laylen said, his eyes wide with shock. "It's okay. I'm okay. Everything's okay."

I blinked a few times, blinking my way out of my raging state. "Sorry, but he needs to stop lying."

I waited for Alex to freak out on me in normal Alex style. But all he said was, "Let's get out of here." Then he turned away from us and headed down the alley.

Laylen and I traded curious glances, and then we followed after him.

Chapter 25

We didn't go to Adessa's. Alex pointed out that it probably wasn't safe for us to go there, since Nicholas was roaming around with a group of Death Walkers, and he knew where our little I hideout was. Laylen and I agreed with him, and that we should probably warn Adessa and Aislin to get out of the house and somewhere safe. But since none of us had our cell phones, we had to go find a phone.

Here's the problem. Phone booths are practically extinct. So after roaming around the hectic streets of Vegas, searching for a phone booth, we finally gave up and entered a store to ask if we could use their phone. But people are kind of rude when it comes to letting "noncustomers" use their phones, so getting someone to let us was becoming a total project. And we were all tired. And hungry.

A great combination, let me tell you.

I was really hating Vegas at the moment.

People kept staring at us funnily too, probably because I had dried blood all over my hands and mud stuck to my clothes. Plus, Laylen had a huge blood stain on his shirt. Afraid someone was going to think we'd killed someone, we all took a second to go into a gas station bathroom and clean up a little. I washed up the best I could. I even rinsed out my hair in the sink, but there was nothing I could do about the fact that I didn't have any shoes on.

After I finished cleaning up, I met Laylen and Alex back outside. Laylen had scrubbed down his shirt, but I could still faintly make out a small stain. Alex had run water through his hair and somehow had miraculously styled it into place.

Apparently while they'd been waiting for me to clean up, they'd come up with a plan. Well, Laylen came up with a plan, anyway. Laylen suggested to Alex to go work his "Alex charm" on the cashier girl inside the gas station, and see if he could persuade her to let us use her phone. I felt bad for the poor girl, and for a brief second I wanted to smack Alex on the back of the head for doing such a mean thing, especially because I once was in that poor girl's position. But my sore bare feet and hunger pains kept me from stopping him.

So Laylen and I waited outside the gas station, which was located in a less busy, but sketchier area of Vegas, while Alex went in to work his "Alex charm" on the poor girl. And within seconds, he had the phone pressed up to his ear.

"So you're okay, right?" Laylen asked, as we stood in front of the glass entrance doors, keeping our eyes out for any Death Walkers, vampires, a man with a scar, etc.

"What, with Alex flirting with that girl," I replied, ringing some of the left over water out of my dark brown hair. "Yeah, why wouldn't I be?" The expression on Laylen's face let me know right away that that was not what he had been talking about at all, and I felt like such an idiot. "Oh, you mean with the bite," I said, feeling stupid. "Yeah, of course I'm fine."

"You don't feel..." He hesitated, leaning back against the door. "Weird or anything?"

I shook my head, cupping my hand over the bite marks on my wrists. "No. No weirdness." Actually, that was a lie. During the bite-session, there was this fleeting instant where I pictured Laylen and me kissing, which was completely weird. I knew it was only the bite that had struck up the picture in my mind, but there was still a lingering feel-good sensation that the image had brought up inside me. But I knew it would wear off soon enough.

"So no weirdness, then?" He still seemed disbelieving.

"Besides this conversation?" I joked.

He laughed, and it felt good that I had been the one to make him laugh. Also, maybe I could take this as a sign that my people skills were improving.

I know, who would have thought, right?

"So, how are you feeling?" I asked. "No weirdness with you?"

He shook his head as he absentmindedly touched his mouth on the spot where his fangs had slipped out. "I feel okay I guess. Except my teeth feel a little strange."

"Strange how?" I wondered.

"I don't know. I can feel them now, up there, and it's...I don't know." He touched the tip of his finger to his tooth. "I've never had them out before."

I gaped him. "What? You've never brought out your fangs before...ever?"

"Nope," he said. "I told you I never brought them out."

"Yeah, but when you said 'never' I thought you were talking about hardly ever, like maybe once and awhile."

"Nope. Never as in never."

"So you've never bitten anyone before? *Ever*?"

He shook his head. "No, you're the first."

Wow. I stood there, taking in the heaviness of the situation. What if, because he brought them out, he changed? What if he started to become blood hungry? It would be my fault because I made him bite me. But he would've died if he hadn't. Especially since Alex had been moving at the pace of a turtle, which I was hoping wasn't done intentionally. But Alex is Alex and you can never put anything past him.

I chose to keep all of this to myself, though. There was no use letting Laylen in on my thoughts of whether or not he was going to go insane and start biting people. I was just going to have to make sure to keep an eye on him.

"Okay," Alex announced as he stepped outside, a bell dinging as the door swung shut. "Aislin and Adessa are leaving the house now—well, Aislin is, and Adessa's going to go stay with some friends of hers until we let her know it's safe for her to return home."

"And where are we going?" I asked, glancing anxiously at a large Chevy truck turning into the gas station parking lot.

"*We* are driving," he answered.

"Driving?" I repeated. Driving seemed like such an amateur thing to do. "Why can't we just have Aislin transport us? Or maybe I could get us somewhere since I can now use my Foreseer power to travel to places."

"No." He moved right in front of me, his bright green eyes gleaming in the neon pink glow of the flashing "Open" sign. "We're not transporting because there's no way we can get to Aislin or Adessa without the fear of them being followed."

"But I could—"

"And we're not using your Foreseer abilities anymore until we know for sure that you know how to use them."

"I know how to use them. I got us to the Black Dungeon perfectly fine, didn't I?"

"Yeah, but you're tired." He gave me an intense look, before looking away at the silent street. "I can feel it."

I focused on the electric buzz, and it did seem very faint—a soft hum instead of fiery sparkles. "Well, so are you," I pointed out.

"Exactly. We all are." He looked at Laylen. "So for now, I think it would be best if we drove. It gives us a chance to rest. And besides, since our location will con-

258

stantly be changing, it'll make it harder for Nicholas to track us down. Showing up in a moving vehicle is basically impossible to do."

"But what about when we stop?" I asked.

"We'll make limited stops, and I won't make the decision to stop until a few seconds beforehand." Alex ran his hands through his very messy and not in an-intentionally-done kind of way hair. "That way he'll have very short notice on where we'll be at."

"You think that'll work?" Laylen asked, moving away from the gas station entrance doors so a man wearing a red baseball cap could go inside.

"Honestly?" He shook his head. "I have no idea if it will, but it's all I got right now, so..."

"So, where's this car we're supposed to be driving?" Laylen asked. "And where are we going to be driving it to?"

"That's for me to know." Alex started across the gas station parking lot.

I headed after him, the gravel cutting into my bare feet. "You're not going to tell us?" I asked, not surprised but irritated.

He came to a stop so rapidly I just about ran straight into him. The electricity awoke from its lazy slumber, reacting excitedly.

He turned around with very serious expression on his face. "Look," he said. "I understand it's your nature to want to know things, but it's best if only I know where we're going. If Nicholas is trying to track you, it'll be easier for him if you're thinking about where we're headed."

Whether his plan made sense or not, I gave in because I didn't have a better idea. "Okay then," I said. "Let's go get a car."

Turns out Adessa had a friend who would lend us their car, or an SUV I guess I should say. The beastly thing could in no way qualify as a car. The colossal SUV—a shiny black Chevy Tahoe—had tires as tall as my legs and a lift to add even more height. I practically had to high jump into it. Then after I made it inside, I had to wait around while Alex and Laylen argued over who was going to drive the beast.

Finally, they decided that Laylen would go first since apparently he felt very wired and awake. So we pulled out of the parking garage and onto a main road of Vegas, where Alex told Laylen to drive to the freeway and head east.

As I sat there on the sticky backseat, staring out the window—at the stars of course—I couldn't help but think about how much trouble we were in now that it seemed Nicholas was helping Stephan. With Stephan having a Foreseer on his side, it was going to make tracking us down much easier. In fact, I was surprised he hadn't already, which made me question just what Nicholas was up to. He had me right there when he pretended to help me, so why not turn me over?

At least we were in a moving vehicle now, and if what Alex said was true then we were safe for the moment.

The longer we drove, the dimmer the florescent lights of Vegas became, until they were completely tucked away behind the sandy hills. I let out a yawn as I stared up at the silver stream of stars, questioning my whole existence. Why was I here? I mean, if the star's energy was being used to open the portal, then didn't it mean I was as well? It was in me, therefore I would be responsible for the portal opening and ending the world.

Well, that was a heavy thought.

"You should get some sleep."

I tore my eyes away from the stars and my very unsettling thoughts and found Alex watching me from the front seat.

"It's late," he said. "And we have a ways to go."

"I'm not really tired," I said, even though I yawned about ten times in the last few minutes.

"Well, you should try to get some sleep, anyway, just in case something happens." He ran his fingers though his hair and turned away. "And I know you're tired. I can feel it."

This whole new "I-can-feel-you're-tired-and-you-can-feel-I'm-tired" thing was weird. But I guess everything between Alex and I was a little weird, so...

I rested my head against the cool, hard glass of the window, and within seconds my eyelids had drifted shut.

Bright light. Bright light everywhere.

I belonged here—I could feel. I belonged in the bright white light.

Peaceful, calm—this was my end.

The light sparkled across my skin, enveloping me in a blanket of warmth.

I'd been here before, in a vision. Nicholas had said it was my end. And as I stood here in the bright light, I knew he was right. This is where I would end up...

Forever.

My eyes shot open, and for a moment I couldn't figure out where I was. Somewhere dark. And warm. Then it dawned on me. I was in a car, headed to who knew where. I was also lying down on the seat, the leather pressing warmly against my cheek.

The whole light dream I had was making me freak out a little, especially because Nicholas had told me that the light vision I'd gone into meant my future was dead. And now I was dreaming about it. That couldn't be good.

From the front seats, Alex and Laylen were chatting about cars, like they were two normal guys, which I guess was a good thing—at least they weren't fighting. But it was still strange to hear a normal conversation that didn't center on Death Walkers, Foreseers, or the end of the world.

"No. There's no way your GTO could beat my Camaro," Alex was saying, sounding a little worked up. "Are you freaking kidding me with this?"

"No, I'm not freaking kidding you with this," Laylen replied calmly. "I bet you hands down that my car could take your car any day."

"Bull," Alex said. "You know I would win, you just won't admit it."

I decided that I'd rather be sleeping than listening to this. But right as I was shutting my eyes, Laylen said something that made me open them right back up.

"I'll tell you what," he said. "I'll admit that you might be right, if you'll admit that you like Gemma."

"If I told you that then I'd be lying," Alex said, sounding as if he meant it. "Well, at least not in the sense that you're implying."

Ouch, that stung.

They were silent. The only sound came from the rumble of the tires and the low hum of the song purring from the stereo speakers—"Epiphany" by Staind.

"Okay, Alex," Laylen said, in an "I'm-going-to-lay-it-out-for-you" kind of way. "*I* think you like her. In , I think you always have and always will. Now, whether or not you'll admit it is your problem. All I care about is that you lay off her. You can be a real jerk to her—to everyone really but it's worse for her because she's new to feeling things."

263

This conversation, for some reason, was making me feel very uncomfortable. But I didn't know how to block it out. Cover my ears? Yeah, then they'd know I was awake and listening.

"You need to shut up," Alex said, his anger blaring in his voice. "I don't feel that way about her. Never have, never will."

"Yeah, because you don't care about anything," Laylen told him. "You never have. Well, I take that back. You used to be normal until Gemma was sent away, then you basically just shut off. Maybe you should just think about why that is. Why would you change right when she left?"

"Because everyone will hurt you if you let them in," Alex muttered as if he was quoting someone.

"What?" Laylen asked. "What does that mean?"

"Nothing. Just drop it." Alex turned up the volume of the music, and the conversation was dropped.

I laid there for awhile with my eyes open, pondering everything. My feelings. My mom. What Alex had said. "Everyone will hurt you if you let them in." I wondered if he really believed it.

I felt very strange, my emotions running all over the place, almost like the prickle was malfunctioning or something.

And maybe it was.

Maybe I was broken.

Chapter 26

When I woke up, the first thing I noticed was that the SUV had stopped. I sat up in the seat, wondering if we made it to wherever we were heading, or if something had happened. After blinking away my sleepy disorientation, I realized we were just at a gas station, getting gas.

Laylen was outside, pumping gas into the SUV, and Alex was nowhere in sight.

I stifled a yawn and then stretched, wondering what time it was. The sun was beating hotly from up in the sky, and the streets that bordered the gas station were bouncing with traffic. There was an old white and green Victorian house across the road that had a sign that read Isabella's Herb Shop. I wondered if it was the same kind of herb store as Adessa's

Someone knocked on the window, causing me to jump. Laylen smiled at me through the glass and motioned to me to open the door.

"Well, good morning, Sleeping Beauty," he said, after I open the door and climbed out into the sunlight. "Sleep well?"

"Surprisingly, yes." I stretched out my legs and arms. "How long was I out?"

"For about eight hours."

"Eight hours?" How the heck had I slept for eight hours with everything that was going on?

"Yeah, you were really out, too." He flashed me a grin. "Snoring and all."

"I don't snore," I protested. At least, I think I don't.

He gave me another teasing smile, before sliding the debit card into the machine.

"Wow, you seem like you're in a good mood," I remarked with a curious tone.

He shrugged, glancing over at a tall woman with long black hair walking across the parking lot. "As good a mood as any, I guess."

He was acting a little...off. "Are you feeling okay?"

He shrugged again, rubbing his lips together, and then looked at me. "I'm fine."

I stared at him, picking up on something. I couldn't explain it, but after the whole first-time-biting thing, I had to worry a little. But before I could press him further, Alex strolled up, carrying a plastic bag.

"If you need to go inside for anything, then you'd better do it," Alex told me, tossing a bag of food and drinks onto to the front seat of the SUV.

Seeing him made what he said last night replay in my head, along with the hurt feelings I felt. "Okay." I headed inside.

"Make it quick," Alex called after me. "We don't want to be stopped for too long."

I nodded, shocked he was even letting me go in by myself.

The gas station was fairly packed, which made my senses go on high alert, especially because I stood out like a sore thumb. My clothes were filthy, I had no shoes on, and my hair was a tangled mess—well, at least more of a tangled mess than it usually was—so people couldn't help but gawk at me as I walked by them. I made my way down the candy aisle, past the drink cooler, and stepped into the restroom. I splashed my face with cold water and washed my hands. Wherever we were, the air felt humid and hot, making my skin feel gross.

I glanced up in the mirror and let out a groan at my reflection. My violet eyes. The one thing that was always going to make me stand out—deem me different. I was painfully realizing that no matter how much I wanted a normal life, it just might be impossible, and maybe I needed to start accepting that I was a star carrying, vision seeing, violet-eyed Gemma.

And that my life might not be long lived.

After my light vision, and my light dream, I had to wonder. They both might have been showing me a part of my future. The thought was scary, but I had to hold onto the fact that not everything I saw or dreamt had played out exactly as I had seen it. Things changed.

For the moment, I really needed to focus on figuring out how to get a hold of the Ira so I could go into The Underworld and save my mom. The problem was I couldn't just walk into a store and purchase an Ira. The only person that I knew of who had one was Nicholas, and now that he might be working with Stephan, getting one from him seemed more impossible than it did before.

"Stupid faerie." I kicked the wall, frustrated. Of course, kicking a tile wall while wearing no shoes was not the grandest idea, and I ended stubbing my toes. "*Ow.*"

One of the bathroom stall doors opened up and an old lady, wearing a long green dress and tan shoes, and looking really alarmed, scurried out of the bathroom.

"Whoops," I mumbled to myself. I guess it was time to go back anyway. Standing in a bathroom wasn't doing me any good. And I was supposed to be hurrying.

I headed for the door, hearing one of the stall doors squeak open. Instinctively, I glanced behind me, and then stopped when I didn't see anyone. The door was swinging, and I wondered if I scared someone else enough that they were afraid to come out.

I sighed. It was definitely time to leave. I turned around, and then stumbled backward, because standing right in front of me was a very obnoxious faerie with golden eyes and sandy hair.

"Well, I have to say that this is not where I pictured us meeting up again," Nicholas said, glancing around the women's restroom. "Although it'll do, I guess."

I backed away from him, knowing full well that I was cornered. "Stay the heck away from me."

He moved for me, a sneaky smirk spreading across his face. "You seem afraid of me, Gemma."

My back hit the tiled wall. "I know why you're here. I know you're working with Stephan."

"You do, do you?"

"You were at the City of Crystal with the Death Walkers," I said heatedly. "And I heard you talking to them. How can you talk to them?"

"I can't," he said, and I shook my head. Let the running around in circles begin.

"Yes you can," I snapped. "I heard. And I heard you talking about capturing me for Stephan. Why would you do that? Don't you know what he wants to do with me?"

I was hoping he would say that he did, and then we would have one of those moments where the villain unleashes all his evil plans.

"Why would you think I was helping Stephan? I can't stand him as much as I can't stand his son." He moved in front of me, leaning in close. "And honestly, if I captured you, I'd rather keep you for myself. There's so much..." He sniffed me. Yes, actually sniffed me, like he was smelling a flower or something. "Power flowing off you."

My mouth dropped. He could feel the electricity.

"Your Foreseer gift...it's absolutely breathtaking," he said, moving back a little.

Oh, he was talking about *that* power.

270

"That's great," I said, looking for a way out of here. I could try to dodge around him, but I didn't see myself making it that far. The only thing I could think of to do was use my "breathtaking" Foreseer ability to move myself from the bathroom to the SUV. But could I do it quickly enough?

All I could do was try.

"Tell me, Gemma." Nicholas was so close to me that the flowery rain smell that was always radiating off him was strong enough to make me almost pass out. "Why are you so afraid of me?"

"Besides the fact that you're working with the man who wants to hurt me?" I asked, trying to picture in my head the massive black Chevy Tahoe parked outside next to the gas pumps.

"You've never liked me from the first time you met me," he remarked, in a playful way, like this was all a game to him, which it probably was.

I shrugged, still focusing on the SUV. *Come on. Come on. Come on.* "I don't know...I guess you just rubbed me the wrong way."

He said something else. But I didn't hear him. I was going...fading...almost there. Then I was being shoved up against the hard tiled wall of the bathroom. The muscles on my back burned in protest, and I let out a whimper.

"Don't even think about it," Nicholas snapped angrily. "You're coming with me." Then he hit me over the head with something.

271

Chapter 27

The next thing I was aware of was that I had a killer head-ache. My head was throbbing so badly I swear my skull had to be cracked. I also noticed my wrists were restrained by something cold and metal.

My eyelids whipped open. I was in an unfamiliar room, and wrapped around each of my wrists was a metal cuff, connected to a chain that extended to hooks secured into a dark green wall behind me.

Crap.

This was bad.

This was very, very bad.

The first thing I did was try to Foresee my way out of this place. I closed my eyes and concentrated on the gas station, but I wasn't feeling it. I wasn't feeling anything, except worry and fear, and the fact that I was in some serious trouble.

What had that crazy faerie boy done to me? Why couldn't I use my Foreseer power? I tried again, concentrating harder, willing myself away from this place.

"There's no use trying." The taunting voice belonged to Nicholas.

I opened my eyes again and found him standing right in front of me. I scooted back to the wall, dragging the chains with me, the metal clinking against the hardwood floor.

"Where am I?" I asked, aiming to keep my voice steady but failing miserably.

"My house." He gestured around the room, which was basically bare except for a table that lined the far wall and a wooden stool perched in the corner.

"Why did you bring me here?" I asked, yanking at the chains.

"Why not?" he asked with a smile that could only be described as dangerous.

This was *not* good. There were so many things about being here alone with him that could be bad. Not only because he could be handing me over to Stephan, but also because he was in control.

He squatted down on the floor so that he was eye level with me. "Tug at those chains all you want; you're not going to get away."

I jerked my arms again, wanting desperately to prove him wrong. But the chains were secured tightly, and yanking them was making the metal cuffs cut into my wrists.

He laughed at me, and I slid my leg out from underneath me and gave a try at kicking him. He hopped back, a flicker of fury flashing across his face, but he quickly collected himself and smiled again.

274

"You're so feisty," he said, his golden eyes glinting dangerously.

I glared at him. "Let me go."

"Now, why would I do a stupid thing like that?" He stood up, gesturing at the floor around me. "I could keep you here forever, you know—the room is surrounded by *praesidium*."

As I glanced around room, I became aware that trimming the floor were lavender crystal balls about the size of marbles. Now, I didn't know what they were, but I knew they had to be bad.

"What's *praesidium*?" I asked, fearing the answer.

He gave a long pause. "Well, I guess since you asked; *praesidium* is another kind of crystal ball Foreseers use. Only instead of channeling energy, it takes it away."

Oh God. That's why I couldn't use my Foreseer power. The bad situation seemed to be getting worse.

"What are you going to do with me?" I asked, my voice cracking.

He grinned deviously. "I think the question is what am I not going to do with you?"

I tried my best to ignore my quivering nerves. "If you give me over to Stephan, you know what he's going to do to me, right? He's going to end the world—everyone will die."

"I don't need you to explain what Stephan is planning to do. I understand, even more than you do, what he's planning to do with you."

275

"So you're just okay with letting him kill everyone," I said, hoping he would let some of the details slip out. "Do you even feel anything at all?"

"I think the real question is do you feel anything." He leaned over me, his eyes nearly glowing. "Which I think is what this whole thing is about."

My stomach rolled. He knew more than I thought he did. "Why are you doing this? Is there a reason? Or are you just plain evil?"

"Am I just plain evil?" He sounded mad. "Before you go opening your mouth and saying things you don't understand, maybe you should consider how much you know about Stephan. Or about his precious son, Alex. You trust him so much, yet he is the son of the man who has ruined your life, and many others as well."

"Did he ruin your life?" The way he said it made me wonder.

He didn't say anything, and I thought I struck a nerve.

"What did he do to you?" I asked, keeping my voice low and swaying.

He stared at me with a look of intensity and I thought he was going to tell me, but then that playful sparkle returned to his eyes and he backed away from me with a stupid grin on his face.

"I think I'm going to go take a walk." He slid his hands into the pockets of his tan cargo pants. "I'd say wait here, but I don't think you'll be going anywhere."

"Nicholas, please," I begged, jerking on the chains again. "You can't hand me over to Stephan."

But he already left.

I let out a frustrated scream, tugging on the chains with every ounce of strength I had in me, disregarding the pain of the metal cuffs cutting deeply into my skin. I tried to break free until my wrists were bleeding; until I was so exhausted that I had no strength left in me. Until all there was left to do was wait.

What I was waiting for, I didn't know.

Chapter 28

It seemed like hours went by. There were no windows in the room, so I couldn't tell if it was dark outside. And where exactly was I? The Kingdom of Fey or the City of Crystal—where did Nicholas live?

My wrists were sore, my head was throbbing, and I was scared and tired. I wondered what Alex and Laylen were doing. What did they do when I didn't return to the car? Were they looking for me? Would they even know where to find me?

I'd just rested back against the wall, giving up all hope that anyone was ever going to be able to find me, when the door opened up.

My heart leapt, hoping it was Laylen. Or Alex. Although, I couldn't feel any electricity, so I doubted that was the case.

Of course, the only person who came strolling in was Nicholas. He was carrying something in his hand, and he didn't look happy at all.

He walked over and sat down in front of me. "Tell me, Gemma, has anyone told you anything about the Fey world?"

"Umm...no?" Was this a trick question?

"Well." He crossed his legs. "We have been around forever. Most people who know of our existence think of us a tricksters, which, most of the time, we are. But we can also be very serious, at least when it comes to our kind suffering."

I wasn't sure where he was going with this, so I just stared at him vacantly.

"I'm not sure if you've heard of him or not, but there used to be a Keeper who called himself Malefiscus," he said.

I swallowed hard. "I might have heard his name mentioned before."

"Good, then I don't have to explain who he is. And I assume you know what kind of a person he was and what he did."

I slowly nodded. "I do."

"Well, during his time of chaos, he tortured everyone, including the Fey. And the Fey leader at that time decided he had enough—that too many Fey were dying—so he made a bargain with Malefiscus. Leave the Fey alone, and we would owe him one favor. Malefiscus agreed and the promise was bound with a Blood Promise."

"A Blood Promise?"

He ignored me, continuing on with his story. "Not too long after the promise was made, though, Malefiscus was caught and sentenced." He paused. "Everyone thought he died—and who knows, maybe he did, but his bloodline

279

did not die with him. It carried on and now resides in a man named Stephan Avery." He opened his hand and placed what he was holding onto the floor between us. A smooth, round stone, with a circle wrapped by an S painted on it—the Foreseer's mark. "Because his bloodline carried on, so did the Feys' promise to grant a favor. Only now the favor is owed to Stephan. No one knew of this, though, until he showed up just a few days ago, demanding his promise in the name of Malefiscus. But he didn't want just any member of the Fey to honor this promise. He wanted the faerie who possessed the gift of Foreseeing— he wanted me. Or, more specifically he wanted me to track down a very pretty, but very tortured girl with beautiful violet eyes and a fiery personality."

If he hadn't mentioned the eye color, I wouldn't have known he was talking about me, because none of the other parts of his description seemed fitting.

"This was after I met you," he continued. "After I'd taken you to Dyvinius."

"What does he want you to do to me?" I was afraid to know the answer, especially because I was in a very vulnerable situation right now, being chained to a wall and all.

"A few things," he said. "But in the end, it all comes down to one thing—I am supposed to bring you to him."

I swallowed hard. "Are you going to?"

"At first I wasn't sure. I know what Stephan is planning to do—that was made clear from the beginning." He

280

pressed his lips together, considering something. "But in the end, I really don't have a choice. I am bound to a promise I cannot break."

"Are you sure you can't break it?" I asked, practically pleading. "Because there might be a wa—"

"No, there is no other way." He talked over me. "If I don't turn you over, then my people will suffer."

"But if you do turn me over, the whole world will suffer," I told him. "I've seen it."

He gave me a mocking look. "Are you sure about that?"

"Yes," I said confidently.

"And how can you be sure? How can you be sure of anything?"

"I..." He had a point. How could I be sure of anything?

He scooted the stone closer to me and I scooted back.

"What is that?" I asked, pointing a shaking finger at the stone.

"Something that's going to temporarily take your Foreseer power away."

"What?" I cried, scooting back from the stone even more. "How?"

"Don't worry," his voice purred. "It won't hurt. And it's only temporary. For the moment, Stephan needs you free of your powers, but eventually you'll get them back."

"Please don't," I begged. "You can't give me to him."

"I already said, I don't have a choice." He looked livid as he rolled up the sleeve of his black shirt. Across his arm was a mark. Not the Foreseer's mark, but a different one — a red symbol traced by a black triangle.

"What is that?" I whispered, although I think deep down I already knew.

"The Mark of Malefiscus," Nicholas practically growled. "I am forever branded with the mark of evil. And between the Blood Promise and the mark of evil, I have to hand you over."

"How did you—how did you get it?" I asked, trying not to shake from head-to-toe. "Are you related to Stephan?"

He shook his head. "No. Like Malefiscus, Stephan is capable of making marks, not just on himself but on other people."

My breath caught again. If Stephan could put the mark on people...What if he'd put the mark on Alex? I wasn't sure if I believed that or not. Yes, Alex had done some questionable things, but now...I don't know...he went to the City of Crystal for me.

Nicholas picked up the stone and held it in front of my face, just out of my reach. "Until we meet again," he said.

"No!" I screamed as the stone began to hum. It did not glow, though, or create smoke. It just hummed. Louder and louder, until the humming clawed at my ear drums.

I threw my hands over my ears. "Nicholas!" I yelled. "Please don't do this."

"It's not my choice," Nicholas shouted over the humming. Then, suddenly, his eyes were rolling back in his head. He let out a deafening scream that rang loudly through the room. The stone fell from his hands and hit the floor with a clank. The next thing I knew he was lying on the floor. He wasn't dead—I could see his chest rising and falling with each breath—but definitely unconscious.

I stared at him, bewildered. What happened? Had the stone backfired its power on him? Then I felt a warmth against my neck. I reached up, and slipped my locket out from underneath my tank top.

"Oh my God." My necklace. My beautiful, amazing, wonderful necklace. The stone's magic must have taken Nicholas's Foreseer power away from him instead of from me.

I tucked the locket back under my shirt and immediately started searching for a way to escape. I didn't know how long Nicholas was going to be out so I needed to hurry. What I needed was the key to the cuffs.

I inched my way over to Nicholas, as far as the chains would allow me to go, which was close enough that I could reach Nicholas's foot. I grabbed hold of his shoe and started dragging him toward me. My word, faeries were heavy. It was like trying to pull a bag of bricks. But I managed and almost started jumping up and down when I found the key tucked away in the pocket of his pants.

"Yes," I cried, unlocking the cuffs and then letting out a breath of freedom. I ran for the door, unsure of how far I would have to go to be able to use my Foreseer powers to get me out of here. But then a sudden thought raced through my mind that made me pause just outside the door. The Ira ball. What if it was here?"

I glanced back at Nicholas, sleeping away. How much time did I have? I wasn't sure, but I had to try and find it. I raced back into the room, ran over to the table and threw open all the drawers. Each one was vacant.

Other than the table, this room was empty, so I ran out of it and into the next room, where I began ripping everything apart. I dumped out drawers, threw the cushions off the sofas, tossed books off the shelves, but I still couldn't find it.

Frustrated, I kicked a small garbage can that just happened to me in my leg's reach. It tipped over and something round and moss colored rolled out of it and across the floor. The Ira.

I swiped it up and stuffed it into the pocket of my shorts, which was a tricky thing to do since the thing was about the size of a softball. But I didn't want to be touching it with my skin when I used my Foreseer ability to try and get back to Laylen and Alex.

Worried I might still be too close to the *praesidium*, I decided to leave the house. I looked around until I found the front door, threw it open, and ran outside. I almost ate it when my feet hit a slick surface—crystal, and it was as slippery as trying to walk across an icy parking lot. I slowly made my way across it, slipping and sliding with every step I took. Finally, I couldn't take it anymore and crossed my fingers that this would be far enough away.

I cast a glance back at the house, which now that I looked at it was not a normal house, but a dome house that had been carved out of snow-white crystal. The roof was dotted with bright red gemstones, and the tree that towered beside it had leaves that glowed like nightlights.

Just as I was closing my eyes to take off, the front door to the dome house swung open, and Nicholas stepped out.

"Gemma." His voice echoed over the ice. "Don't even think about leaving." He started to run toward me, moving slowly— feebly—like the stone had drained him of most of his energy.

I shut my eyes, and quickly conjured up a mental picture of the massive SUV, hoping Laylen and Alex would still be at the gas station.

"Gemma." Nicholas's angry voice sounded closer.

I squeezed my eyes shut, picturing the leather backseat of the SUV and how I had been lying down on it. I heard Nicholas call out my name again, but I was already gone.

Chapter 29

I landed on my back. My eyes were open and I was staring up at the vinyl ceiling of the black SUV. I shot upright, breathing heavily as I immediately skimmed my surroundings. To my amazement, the SUV was still parked at the gas station, only now instead of being parked to the side of a gas pump it was in a parking space in front of the gas station. The sun was still shining brightly, so I must have not been gone for too long.

But where were Laylen and Alex?

Right as I thought it, I spotted them standing not too far off in front of the car. They looked like they were arguing, stern expressions set on their faces, their arms flying as they spoke heatedly.

I threw open the car door. "Hey," I yelled and they both jumped.

As soon as they saw it was me, they ran over and hopped into the car.

"Where the heck have you been?" Alex asked, not in a rude way, but in an extremely freaked out one.

"We have to go." Not knowing how long it would take for Nicholas's Foreseer power to return to him, I knew we needed to get on the road fast.

Alex and Laylen looked at each other, and then a few moments later the tires were spinning as we peeled out of the parking lot, leaving the gas station behind in a cloud of dust.

I think it took Alex about a minute before he started firing off questions at me. Where were you? What happened? Why are your wrists bleeding? Are you okay? The last one threw me for a bit of a turn, but I answered each one, and made sure to include all the details about the Fey and the Blood Promise. I even took it upon myself to be the one to tell him that his father was definitely a descendent of Malefiscus. I also told him about Nicholas's new mark.

I thought when I told Alex all of this, he would freak out. Well, I mean freak out in the sense that he would deny, deny, deny, and refuse to believe such a thing about his father. Yeah, he did change a little bit over the course of the last few days, but some of the things I told him were big.

So I was shocked when he shrugged and said, "Of course my father is a descendent of Malefiscus. I already knew that."

Laylen's head whipped in Alex's direction. "What? I mean, yeah we all guessed he was, but....you knew?"

Alex slumped back in the chair. "When I was little, my father would tell me stories of Malefiscus."

"Everyone's parents did," Laylen pointed out as he merged the SUV into the left lane so he could pass a very slow moving minivan.

"Yeah, but my father would tell me different stories." His jaw tightened. "Darker stories."

"How dark?" I asked, leaning forward on the console.

"Stories of how one day a descendent of Malefiscus," he ran his fingers through his hair, letting out a stressed breath, "would bear Malefiscus's mark."

"Those were the kind of stories your father told you when you were little?" I stared at him, horrified. Jeez, maybe Marco and Sophia weren't that bad.

He shrugged. "I was a little kid, so I thought it was normal. I honestly didn't even remember his story until you mentioned your vision and how he…" He swallowed hard. "How his parents cut off his mark. I knew then that my father had to be the descendent he always told me about."

I shook my head at him. "And you didn't bother mentioning any of this to us because…"

"Because I don't bother mentioning a lot of things to you." Alex stared out the window with his arms folded.

As I sat there thinking about Alex and the way that he was, the thought that he might have been marked by Stephan, just like Nicholas had, crept back up into my mind.

"So did you know your father could mark people with the Mark of Malefiscus?" I asked, looking at Alex.

He shook his head. "That I didn't."

I rested my arms on the console and leaned forward even more, trying to get a better look at his face, so I could watch his expression when I asked the next question.

"He didn't...I mean, he didn't mark...you, did he?" I felt horrible for asking it, but we needed to know.

He just stared at me, unblinking, not saying a word.

"Sorry, but I had to ask," I muttered.

He kept staring at me with this serious look in his eyes. "Do you think I have the mark?"

"I don't...a...I don't know." I sounded like a babbling idiot. "I don't know what to think anymore, not with everything that's happened." I tried to make eye contact with Laylen so I could signal to him to help me out with this, but he was focused on the road.

"So what do you want me to do?" Alex cocked an eyebrow at me. "Strip off all my clothes and prove to you that I don't have the Mark of Malefiscus anywhere?"

"No," I said, and then I turned my head away and bit down on my bottom lip, hoping he couldn't feel my increasing body temperature.

"Okay, then, I guess you'll just have to believe me." There was a hint of laughter in his voice.

Believe him. Was that possible? A week ago I'd have said there was absolutely no way I could believe him. But,

I don't know, things change. The idea of believing him didn't seem as absurd as it once did.

"Well, what are we going to do now?" Laylen asked suddenly.

"We're going to keep driving east." Alex dropped open the glove box. "We'll make a plan when we meet up with Aislin."

"A plan to go to The Underworld and save my mother, right?" I said.

"If we can get the Ira back, then yes." He started digging though the glove box and I slipped the Ira ball out of my pocket and placed it on top of the console in a *Ta-da!* way. He glanced over his shoulder and his eyes widened. "Where the heck did you get that?"

"I swiped it from Nicholas's house before I left," I said proudly.

"Nice job." Laylen flashed me a smile through the rearview mirror.

"Impressive," Alex added, looking very much impressed. He picked up the Ira, lifted up the lid to the middle console, and dropped the Ira down inside. Then he returned his attention back to rummaging around in the glove box.

"What are you looking for?" I asked, flopping back against the seat.

"For this." He pulled out a first aid kit. "Your wrists need to be cleaned up. What happened to you, by the way?"

I glanced down at my semi-mutilated wrist. "Nicholas chained me up to the wall and every time I jerked at the chain, the metal cuffs cut into my skin."

Alex's jaw tightened. He hopped over the console and into the backseat, opened up the first aid kit, and took out a roll of gauze and a bottle of peroxide.

He held out his hand. "Here, let me see one of your wrists."

I gave him my left one first because it looked like it'd taken the worst of it. I sat there, letting him dab my skin with a cotton ball soaked with peroxide, and tried hard not to wince. But then the sparks tickled at my skin, and it numbed some of the pain away.

Even dressed in his worn out clothes, Alex was still as gorgeous as ever. I thought about Stephan being his father. Maybe that had contributed to why Alex was such a jerk most of the time and why he was the way he was. I thought about the younger Alex I saw and how he was so much different—so much more caring. Could it be possible that that Alex still existed?

After Alex finished cleaning my left wrist with peroxide, he asked for my other wrist. He dotted the cotton ball on my cuts, but when he was done, he didn't wrap my wrists with gauze like I thought he would. In fact, what he did next shocked the heck out of me. He raised my wrist to his mouth, so there was only a sliver of air between his lips and my skin. Then he blew softly on my wound, causing my heart to flutter and the electricity to shimmer. I closed my eyes and focused on my breathing. He switched to the other wrist, doing the same thing, and I tried not to gasp. When he released my wrist, I opened my eyes, and found him watching me with the most intense expression on his face.

There was something different that happened between us then. I don't know how to describe it. The prickle was there, on the back of my neck, but I couldn't quite place my finger on what feeling was trying to emerge. I didn't move away when he leaned toward me, even though I knew he was going to kiss me. In fact, I was more than willing to let him kiss me. I wanted him to. But then the car came to a brake-slamming stop that sent me flying forward, but Alex caught hold of me before I made it too far.

"Sorry," Laylen apologized. "I thought I saw a deer in the road."

I glanced around outside, but all I could see was the sage brush covering the flat land. There was nowhere for a deer to hide.

"Do you need me to drive so you can get some rest?" Alex asked.

Laylen shook his head. "No, I'm good."

He sped up the car again, and Alex bandaged each of my wrists with gauze. I didn't pay attention to him much, though. I was too distracted by Laylen and how strange he had been acting. Ever since he bit me, he had been acting a little off. He hadn't done anything major, like run the streets biting people, but I was still worried that something was wrong. But I didn't want to bring it up to Alex because I figured he would be unsympathetic. But I'd make sure to keep an eye on him.

Just in case.

Chapter 30

We drove for days. Yes, days. We drove all the way to the other side of the country, to the beautiful, but very humid, state of Maryland. The air was so heavy and moisturized there, it was like being in a sauna.

Not too far off from the little beach house we were hiding out in was the ocean. From the room I was staying in, I could sit out on the deck and watch the ocean's waves crash against the sandy shore. It was a fascinating thing to watch for someone who had never seen the ocean.

The house belonged to a friend of Adessa's, which was a good thing because that meant Stephan didn't know where it was, nor Nicholas. When we arrived, we informed Aislin and she transported here. She had also put up some location charms, which were supposed to help make tracking us down more difficult. But at this point, I was prepared for the fact that at any given moment someone could turn up. It was only a waiting game. The question wasn't *if* someone was going to show up, but *when* someone would. And who? The list was long.

It was our second night here. We had all been resting from the insanity of the last few days we had. Alex was still recovering from being in the City of Crystal, and I was drained dry from all the bouncing in and out of visions. Everyone, including me, figured it'd be best to rest for a few days, and then I was going to give it a go at using the Ira. I wasn't going to lie and say I wasn't afraid of going to The Underworld. I'd been there before and that had been in a vision. Real life was going to be a lot worse because I wouldn't be invisible. But I had to do it.

There was something else concerning me besides my future endeavor to The Underworld. Laylen's moods seemed to be getting stranger. One minute he was perfectly fine, and the next minute he was upset over something. If I didn't know any better, I would be wondering if he was experiencing a prickling sensation on the back of his neck that was releasing an abundance of his emotions. But Laylen had never previously been unemotional, so I knew he couldn't be suffering from a soul-detaching-Keeper-gift that a certain red-headed Keeper who had raised me possessed.

No. Something else had to be up with him.

I was sitting out on the deck that extended out from my bedroom. The sky was jet black, and the moonlight reflected like an orb against the dark ocean water. The stars were twinkling in their own beautiful way, and the lull of the ocean was having a calming effect over me.

If I hadn't been sitting out there, I wouldn't have seen him walk across the sandy beach, heading away from the house to who knew where. The light of the moon hit his blond hair, making it look white, but I could tell by his height and the way that he walked that it was Laylen.

"Where is he going?" I mumbled to myself. I stood up and yelled, "Laylen!"

He turned and looked at me, and then...he ran.

"Laylen!" I shouted, causing a rising uproar amongst the neighbor's dogs. "Where are you going?"

But he already disappeared into the darkness of the night.

"Crap." I went into my room, slipped on my flip flops, and ran out of the bedroom. I was so mad at myself. I knew something had been wrong with him, but I never said anything, and now he was running away.

I reached the front door and realized I had two options here. One, that I take off on foot, all by myself, in the middle of the night, and roam around a strange town, looking for a vampire who was struggling with some issues. Or I could go wake up Alex, and he could drive us around in the SUV.

Even as I headed back to Alex's room, I wasn't sure he would help me. Yeah, Laylen and Alex had been getting along—in fact, everyone had been getting along—but I was still skeptical that Alex would jump out of bed and say, "Yeah, let's go find him."

When I got to Alex's door, I hesitated before knocking. It took him a second to answer, but the door did swing open, and a tired-eyed, shirtless Alex with some serious bed-head stood in front of me.

He blinked wearily at me. "What's up?"

"I just saw Laylen leaving." My words came out rushed. "Down the beach. And when I called his name, he ran."

His eyebrows dipped down. "Where was he going?"

"I don't know....but he's been acting kind of weird since he...since he bit me."

"You've noticed that too?"

"Wait, you've noticed it?"

He nodded. "Yeah, he's been acting just like..." He trailed off, looking away from me.

"Like me," I said, like it was obvious, which it was. There was no use tiptoeing around it.

"Well, I wasn't going to put it that bluntly, but yeah, he's been acting like you." He gave me a funny look. "Or the old you. I'm not really sure about the current one."

"Okay." Let's get off that subject. "Well, if something is wrong with him, then we need to go find him."

Alex nodded and walked back into his room. I tried not to stare at him too much as he slipped a black t-shirt over his head. He put his shoes on, grabbed the car keys off the dresser, and then we were heading out the door.

"Okay," he said once the engine was running and we both had our seat belts buckled up. "Which direction did he head in?"

"To the left," I told him, and he backed the SUV down the driveway. "So where do you think he's going?" I asked

Alex as we drove past the brightly painted beach houses that lined the street.

"I'm not sure," he said a little too quickly.

My head whipped over to him. "You're lying. I can tell."

He shot me a dirty look, but then erased it; I guess he changed his mind about fighting with me. "Fine...I think when he...bit you it might have awakened the blood thirst inside him."

I gave him an unconvinced look. "There's no way that could be true." But I didn't fully believe my words myself.

He raised his eyebrows at me questioningly. "Think about it. You were his first bite, and if anyone's blood's going to make a vampire go all blood crazy it's going to be yours."

"Why would mine do that?" I was offended. "There's nothing wrong with my blood."

"I'm not saying there's something wrong with it, just that it's very...energized," he said, then quickly added, "Or at least I can imagine it is." His grip tightened on the steering wheel, and I stared at the hand I saw him cut in the vision—the one when we were little and we made some kind of vow to each other. *Forem.*

I traced the barely visible scar on my hand. "What does *forem* mean?"

He dropped one of his hands from the steering wheel and tucked it to the side of him. "Why do you keep asking me that?"

"Let me see your hand."

"Gemma, quit being weird."

I looked down at my hand. The scar was so faint, I never even noticed it until I had seen the vision. "I saw a vision of us when we were little. You and I were hiding in that hideout—that's how I knew where it was. Someone was yelling for us—I think it was you father—and I was scared to death because I didn't want to leave, so you cut my hand and yours, and we pressed them together and said *forem*." My voice trembled. "Right after that, I saw Sophia detach my soul."

It went so quiet that I could hear the roar of the ocean. I wasn't sure why I told him about the vision; I just did. I wasn't expecting anything, but when he looked at me, his eyes were so full of sadness I thought he was going to say that he was sorry I had to see that.

"Gemma, I'm—I'm—" His eyes widened, and he was no longer looking at me, but to the side of me, out the window.

I followed his gaze, and saw Laylen rounding the corner of a bar, the flashing neon signs glowing against his pale skin as he walked by them. He was not alone, either. He was with a woman. Her long hair was tied up in a ponytail, and her tan skin was like a shadow against the night.

Alex made a sharp turn and ramped the SUV over the curb.

299

"Who's that he's with?" I asked, clicking my seat belt loose as the car came to a stop.

"I have no idea." He turned off the engine, and we both hopped out.

There was a group of men loitering at the entrance of the bar, and the smell of their cigarette smoke stunk up the air. They made catcalls as we walked across the parking lot, and I moved around to the other side of Alex, putting him between the rough looking men and myself.

One of them made a very inappropriate comment — which I will not repeat — and Alex's eyes lit with rage. He started to move toward the men, but I grabbed his arm.

"Now is not the time." I tugged at his arm. "Come on."

He actually listened, but his eyes did glint murderously when one of the men shouted something about him being a wussy boy.

Those men should really consider themselves lucky, seeing how I'm pretty sure Alex could beat the crap out of all of them without even getting a scratch. (He is a Keeper after all.)

But all thoughts of those men immediately exited my mind when we rounded toward the back of the bar, and standing underneath the back light, right next to the dumpster, was Laylen.

And he was biting the woman.

300

Chapter 31

"Laylen," I called out, and he immediately let go of the woman. Her limp body hit the asphalt with a thumping noise that shot goose bumps all over my skin.

Laylen's blue eyes were wide and he looked horrified as he glanced down at the lifeless body of the woman and then back at us. Alex stepped toward him, but Laylen put up a hand, his fangs gleaming in the light.

"Stay away from me," he hissed.

Alex pointed down at the woman. "I'm just going to check to see if she's okay." He took a step forward again, making sure to move cautiously.

Laylen didn't protest. He sunk to the ground and cradled his head in his hands. While Alex made sure the woman was okay, I carefully made my way over to Laylen. He looked so broken that I wasn't sure if I could handle this or not. I was no pro in dealing with human emotions—heck, I could barely deal with my own most of the time. So as I knelt down on the asphalt beside him, I tried to will the prickle to show up and release some kind of emotion that would let me know what to do.

It never came, though, so I guess I would have to figure out this one on my own.

"Laylen," I said, gently touching his arm. "Are you okay?"

He pulled away. "Don't touch me."

"She's okay," Alex said, and he came over and stood behind me. "She's just unconscious."

"See, she's okay," I told Laylen.

Laylen raised his head, and I almost shrank back from the anger in his eyes. "It doesn't matter. It's still there."

"What's still there?"

"The...the hunger."

I glanced up at Alex, my eyes pleading with him to help me out. I didn't know what to do.

He gave me this look, and I thought he wasn't going to help me, but then he knelt down on the ground next me and said. "Look, she's not hurt, okay. So let's just go back to the house and forget this ever happened."

Laylen glared at him with his fangs out. I had to admit, he looked terrifying. But for his sake, I made sure to stay calm.

"Hey," I said, telling myself I could do this. I could be sympathetic and make him feel better. "It's going to be okay. She's not dead, only passed out, and when she wakes she'll probably feel really..." I searched for a word that would describe what I felt when he bit me. "Euphoric."

"It doesn't matter how she feels," he said, his voice pained. "I bit her, which is something I've spent the last few years trying not to do."

God, this was all my fault. "Laylen, this isn't your fault. Please just come back to the house with us—we'll figure something out, okay?"

Honestly, I didn't think my little speech was that persuasive, but apparently he thought it was, which was all that mattered. He got to his feet and then all three of us went back and climbed into the SUV. We drove back to the beach house in silence. I made sure to keep an eye on Laylen, fearing he might freak out and try to run away again.

He seemed calm, though, but still not his normal self, which had me worried.

What if Laylen, the only person who'd ever told me the truth—who was always there for me—was gone?

When we arrived back at the beach house, Laylen went straight into his room and said he was going to bed. I was afraid he might leave again, but Alex promised he would watch him. We had woken up Aislin—not intentionally, but nonetheless we had to explain to her what had just happened. Then I sat on the couch, listening to Alex and Aislin argue over what to do with "him." I didn't like how they were talking about Laylen, like they feared he might go off the deep end and kill us all. I, in no way, believed this could ever be possible. And when they started talking about leaving him behind—going someplace else without him—I lost it.

It was late, and I was tired. The prickle had been nagging at the back of my neck and I finally shouted, "Would you two just shut up!" They both looked at me with surprised expressions, which I couldn't blame them for—I surprised myself. I lowered my voice. "Look, he's not going to freak out and kill anyone, okay? So just drop it."

"Gemma," Alex said, his tone letting me know I wasn't going to like what he was about to say. "We can't know for sure whether he's dangerous or not. He's bitten someone now, everything has changed."

"When he bit me, you didn't have a problem with it," I pointed out.

"Oh, I had a problem with it." A look passed over his face like he regretted what he just said. "Look, we have too many other problems to worry about. And right now I think we really just need to focus on getting into The Underworld."

I shook my head. "No. I won't leave him. You two do whatever you want, but I'm staying."

He held my gaze, and I could see the cocky attitude rising in him. It was something I hadn't seen lately. "You know you can be really stubborn sometimes."

I shrugged. I wasn't going to even try to argue with that. I knew that I was. "Stubborn or not, I'm still not leaving him." I held Alex's gaze with sheer and utter

304

determination, forcing myself to ignore my normal instinct to look away—let him win.

"Fine," Alex said. "We'll stay with him, but if anything happens it's on you."

I almost laughed, because he said the same thing to Laylen once about me.

"Fine, it's on me." I stood to my feet. "Now I'm going to go check on Laylen and make sure he's okay." Ignoring the dirty look Alex gave me, I left the room.

Laylen was standing out on the deck. He didn't even acknowledge me entering; he just stared ahead at the ocean. I went over and stood beside him, placing my hands on top of the deck's railing as I looked out at the ocean as well. We stayed like that for awhile, silent and unmoving, watching the oceans waves.

"For the last few years," he finally spoke, "I've felt so empty. After I was turned into a vampire, everyone I knew no longer wanted to be around me. And my parents were gone, so…I was basically all alone."

I nodded, knowing how he felt; knowing how it felt, to have no one; to be an outcast. To be all alone.

"I think the worst was Aislin." He rested his elbows on the railing, still not looking at me. "I don't know if you know this or not, but she and I used to be together."

"She mentioned it to me once," I told him.

A gap of silence trickled by and then he looked at me. "You know she just left me—just up and walked away. She never said exactly why, only that her father wouldn't let her see me anymore. I don't believe that it was just her father's doing, though. I think it was her choice too, and that hurt even more."

I swallowed hard, thinking about when Laylen had been dying, and how he told me he could no longer feel the pain of being alone anymore. I thought back to my life and how I had spent every day alone. How when I started to feel emotion, this alone feeling had suddenly risen in me like a giant gaping hole full of pain. I knew this was the same feeling Laylen was describing. I could feel it right now, not as painful, but still there.

Tears started to sting at my eyes. "It'll be okay," I said, not sure if I was trying to convince him or myself.

"Will it?" he asked, and I could see it in his eyes; the hurt, the sadness, the pain.

I don't know why I did what I did next. I mean, I never did it before, at least that I could remember. But maybe that's just it. Perhaps I couldn't remember—at least in the sense of remembering in the form of a memory—but I could feel the memory inside me. I could feel the memory through the prickle on the back of my neck, and it guided me to Laylen, and helped me wrap my arms around him, giving him a hug.

There was no hesitation on his part. He hugged me right back. And we stayed that way, just two people who understood each other; two people who knew what it felt like to have no one. But maybe that was no longer the case.

306

Maybe we had each other.

Chapter 32

When I woke up the next morning my eyes were a little swollen and red. After I left Laylen's room, I went straight back to my room and cried. Most of my tears had been for Laylen, but some were for myself. Strangely though, I did not feel as sad as I did last night. Maybe Laylen's and my little hug had filled up some of my sadness. And hopefully it did the same for him too.

I still had a lot to worry about, though. Laylen for starters still had me concerned, along with the fact that I was supposed to be attempting to take myself and Alex to The Underworld this morning. The pressure of actually being able to pull it off was weighing down on me like the hot, humid air. But all I could do about it was hope it would all be okay—that everything would go right.

So, I tried not to think about the fact that Nicholas had said that the Ira needed the power of two Foreseers to function as Alex and I sat in the living room with the Ira balanced on the coffee table.

Aislin was with Laylen, out on one of the decks. She was supposed to be keeping an eye on him while we were gone. But after Laylen's revelation about Aislin abandoning him when he turned—which, may I add, was her father's fault—my confidence in her was low.

"Now are you sure you want to do this?" Alex asked me, which was the same thing he asked me a thousand times already.

I nodded. "Yeah, I'm as sure as the last time you asked me."

He cracked a smile, but it was a nervous smile—he was nervous.

I was nervous. "Do you have the diamond?"

He patted the pocket of his jeans. "Yep, it's right here."

"Okay then." I took a deep breath and reached out for the Ira, my hand shaking with zero confidence, and I froze. "Are you sure *you* want to do this?" I asked him. "Because I could go alone."

According to my vision, though, I already knew what his answer would be.

"I'm sure," he said, nodding. "Besides, I was there in your vision, remember?"

"Yeah, but it doesn't mean you have to go," I pointed out.

"Yes, it does." He grabbed a hold of my hand, my fingertips buzzing electrically. "Now let's go."

I took another deep breath, concentrating as I placed my hand on the Ira. It was shocking how much energy radiated from it. Between Alex holding my hand, and the power flowing off the Ira, I felt like I might burst from the energy zooming through my body.

The first thing I saw in my mind was the lake. Panicking, I quickly shoved the image out of my mind, and tried to focus on the tunnel I was in during the vision. The dirt walls, the damp air, the darkness. I hadn't expected it to be easy. Maybe Alex's touch had given me the extra boost or something. Or maybe it was just my unique Foreseer ability that had made it so that when I opened my eyes we were there.

The tunnel was as dark as I remembered it being. The damp air caused my clothes to cling to my skin. The ceiling and walls dripped with water, and emptiness haunted all around.

"Do you know which way to go?" I asked Alex, still holding onto his hand.

He glanced up and down the tunnel. "I'm not sure...didn't you see where we went the last time?"

I shook my head. "No. The only reason I found the cave where the vision took place was because Nicholas and I had been running from a Water Faerie, and I can't remember which way we went...I don't even know if we're in the same place."

Alex let go of my hand and dragged his fingers through his hair. "Okay, left or right?"

Just as he asked it, a scream rang out from down the tunnel from our left side, sending a spasm of shivers through my body.

"Right," I said quickly.

He nodded, and we headed down the tunnel to our right.

The Underworld is not a welcoming place. Obviously. With everything I've told you about it, I'm sure you fully understand that a place where the dead walk and torture punished souls could not be in any way welcoming. But to be there, for real and not in vision form, was about as frightening as being chased by a bunch of glowing-eyed Death Walkers and a man who wants to freeze over the world with ice.

As we crept down the tunnel listening to the horrific screams that seemed to be shooting at us in every direction, I couldn't help but wish I could leave—run away where it was safe and warm and scream free. But I knew I had to be stronger than that, because this is where my mother had lived for the last fourteen years, and I had only been here for about five minutes.

I stayed close to Alex as we walked. Before we left, he had tucked a knife in his pocket, which brought some sense of security, but not much. Our shoes hit the moist dirt floor and created soft pitter-patters up and down the tunnels. Water was dripping in my hair. But these were all mild things. The real problem started when a white, floating figure appeared in the tunnel, just a little ways in front of us.

"Alex," I hissed, pointing at the Water Faerie.

He put his finger to his lips, shushing me, and kept walking. We kept getting closer and closer to the Water Faerie. My heart thumped louder and louder in my chest. My legs shook, and my breathing faltered. Then it was there, right in front of us, a ghost-like figure of a Water Faerie. Its eyes were two empty holes, its white fabric body trailing on the ground, and when we passed by it, it opened its gaping-hole of a mouth and let out a breathless scream. I clutched onto Alex's arm as the Water Faerie turned and followed after us. It didn't try to touch or communicate with us; it just trailed behind, tormenting us with its presence.

Then came another one, then another, and suddenly Water Faeries were everywhere, flying around us like freakishly large butterflies, only they weren't butterflies but undead Fey. Pieces of them kept swinging in my face, and I wanted to shoo them away, but my pulsating fear stopped me from doing so. We just kept walking and walking, further down the dark tunnel, and I prayed to God that it was the right way, because turning back meant we would have to endure the faeries' torment even longer. It was as if they got some sick pleasure in my uneasiness, swirling and dancing over my head. They were probably laughing on the inside.

And just as I thought I couldn't take it anymore, the tunnel opened up into a room. Well, not a room but a cave. The cave. The rock-shaped throne was in front of us, but the Queen wasn't sitting in it. It was then that I realized something was wrong. We weren't supposed to enter the cave ourselves, but be brought in by a faerie. I froze and Alex tensed up beside me.

"What is it?" He gave me a quizzical look. "What's wrong?"

"This isn't how it works," I said, fear skyrocketing in me, which seemed to be causing chaos to rise among the Water Faeries. "We don't come in here by ourselves. We're brought in by a Water Faerie."

Someone cleared their voice from behind us and we both turned around. It was the Queen. Her long white hair draped down her back, and her hollow eyes were tinted with a spark of delight.

"Well, it looks like I have some unexpected visitors," she said. "Coming here willingly to be tortured in my world—let the Fey take you, as they will? I have to say, you two are brave little souls."

This was all wrong. This was not what I had seen. Something had shifted.

And Alex and I were screwed.

Chapter 33

Back during my first visit to the City of Crystal, Dyvinius had explained to me how visions work. He said that if a vision wasn't read correctly then the world as we knew it could shift. I never considered that we just might be playing with fire when Nicholas and I had been bouncing around in and out of visions. And the vision where I took Nicholas and myself to The Underworld had never really been finished. Nicholas had freaked out and made me take us back to Adessa's before I was able to see the entire outcome of the vision. I had been so stupid not realizing this, and now I had dragged Alex into a mess he hadn't known he was getting dragged into.

Crap. I couldn't believe this was happening. What other things had changed because I hadn't been careful? Playing with visions was such a risky thing. And now I had no idea what was going to happen.

"I have to say," said the Queen, "it isn't every day that someone voluntarily enters my world. Usually it's with much force and fussing. And yet you two are here, entering it with your own free will. Tell me, what has brought you here?" She wasn't being kind; she was taunting us—I could hear it in her voice.

"We came here to get something," Alex told her in a firm voice.

"Ah, I see." She eyed us over with her empty eyes and then turned around and motioned to us to follow her.

While she had her back turned, I leaned over and whispered in Alex's ear, "This isn't right."

He gave me a look like I was insane. "What isn't right?"

"This isn't how I saw the vision go," I whispered, and his eyes widened.

We followed the Queen back down the tunnel, past the cluster of floating Water Faeries, and up a set of marble stairs, which led us to a room that had a long antique table trailing down the center and a massive chandelier hanging from the ceiling. There were no crystals decorating the chandelier, but pieces of thorn-covered wire that were bent and turned in every direction. Covering the dirt walls were twisted pieces of vine that looked like seaweed.

"Have a seat," the Queen told us, gesturing to the chairs trimming the table.

Alex and I did what she asked, and then she took a seat at the head of the table. There was a long pause while she sat, watching us.

"So you've come here for something, have you?" she finally asked.

"*Someone*, actually," Alex told her. "Her name is Jocelyn Lucas."

I could tell right away that the Queen knew who we were talking about—you could see it in her face.

"Tell me, boy, what is your name?" the Queen asked.

"Alex Avery," Alex said with some hesitance.

"Ah, I see. You're a Keeper." She moved her attention to me. "And you? What is your name?"

"Gemma Lucas," I told her, forcing my voice to come out steady.

Darkness masked her face. "So you are, what? The daughter of Jocelyn?"

I nodded. God, I hoped she knew nothing of the star.

"I see." The Queen tapped her sharp fingernails on the top of the table. "So what did you expect? That you would come down here and demand I give you my best slave, all because you asked?"

"No," Alex said, "We've actually brought something to trade for Jocelyn's freedom."

"I can assure you, Alex, that you have nothing I want," the Queen replied with a disdainful manner.

Alex slipped the sapphire teardrop diamond out of his pocket and held it up for the Queen to see. "Not even for this?"

She looked surprised, which I took as a good sign...at first. But then she started to laugh, the high pitched laugh that rang sorely against my eardrums and shook at the chandelier.

I gave Alex a glance, and he shrugged.

The Queen stopped laughing and her laughter swiftly shifted to anger. "You think that you can come down here and try to make a bargain with me with something the Keepers took from me to begin with?" She rose from her chair, towering over us. "How dare you insult me. You are just like your father. Taking whatever you want and doing whatever you please."

I wanted to bang my head against the table. Was there anyone who didn't have a grudge against Stephan? Probably not, but still...

"I have been waiting for the day when I would see your father again and settle what he started a long time ago." The Queen sauntered toward us, her eyes locked on Alex.

Alex, being Alex, held her petrifying gaze. "I understand that you may have had some issues with my father, but I can assure you that—"

"Silence." The Queen's loud voice caused the dirt walls to quake. "I don't want to hear any excuses. I always swore to myself that one day I would get even with Stephan, whatever it took. And here you are. It's the perfect opportunity. A much smaller version of him, of course, but still, it'll do."

"He's nothing like his father," I said abruptly, and then shrank back when the Queen focused her attention on me. My body quivered but I pressed on. "And he only came down here because I asked him to—so I could get my mother."

The Queen's face was not full of anger, but of inquisitiveness. She walked back to her chair, but didn't sit down. "You know, Jocelyn has never mentioned having a daughter, so I find it rather peculiar that someone would show up with the son of one of my sworn enemies and claim to be her daughter."

"Well, I am," I assured her. "And I want to take her back with me."

"Take her back?" She started laughing again. "Oh, I'm afraid there's no way I can do that. You see, you can't take her back with you, because you yourself are never leaving."

"No, we can leave," I told her, but my certainty that I really could was questionable. "I came here through the Ira, and you can't keep us here—there are laws that say you can't."

Alex shot me a look that warned me I was treading on very thin water.

"Oh, I'm afraid that's where you are wrong," the Queen said. "The Ira was created for the leader of the Foreseers to enter The Underworld. Therefore the law of release only applies to him." She smiled a big empty smile before gesturing her hand around the room. "So, Gemma and Alex, let me welcome you to your new home."

318

Chapter 34

"Let me welcome you to your new home." The Queen's words kept running through my head like a plague. You could see it on her face that she got some sort of sick, twisted pleasure when she told us we couldn't leave. Which wasn't surprising. She was the Queen of a world that ran on fear.

But don't get me wrong, I still tried to get us out of there. I tried so hard to blink us out of that horrible place that I gave myself a splitting headache.

After the Queen declared we were never allowed to leave, she locked Alex and me in a cement chamber that had a single bed in it. It was like being in a jail cell, except there were no bars on the door.

The Queen was probably going to keep us here until she was ready to begin our torture sessions, where we would end up being faerie food. Or at least our fear would. Fear was not a new emotion for me—I had felt it many, many times. So I knew that in order to bring it out of a person, something bad had to happen.

"I'm really starting to wonder just how long the list of people who my father has pissed off is," Alex said.

We had been sitting on the bed, staring at the cement walls for awhile, so the sound of his voice startled me a little.

"Probably pretty long," I said, and he shot me dirty a look. "Sorry, but it's probably the truth. I mean, he walks with the Death Walkers, betrays the Keepers, forces faeries to help him all because of a Blood Promise made ages ago. And he's also pissed off the Queen of the dead for who knows what reason. That list right there is really long."

Alex let out a sigh. "Yeah, you're probably right. We probably will be running into a lot more people who hate him."

I was right. What the…

"Why are you looking at me like that?" he asked.

I kept looking at him the same way. "Like what?"

"Like I just shocked the heck out of you."

I shrugged. "I don't know…because you said I was right?"

He stared at me perplexedly, as if he was trying to figure something out.

"So what are we going to do?" I asked. "I mean, are we going to be able to get out of here?"

He let out a loud breath as he ran his fingers through his hair. "I don't know, Gemma. I don't even know what exactly happened. I mean, do you have any idea why this didn't work out like how you saw in the vision?

I massaged the sides of my temples, trying to force my headache away. "Because I didn't finish seeing the vision, at least that's what I think happened. Nicholas forced me to take us away before I saw the whole thing play out." Someone screamed not too far away, and I shivered. "I'm sorry," I said.

Alex cocked an eyebrow at me. "Sorry for what?"

"For messing this up."

He shook his head, dragging the knife he brought with along him on the frame of the bed. "You didn't mess this up. I did, by being my father's son."

"Well, I think we can also put a little bit of the blame on Nicholas." The mention of faerie boy's name caused an acidic taste to burn in the back of my throat. "For not giving us all the details about how the Ira works. Although, we never should have trusted him to begin with."

"Yeah, I know." Alex leaned back against the cement wall and folded his arms across his chest.

"What will they do to us?" I asked quietly. "The Water Faeries—what will they do to instill fear in us?"

"I'm not sure," he said, and I knew he was lying by how he avoided looking at me.

"Just tell me," I said tiredly, and slumped back against the cement wall. "I think I need to know what I'm in store for."

He locked eyes with me. "You really want to know?" he asked, and I nodded, even though I felt like I was being choked. "Okay, well to put it simply you're in store for a lot of pain."

I nodded, the choking feeling practically strangling me to death.

It got quiet. Noises of dripping water filled our little concrete prison in a way that was almost maddening. Pain. I was going to be in a lot of pain. But was he talking about the physical kind of pain, or the emotional kind?

"Look," he said, before I could ask him to clarify which kind of pain he was referring to. "No matter what happens, I need you to hold on, okay? No matter how bad things get, don't give up."

The idea of not giving up was suddenly eating away at me. "But wouldn't it be better if I didn't hold on? If I just let myself go?"

He looked alarmed. "What's that supposed to mean?"

"I don't know…" The prickle was starting to poke at me. Poke, poke, poke. I scratched viciously at the back of my neck. "It means, wouldn't things be better if I was gone?"

His eyes widened, and he looked as if he was freaking out. Not the reaction I was expecting, but okay. "Wh— why are you saying this?" he asked.

The prickle was really going at it. "Because it would be better for a whole lot of people if I was. I mean, if I might be the one who's going to open the portal instead of closing it, wouldn't that make me be responsible for everyone's deaths?"

"Where did you get the idea that you're what's going to open up the portal?"

"It's kind of obvious, once I really thought about it. I mean, Stephan's working with the Death Walkers, bears the Mark of Malefiscus, and I saw him in that vision where the world had ended in ice. What do all those things have in common? They're all bad. So why would Stephan want the star's power for anything good?"

Alex rubbed his hands across his face, I think maybe to hide the fact that he thought the same thing I did. When he dropped his hands, though, the look on his face took me aback.

"I don't care what you think the star's energy is being used for." His bright green-eyed gaze burned into me. "We came down here to save your mom, so we could try to piece this all together and come up with a plan to stop it. And until we get all that done you can't give up. You can't give up before we've really even tried, okay?"

Who was this guy sitting next to me, staring at me with such an intense look of determination in his eyes? Yeah, I knew it was Alex, but not the Alex who I first met.

"Okay," I said, forcing my strange "giving up" feeling away for the moment. "I won't give up until we've tried."

He nodded, and we both sat there in the silence again, staring at the cement wall in front of us. Alex put his knife back in his pocket, slid his hand over, and set it on top of mine. I shut my eyes and let the buzzing take me away from this horrible place. I let it deafen the screams. I let it sweep me away.

Chapter 35

Alex and I stayed the way we were until the door to our cell swung open. When I opened my eyes, I saw that a Water Faerie was hovering in the doorway. I thought about running—knocking the Water Faerie down and bolting for an exit. Although there wasn't anywhere for me to go…"Oh my God," I breathed.

Alex looked from the Water Faerie to me. "It'll be okay, Gemma. Just make sure you hold on."

I grabbed his arm, my eyes widening as I whispered, "I think I might know a way to get out of here."

"What?" he said loudly, and I shushed him.

"It's time." The Queen appeared in the doorway. "Both of you follow me."

I got to my feet, but Alex just sat there staring at me, still shocked by what I said. He was probably wondering how the heck I could know there was a way out of here. The only reason I did know there might be a way out was because of Laylen's and my trip to see Vladislav. See, during our visit, when we asked Vladislav if anyone had ever escaped The Underworld, he said yes, and then added that most of the people who do try to escape drown during the

324

attempt. So there was another way out of here besides through the Ira. There was a way by water.

But where was the water? The Underworld was supposed to be below the lake, so…I glanced up at the ceiling, at the water dripping down from it.

"Hurry up!" the Queen roared.

Alex got to his feet, and we followed the Queen out of the cell and into the tunnel, which was lined with jail cell doors. We had gone a ways when Alex grabbed my arm and pulled me back.

"What do you mean, you know a way to escape?" he whispered. "Where is it?"

"When Laylen and I went and saw Vladislav," I said, speaking so quickly I tripped over my words, "he said people had escaped before. But most of them drowned."

He took in what I said. "So we need to find water."

I pointed up at the ceiling, at the water seeping through the cracks. "We need to go up."

Alex reached up and touched the muddy ceiling with his fingertips. "So there has got to be an exit somewhere that takes us up."

"What are you two doing back there?" The Queen's fuming voice boomed down the tunnel. "Get up here now."

We hurried and caught up with her. Alex still had his thinking face on, and I could tell he was trying to come up with some sort of plan to get us out of here. I still felt a little skeptical, though, because we still had to find where the way out was, and we also needed to figure out a way to get away from the Queen and her Water Faeries.

But all thoughts of escaping left my mind, when we reached where the Queen was taking us. In fact, all of my thoughts disappeared and were replaced by one thing.

Fear.

They say torture is...well, torture. But this was so much worse than I'd expected. Water Faeries were floating around everywhere. But that was the easiest part to take in. The worst were the people's screams that filled up the room. I knew Alex told me that the people who were sentenced here were bad, but it didn't mean that what was being done to them was right. Each one of them was strapped down on a wooden table, being tortured in various ways, but each one looked equally painful. My stomach rolled at the sight of one man in particular that had his arm twisted in a way that an arm should not be twisted.

"Don't look at them," Alex said, and I looked away from the torture chamber.

But not looking at them couldn't block out the sounds...the cries...the pain.

The only thing I could be thankful for at the moment was that the Queen took us to a different room that had cement walls thick enough to muffle out the screams. In the room, there was a single chair that had straps attached to the arms.

The Queen turned to face us. "Tell me, Gemma. What is it your most afraid of?"

I swallowed hard. She was so asking the wrong person this question. Fear was such a new thing to me, and the only thing I could think of that would qualify as my most-afraid-of thing was Stephan and the Death Walkers.

"I don't know," I said, sounding weak. I hated that I sounded weak.

"You don't know?" She looked at me intriguingly and a toothless grin spread across her face. "Well, I think it's time you found out." She raised her hand in the air and snapped her fingers. Two Water Faeries flew up to me and grabbed me by the arms. I tried to pull away from them, but their bony fingers had freakishly strong grips.

"Stop!" Alex called out. "I'll go first."

"Oh no," said the Queen with amusement in her voice. "I have a feeling that you watching her get tortured is probably going to bring out just as much fear, as if it were you getting tortured yourself."

Alex started to protest, but the Queen silenced him. Then two Water Faeries came up behind Alex and grabbed him by the arms, holding him where he stood. He tried to fight and pull away, but like I already mentioned, the Water Faeries are freakishly strong. Apparently, even stronger than a Keeper.

The two Water Faeries dragged me over to the chair, and one held down my arms while the other strapped me to the chair. Once they let go of me, I tried to yank my

327

arms free from the straps, but the only thing that accomplished was my sore wrists aching even more.

"Oh, good. She's already getting scared," the Queen said, pleased. There was this long gap that passed before she said to the Water Faeries, "Well, get on with it."

They hovered beside me, and suddenly they were in front of me, their eyeless holes so close to my face that I now realized they had actual eye sockets, just no eyeballs. I almost threw up.

"Now, which way to go here?" the Queen dithered. "Oh, I know. Since you guys were so kind to bring it back to me." She reached into the pocket of her white dress and pulled out the teardrop-shaped sapphire diamond. "Let's use this to torture her soul."

Was she serious? Torture my soul. My soul. No freaking way.

Panicking, I yanked at the straps, pulling and tugging as hard as I could. But it was useless. The Queen handed the diamond to one of the Water Faeries and it came face-to-face with me. As it reached its bony fingers toward my mouth with the diamond resting in its hand, I couldn't help but let out the most blood curdling scream.

And then....it dropped to the floor.

Chapter 36

Okay, I should probably explain what happened a little bit better. The Water Faerie dropped to the floor, not my soul. Its body hit the cement floor with a loud thump, along with every other faerie in the room, including the Queen herself.

There was this moment where Alex and I just looked at each other with wide eyes, and then Alex was running for me.

"What the heck happened?" I asked as he worked to get the straps unfastened.

"I have no idea," he said, slipping the buckle loose. "Let's go."

I jumped to my feet, and we ran past the lifeless bodies of the Water Faeries and out the door. To our shock, the Water Faeries who had been in that room had sank to the floor as well.

I stood there gaping at the scene in sheer and utter bewilderment.

One of the men strapped to a table begged me to free him. "Come on, little girl," he said. "Just undo the straps, okay? I promise I don't bite."

"Gemma." Alex's voice brought me back to reality. "Come on." His hand was extended out to me.

I glanced at the man, who was still begging me to let him go.

"They're here for a reason," Alex said. "Now come on. We have to go, before they…" He glanced at the faeries' lifeless bodies scattered across the floor. "Wake up, I guess?"

I nodded—he was right. I took his hand, and we sprinted down the tunnel.

"We have to find water," Alex said as we ran toward where the cell doors were.

"Wait," I said, pulling back. "We have to find my mom first."

He shook his head, trying to drag me forward. "No, we have to go. We don't know how long they'll be out."

"I'm not going without her," I said sternly, refusing to budge. "I came down here to rescue her, and I'm not leaving until I do. Besides, this is our only chance to free her — we'll never be able to come back."

"We have no idea where she is," he argued. "It could take forever."

"Fine." I slipped my hand free from his and dodged around him. "You go find water," I called over my shoulder, heading for a cell door, "but I'm going to go find my mom."

Alex let out a frustrated breath, but he followed after me. "Gemma, we need to go now."

330

Ignoring him, I unlatched the first cell door I came across and opened it up. The room was empty. "We'll never get answers if we don't find her..." I hurried to the next cell door and opened it up. Empty again. "Like you said, she knows things. That's why she's down here." I unlocked a third door, starting to wonder if maybe I was on the wrong track with the cell doors. "And if we don't get some answers, the world's going to end. I've seen...." I opened the third door and immediately trailed off, my jaw dropping at the sight of a woman sitting on the bed, wearing ratted old clothes. Her brown hair trailed down her back, and her bright blue irises were as blank as my eyes had been before I experienced the prickle. But despite the blank look, I knew...she was my mother.

Her head slowly turned and she looked at me, but there was no recognition that she knew who I was.

"Mom," I whispered. The word felt so strange coming out of my mouth.

She blinked at me, but that was it. There was nothing there—no life, no spark, nothing.

"Jocelyn," Alex said from over my shoulder. "Are you alright?"

Still my mother stared at us with nothing more than a look of emptiness.

I felt like I might start crying, but knew I couldn't. Now was not the time to shed tears.

"What should we do?" I asked Alex.

He considered this carefully. "Go over and take her hand, but move slowly—see if you can get her to come with us."

I looked at him with terrified eyes. "Maybe you should do it."

He shook his head. "No, this is something I think you have to do."

Whether he was right or not, I took a deep breath and made my way cautiously into the room. My mother made no reaction, just sitting there, her hands resting on her lap.

"Mom," I said, reaching my hand out toward her. "It's Gemma...your daughter."

She looked at me, and then suddenly she was *really* looking at me. She got to her feet and moved in for a hug, but then pulled back quickly, cradling her arms across her chest.

"Gemma," she said, not looking happy but horrified. "What are you two doing down here?" Her voice was sharp and it made me cower back. "You shouldn't be down here."

"We came here to save you." My voice wobbled.

"Well, you shouldn't have," she said sternly. "How did you even get down here?"

"With an...Ira."

Her eyes didn't widen in surprise. In fact, she acted as if she predicted me to say that. "Well you have to leave now."

Easier said than done. "We would, but...my Foreseer power isn't working at the moment."

She shook her head. "I was hoping that would skip you."

What the heck was she talking about? "Huh?"

She started to say something else, but a loud cry, like an angry cat, screeched from somewhere.

"We have to go." She rubbed her forehead. "But how am I supposed to get you out of here?"

"We need to get to water," Alex told her as he entered the room. "There's supposed to be a place somewhere down here that will take us up through the lake. A water route, maybe? Do you know where it is?"

"We can't go anywhere." She frowned. "The Fey will make us suffer if we try."

"The Water Faeries are out for the moment," Alex told her in a gentle voice. "So they can't make you suffer. But we have to hurry before they wake up."

She stared at us in confusion, and then suddenly her eyes lit up. "Oh my God, I completely forgot about that." She brushed past Alex and me and ran out into the tunnel.

Alex and I gave each other a look, and then we chased after her.

"Mom," I yelled. "Where are you going?"

She kept running down the tunnel, her bare feet thumping against the dirt floor. Another cat-like screech rang out from somewhere, and Alex and I sped up our pace and caught up with my mother.

"You forget things sometimes!" she shouted at us as we ran. "Being down here, it messes with your mind and sometimes you just forget."

Forget what? Where the exit was? "But do you remember where it is now?" I asked.

She nodded, and a burst of adrenaline soared through me. We ran deeper into the darkness, weaving and turning through the tunnel. I crossed my fingers that my mom really knew where she was going. The cries and screams seemed to be filling the air more and more, and I worried that the Water Faeries were waking up. My mother seemed unbothered by the screams. She just kept running, and didn't stop until we entered into the cave with the rock-shaped throne that twisted up to the quartz ceiling.

My mom sprinted over to the throne and circled around it as she stared up at the ceiling. "When I first came here, I was told that if you climbed up the back of the throne it would take you to a place where you could escape. The problem was, I never had a chance to get away. And after awhile, I just sort of forgot about trying." She stepped up onto the throne and climbed up the back of it. The twisting shape was like a slide, which made it hard to climb. But even though it was tricky, she managed to make it all the way up with only a few slips, and then she disappeared through a small hole in the ceiling.

I looked at Alex, stunned.

"Alright," he said, hopping up onto the throne. "Let's go." He reached up and pulled himself onto the back of the throne. I followed him, but I moved less gracefully than he did. I even managed to scrape my knee on the rock more than once. But finally, I was pulling myself up into the hole where my mom had disappeared.

It was dark up there, but there was a faint light streaming from someplace. A narrow tunnel stretched out on each side. The floor was muddy and water ran from the ceiling in sporadic bursts that had already soaked into my clothes and hair.

"Which way do we go now?" Alex asked my mom.

She glanced to the left, and then to the right. "I think this way," she said, and stumbled off to the right.

Alex and I ran after her. She seemed sort of dizzy, weaving from side to side as we sprinted down the tunnel. The further we went, the brighter the light became, until finally we were blinded by it.

A second later we stepped out onto a rocky ledge, and my heart stopped. At the edge of the ledge was a drop off. The height alone was astonishing, but the waterfall spewing over the side of the drop off was what sent my pulse racing the most. Well that, and the pool of water with a severe looking undercurrent that the waterfall poured down into.

Never did it occur to me during our talk of our water escape that I would have to dive off a ledge into water that was probably going to suck me under. Oh, and let's not forget to mention the most important part: I couldn't swim.

"So what are we supposed to do?" I asked, my eyes locked on the waterfall. "Just jump? Because I'm not sure if I can make it."

"Yeah." Alex stared down at the water and then back at me. "I think—"

A shriek blared down the tunnel and I could now see them—the Water Faeries. They were still a ways away, gliding down the shadowy tunnel like ghosts.

"Crap," Alex said, grabbing my hand. "Jocelyn, we need to—"

Before he could finish, my mother, who had been standing on the ledge, suddenly jumped.

I gasped and ran for the ledge. "Mom!" I couldn't see her; only the violent water whirling. "Mom..." I whispered.

"Gemma." Alex's voice yanked me back to him. "Grab on to me."

"What?" I shook my head. "No."

Alex looked my straight in the eyes. "Wrap your arms around my neck and hang on."

I wasn't sure I could do this—jump into the midst of raging water, when I couldn't swim.

"I don't think..." I glanced at the Water Faeries, who were so close now I could see the bareness in their eyes. I took a deep breath, summoning every ounce of strength I had in me, and wrapped my arms around Alex's neck, linking my fingers together tightly.

Alex put his arms around my waist and pushed me so far into him I swear the electricity was going to weld us together. "Close your eyes," he said, and I did, but not before I caught a glimpse of the Water Faeries about to emerge from the tunnel.

Another loud shriek, and then we dove.

Chapter 37

The water tore at me from every angle, cold and rough, violently trying to steal my oxygen. I tried to hold onto Alex, but the water was making my hands slip loose. Alex was kicking, trying to break us free from the undertow. But we just kept getting pulled in all different directions.

Eventually the water started to settle, and our bodies became less tangled. He swam us upward, and finally we broke through. I gasped for air, and so did Alex. He opened his mouth to say something, but I was tugged downward by a set of bony fingers that had snatched hold of my ankle. My hands slipped from around Alex's neck, and I was submerged by the dark water again. I tried to kick the Water Faerie off of me, but all it did was tighten its grip.

And then Alex had my arm. I knew it was him because of the buzzing. He was pulling on me, but the Water Faerie was too. My body felt like it was going to tear apart. Then Alex was beside me, underneath the water. Our bodies tangled together, along with the Water Faerie's. There was a lot of tugging and spinning, and then suddenly I was no longer being pulled down, but whooshing upward and bursting out of the water.

Alex swam faster than I ever thought was humanly possible. Especially while hauling me along with him. And before I knew it, we were lying on the shore, out of breath and panting loudly.

"Are you okay?" Alex asked, out of breath.

I coughed up some of the water I swallowed. "Yeah, I...Wait. Where's my mom?"

In the snap of a finger, we were both on our feet and searching. But I couldn't see her anywhere; the only thing in sight was the grey stone castle, the tall-treed forest, and the haunting Water Faerie filled lake.

"Oh my word," I breathed.

Alex followed my gaze and his jaw nearly hit the ground.

Across the dark water, the Water Faeries floated. The sight would have been alluring — they looked like ballerinas dancing. But knowing what they really were, and what they could do, the sight only made a chill slither down my back.

"They can't come up here, right?" I asked.

He nodded, but his bright green eyes were still locked on the water. "I've never seen so many of them up here before, especially when no one has summoned them."

As I watched the Water Faeries swim around, a thought abruptly smacked me in the head. "Wait. What if my mom's still in there?" And then I was running toward the lake, my brain too irrational to process the consequences if I stepped in.

Luckily Alex grabbed me and pulled me back.

"Are you freaking crazy?" he exclaimed, shaking me by the shoulders with a look of what could only be described as terrified. "You can't go in there."

It took my brain a second to grasp the severity of the situation I had just about gotten myself into. "I'm sorry, but what if she's in there?"

His harsh expression slipped to a semi-sympathetic one. "If she is, then there's nothing we can do about it."

"We can go back," I said, my tone razor sharp. "We have to save her."

He shook his head. "There's no way we're going back there after what happened. Now that they know something's different about you, they're going to be all over you if you even step foot in their world again."

"So what?" I was trying with all my might to wiggle my arm free from his grasp. "I don't care. How do expect me to just let her stay down there after I saw how horrible of a place it is?" I could feel the tears stinging at my eyes. "Let me go!"

"No," he told me, just standing there, holding on to my arm, my yanking not even fazing him the slightest bit.

"Let me go," I growled.

He shook his head, tightening his grip. "You're not thinking clearly right now."

I stared him down with a determined look. "You have to let me go. You don't need to protect me anymore now that the star's power is probably not going to save the world."

He stared at me with this strangest look. "I think you—"

Then we heard it. An earsplitting bang that rocketed through air.

"What the heck was that?" I asked, glancing around at the trees.

Alex looked over at the castle, and then at the ground. I followed his gaze and saw what he was looking at. Footprints, printed across the mud, leading toward the castle.

We took off, tromping through the muddy grass and running up the hill, until we reached the door to the castle. Alex seemed a little uneasy as he turned the doorknob and creaked the door open. The stale air immediately surrounded us.

"Does anyone live here?" I whispered as we stepped inside.

He shook his head and dropped his hand from the doorknob.

It looked as if no one had been inside the castle for ages. The banister that guided the stairs had a thick layer of dust on it and cobwebs ornamented the ceiling like a haunted house on Halloween.

Alex went to the bottom of the stairs and glanced up. Another bang shattered the air and his gaze darted down the hall, where the noise had come from.

"What if it's not my mom?" I whispered.

He held up a finger and then crept down the hall. I stayed behind him, keeping my footsteps light. There was another loud noise that sounded like glass being shattered, and then I saw her.

She was in the room where my soul had been detached; the room with the stone fireplace and tiled floor. She was standing in the midst of a pile of broken glass, her bare feet, I'm sure, getting cut by the sharp edges.

"Mom," I said softly as I stepped cautiously into the room.

She'd been staring at the broken glass, but blinked up at me when I said her name. Any acknowledgment she had of me was gone, and I could see it in her bright blue eyes that she, again, did not know who I was. She grabbed a vase from off a nearby desk and threw it at the floor.

"Jocelyn," Alex said, and she looked at him, tears dripping down her cheeks. Alex took a slow step toward her, but froze when she screamed.

Then her eyes slipped shut and she collapsed to the floor.

Chapter 38

This was not how I pictured my reunion with my mom. Maybe I had been delusional, but I always pictured it as much more welcoming and filled with hugs, despite the fact that Alex had warned me that the Jocelyn everyone knew might be no more.

Instead of giving me hugs, she'd lost it and passed out on the floor in the middle of the broken glass.

"Is she going to be okay?" I asked Alex, who was leaning over my mother, checking her wrist for a pulse.

"She's alive," he said, setting her arm down gently. "I don't know what's wrong with her, though."

"She didn't just pass out."

"I don't know, she could have, but..."

"But what?" I hated it when he trailed off like that, leaving his sentences hanging in the air.

"But with where she's been, and how long she's been there, I can't say for sure what's wrong. She could be in shock or something."

I felt so frustrated I could have screamed. I kicked at some broken glass. "So what do we do now?"

He shrugged. "I guess we go back to Maryland—to Laylen and Aislin—and wait until your mom wakes up."

"And what if she doesn't?"

He didn't answer.

Thank goodness my Foreseer gift was working again. Otherwise we would have had a very long drive back to Maryland. I managed to get us back to the beach house without any problems. My mom was still out when we arrived, and Alex carried her back to an empty room, leaving me to explain what had happened to Aislin and Laylen.

All three of us sat in the living room, and they listened to me ramble on and on about our journey to The Underworld. By the time I finished giving them the details, Alex had returned. He looked tired. There were bags under his eyes, his hair was messy, and the lake's water had crinkled his clothes. It had crinkled mine as well, and the fabric felt dry and rough against my skin.

"So all the Water Faeries just passed out?" Aislin asked, her bright green eyes wide.

I nodded. "Yeah, one moment they were trying to do some kind of torture thing on my soul with that diamond we took down there, and the next moment they were on the ground."

"Was it because they were trying to do something to your...soul?" Aislin asked worriedly.

"I don't know what happened exactly." But I wouldn't be surprised if my soul had done it, seeing as how it was broken.

"I don't think it was your soul that did it," Alex interrupted, sitting down beside me. "I think it was because of the overload of fear you shot at them."

"What overload of fear?" I looked at him funny. "All I did was scream."

He looked as though he was choosing his next words very carefully. "I think because your emotions are so new to you that sometimes they come off a little....strong. And with the excessive amount of fear you shot at the Water Faeries, I think it sent them into shock."

"*Strong*," I said, insulted.

He pressed his lips together, doing that thing that he hadn't done in awhile. You know, the one where he is trying to hide the fact that he finds my irritation amusing.

The look—which used to make me angry—was having a different effect on me. It was making my skin tingle, and I was pretty sure it wasn't from the electricity. But I refused to let him know this, or he would probably do it to me all the time, which honestly wasn't sounding that bad to me at the moment.

"So how are we going to get my mom to wake up?" I asked, changing the subject.

The look Alex was giving me was quickly erased. "Gemma, I don't know for sure that she will."

"But you don't know for sure that she won't," I pointed out.

Everyone looked at me, and I could see it on their faces. They felt sorry for me. Even Laylen looked at me that way. But why? Because they all thought my mom wasn't going to ever wake up.

"Gemma," Alex started to say.

"I don't want to hear it," I told him. "She'll wake up. I know she will." Then I stood up and headed back to my mom.

She looked dead. I wasn't even going to try and sugarcoat it, because that's how she looked. She lay in a bed with her eyes shut. Her veins were a dark purplish-blue against her pale skin. The rise and fall of her chest was the only thing that let me know she was still alive.

"Mom," I whispered, staring down at her. The prickle traced down my neck, and suddenly the word "mom" didn't seem so awkward. "Mom," I said louder, tears soaking my eyes. "Mom."

And then I was falling down on the bed next to her, crying. And I cried until I fell asleep.

When I woke up, dawn was hitting the windows. The ocean's waves were swishing outside, and the house was silent. My eyes felt puffy and swollen, and I wondered how long I had been crying before I fell asleep. I sat up and rubbed my eyes.

"Gemma."

Her voice scared the crap out of me, and I fell out of the bed.

"Ow," I said, rubbing my elbow as I got back to my feet.

My mom was sitting up in the bed, staring at me in alarm. "Are you alright?"

I nodded at her, giving her the same look of alarm. "Are you alright?"

She swallowed hard and then started coughing. "I think I need some water."

"Okay, I'll go get you some," I told her.

I quickly went into the kitchen, took a glass out of the cupboard, and flipped on the faucet. While I was filling up a cup of water, I thought I heard someone move up behind me, and I nearly screamed at the top of my lungs when I turned and came face to face with a very tall, blue-eyed, blond-haired vampire/Keeper.

"Holy crap." I pressed my hand to my racing heart. "You just about scared me to death."

"Sorry," he apologized, like it was his fault I was so jumpy. He had on a pair of jeans and a dark red t-shirt, so I was guessing he had been awake for awhile "I didn't mean to scare you."

"It's okay." I glanced around the kitchen. "What are you doing?"

He shrugged, looking so sad it made my heart hurt. "I don't know. I heard someone get up, so I came to check who it was."

"Oh." I shut off the faucet. "I didn't wake you up, did I?"

347

He shook his head. "I was already awake."

"So is my mom," I told him, excitedly.

"Is she...okay?"

"I don't know. But I'm going to go find out." I headed to leave, but stopped at the doorway. "You want to come with me?"

"Wouldn't you rather go wake up Alex?" Laylen said, still standing over by the sink. "I'm sure he has a ton of questions for her."

I had a ton of questions for her, but I needed to make sure she was alright before I started bombarding her with them, which was exactly why I wasn't going to go wake up Alex. "I'd rather you come."

"Okay." He nodded and followed me out of the kitchen.

During our thirty second walk to my mom, I asked Laylen how things had been while Alex and I were gone. He told me they had been fine—that everything was fine—but I could tell that they weren't. He seemed really unfocused. I decided that a little later I would ask Aislin how he had been while we were gone. But first, I needed to check on my mother.

She wasn't in the bed when we entered the room. She was out on the deck, staring out at the ocean. I carefully approached her, the floorboards creaking underneath my weight, but she didn't turn around.

I came to a stop beside her and handed her the cup of water. She took a few swallows and set the glass on the railing. I waited for her to say something, but all she did was look out at the ocean with a lost expression on her face.

"Mom," I said, concerned she might have slipped into a state of shock again.

My mother turned and looked at me. Then her eyes moved to Laylen. "Laylen...is that you?"

He stepped up beside me. "Yeah, it's me."

She smiled, but it looked wrong, like she had to work really hard to make the corners of her mouth curve upward. "You've grown up so much." She looked at me, and in the brightness of the rising sun I could see her eyes held a deep sorrow in them. "And you..." She burst into tears, alarming me. "You're—you're still..." She trailed off, thinking about something as tears continued to stream down her cheeks. Then she let out a sigh. "You're still you."

I wasn't sure what to tell her—that I wasn't still me, but someone trying to figure out how to be me. But I was afraid saying this might break her heart, and she already looked really broken.

"So what's been going on?" she asked, and took another sip of water. "While I've been gone."

What happened? That was the million dollar question, wasn't it? I took a deep breath and started to explain.

I tried my best to get everything right and fill her in on everything that had happened. There was so much though, and truthfully, I really didn't know much. But I told her everything I knew. I told her about my lifeless years and how the prickle came and freed me. I told her about the Death Walkers and how Stephan was working with them. How he had the Mark of Malefiscus and how he put the mark on Nicholas. I explained to her my special Foreseer gift and the visions I saw. And even though I didn't want to, I gave her the details of how Stephan had tried to take it all away from me again. And how the locket—the locket she gave me—had saved me.

She took it all in, processing my every word. When I struggled with certain details, Laylen jumped in and aided me through them. We also had to explain to her what Laylen was, even though it really didn't have anything to do with any of this. But I felt like she should know every-thing—after being trapped in a place of death and fear for as long as she had.

When I was done, she sat there in silence. We were still out on the deck. The sun was beaming down. The ocean was roaring and people were out on the beach, splashing and playing in the salty water without a care in the world.

They were lucky—not having to know the dangers that were out there.

"Gemma," my mom said after I finished talking. "I'm so sorry." She reached over and tentatively took my hand.

I could feel her pulse racing through her touch. "I'm so sorry you had to go through this."

I swallowed hard, feeling my insides lurch. "It's not your fault...I—I know you tried to protect me."

She shook her head. "I should have tried harder."

I didn't want her to feel responsible. She did what she could—I watched her do it. Before I could try to convince her, it wasn't her fault, though, she said, "I need to talk to Alex."

"Alex?" I gave her a quizzical look. "Why do you need to talk to him?"

"Because." She looked at Laylen then back at me. "I need all of you here—including Aislin—before I can explain what I know about what's going on." When I still looked at her strangely, she added, "I need all of you here, because what I'm about to tell you involves all of you. Each of you plays a part in it."

"Plays a part in what?" I asked. "Stephan trying to open the portal?"

"Oh, Gemma." My mom shook her head exhaustedly. "There is so much more to Stephan's plan than just opening a portal and releasing the Death Walkers."

Chapter 39

You know those moments where time seems to stop? Well, I was having one of those moments right now. Laylen, my mom, and I sat there as the words my mother had just said sunk in. Laylen had been right when he said that my mother probably knew things, but I'd never expected her to say there was a lot more to Stephan's plan than just opening the portal, or that she would say all of us played a part in whatever Stephan was planning to do. I'd always assumed it was just me.

Me and the star.

I guess I was wrong.

Laylen got to his feet and told us he would go wake up Aislin and Alex. Then he left my mother and me sitting out on the deck alone. For awhile, neither of us spoke. We just sat there, listening to people laughing out on the beach.

"So, how have you been really?" she finally asked. "And don't say okay, because I know it's not true."

"I don't know..." I said, searching my mind for a way to change the subject. "I don't get something. Why was I able to undo what Sophia did to me? When she detached my soul, I mean."

"That's a question I can't answer just yet," she said, tilting her head up toward the sun. "I will, though, just as soon as everyone gets here."

"Okay." Not the answer I was expecting, but it worked.

Laylen returned seconds later with a very sleepy-eyed Aislin and Alex. Alex and Ailsin each grabbed a chair and dragged it to where my mother and I sat, and Laylen hopped up and took a seat on the railing.

Aislin was the first to speak, seeming kind of nervous. "Jocelyn, I can't believe you're here...It's just so..." She looked like she was going to burst into tears

My mom, despite the fact she had been locked away in The Underworld, still possessed motherly instincts and reached over and placed a hand on Aislin's hand. "It's okay. I'm alright. Everything's alright."

I highly doubted that was true. In fact, I was fairly sure my mom was about to drop a not-all-right bomb on us pretty soon.

Alex seemed less tolerant toward Aislin's emotional behavior, and I even caught him rolling his eyes.

"So, Laylen said there was something you wanted to tell us?" he asked impatiently.

My mother nodded. "There is. But I need you to tell me what you know first. Gemma's already told me what she knows, but I think you might know a little more."

Shocker? I think not.

He pressed his lips together, his arms crossed over his chest as his eyes wandered around to all of us.

"Alex." My mom's voice was persuasive. "I understand your initial reaction is to keep things a secret—it's what you've been taught to do. But it's important that you tell me what you know, so we can stop the end of the world from happening."

He still seemed hesitant. "Where do you want me to start?"

My mother considered this. "Why don't you start from the beginning?"

"But, what is the beginning?" Alex asked, like he was asking a riddle.

My mother was patient, though. "Why don't you start with the day that Gemma's soul was detached. Do you remember what happened that day?"

He glanced at me, and I raised my eyebrows at him, implying to go ahead, because boy was I dying to hear this.

"The day Gemma's soul was taken away..." He shut his eyes for a moment and then opened them back up. "She and I were hiding out in that little fort in the side of the hill, because earlier my father had told us Gemma had to go away."

I touched the palm of my hand where the faintest of scars resided, remembering the vision I saw. How he had cut my hand and his, saying the words *forem* as he pressed them together. It was a word I still didn't know the mean-

354

ing of. One of these days, I think, I was going to have to invest in buying a Latin Translator Pocket Dictionary, if such a thing existed.

Alex must have noticed me touching my hand, because he clenched his own. "But he ended up finding us and took Gemma away. I never saw her again...Well, until my dad made me enroll in school to see if I could get to the bottom of why she started to feel."

"And what happened between all those years when you didn't see Gemma?" my mother asked, urging him for more details.

He was holding back, I could tell, but my mom asked him again and he gave in. "Basically, my father trained me and Aislin to be Keepers, but he focused more on me because Aislin was busy getting taught how to use her witch power."

My mom nodded. "And what happened while your father was training you to be a Keeper? Did he teach you to be emotionally closed off?"

"Emotionally closed off?" I gaped at my mother, wondering if she was losing it again. "No Mom, that was me."

My mom kept her eyes on Alex, and he swallowed hard.

"Not so much emotionally detached," he said, really struggling to keep his voice under control. "He would always tell me emotions are overrated, and that to be a good Keeper I had to keep my emotions under control and only

355

show them on the outside, but not feel them on the inside…something that's not always possible for me to do….at least sometimes." Alex looked more confused than I had ever seen him look, as if he was trying to figure something out, but just couldn't get there. Then he glared at my mother. "I really don't get what any of this has to do with the star's power and the end of the world."

"It has everything to do with it," my mother told him and rolled up the sleeves of the ratty old shirt she was wearing. "I just have one more question before I explain what *I* know. The day Gemma started to feel, were you there at her house?"

I'm pretty sure that everyone's eyes, including my own, widened in shock.

"Why the heck would you think that?" Alex asked, baffled. "I wasn't allowed to be near her."

"I understand that." My mom's voice was calm. "But I need to know if, by some chance, you decided to break the rule your father set of not being allowed to go near her."

Everyone waited for him to answer, but I'm sure I was the one most eager to hear what he was going to say.

Alex gazed out at the ocean, his bright green eyes twinkling in the sun like emeralds. "It was something I couldn't help…going there."

"I understand that," my mom said. "More than I think even you do."

I didn't get what was going on here. Why hadn't Alex told me this? Then again, why was I getting surprised over this? This was Alex. But, I don't know, I thought he'd been a little better about not keeping secrets. I guess I was wrong.

"So, you were at Marco and Sophia's the day my emotions returned?" I asked Alex, angrily. "And you never told me?"

He avoided looking at me as he shrugged. 'It wasn't that big of a deal. I mean, so what if I went there?"

"Alex, I'm fairly sure you're the one who brought Gemma's emotions back to her," my mom said as patiently as ever. "See, there's a connection between you two, which is where the electricity comes from."

"What's the connection?" My words rushed out.

She took a deep breath and said two simple words. But they were two words that would change everything.

"The star."

Chapter 40

"The star." I repeated my mother's words. "How does that connect us? I mean, it's only in me, so I..." I trialed off as a thought occurred to me. Electricity that flowed between two people—it was something that always seemed so impossible, yet every time I was around Alex, there it was. I could feel it buzzing right now, hot and shimmering. But I only felt it with Alex and never anyone else, which meant what...oh. "Does Alex have a star's power in him too?"

"Are you crazy?" Alex practically yelled at me. "Why would you even think that?"

I glared at him. "Why would someone ever think I was carrying around a star's energy inside me? They wouldn't. But yet I am."

"I don't know..." He had this look on his face like he was trying to cause trouble. "They might, considering how you are."

"What, *unemotional?*" I said furiously.

"Okay, you two," my mother interrupted, which was a good thing because I could feel the electricity on the rise, so things were about to get really heated. "Alex, Gemma's

358

right. You do have a star's energy in you. Not a separate star, but the same one."

Alex was shaking his head. "No. There's no way. How could a star's power accidentally get transferred into Gemma and me?"

"Because it wasn't an accident," my mother said, and motioned her hand around at all of us. "None of it was. All of this—all of you—happened for a reason. Gemma having the star in her—you having the star in you. Aislin being a witch, and Laylen being a vampire. None of this was an accident."

My heart was beating a million miles a minute, like an insane humming bird was in my chest. I glanced at Laylen, remembering how Nicholas said Stephan had created him, and how Laylen had told me he couldn't recollect how he had been changed. Memory loss, just like me.

"So what you're saying," Laylen said, speaking slow-ly, as if he'd forgotten how to form words, "is that I was bitten on purpose—that Stephan had a vampire bite me?"

My mother nodded and then looked at all of us grave-ly. "Stephan has been planning this out for years—ever since he found out the portal could be opened." She sighed, looking drowsy. "Stephan's been looking for a way to free Malefiscus since the mark first appeared on his face. No one knew about his mark, though, because his parents cut it off and tried to keep it hidden. I didn't even know he had it until it was too late." She swallowed hard. "Stephan is a descendent of Malefiscus, but I'm not sure how. I don't think either of his parents bore the mark."

"I still don't get it, though," Alex said. "You say all of us play a part. But play a part in what?"

"Well, for starters, in freeing Malefiscus," my mom explained. "Stephan's been trying to free him even before he was told he could by a Foreseer. It was through visions that he finally figured out the exact details of what he had to do to pull it off—a sort of step-by-step guide."

"But I thought Malefiscus being immortal was just a myth?" Laylen asked, putting his feet up on the bottom railing.

My mother shook her head. "He could create marks, just like Stephan can. Although, I'm pretty sure Stephan himself hasn't been able to create the Mark of Immortality...yet."

"Yet?" I asked. "Does that mean he will?"

"It's only a matter of time," my mom said, nodding. "He'll find a way eventually."

I thought about the Death Walkers and how difficult they were to kill, and how the Sword of Immortality was one of the few things that could kill them. And how, in the end of the world vision I saw, Stephan had had the sword. As of now, we still had the sword, but did this mean we would end up losing it?

Aislin, who had been sitting silently in her chair, looking very much freaked out, suddenly sputtered out, "But why does he need a witch and a vampire? And why did he have to create them?"

My mother took a shaking breath, grasping her hands together. "Not a lot of people know this, but during Malefiscus's reign, it wasn't just the Death Walkers who were terrorizing people. There were some witches, vampires, Fey, and even a couple of Foreseers who had joined him." My mom took another sip of her water, and when she placed it back on the railing it tipped over and tumbled off the side of the deck. She shook her head. "When Hektor finally captured Malefiscus, the Keepers had to come up with a way to make his followers surrender. So they put Malefiscus in a portal and sealed it with the blood of three individuals; a Keeper who also was a vampire, a Keeper who was also a witch, and a Keeper who was also a faerie. That way the Fey, witches, and vampires who followed Malefiscus would be bound to the portal as well, without the Keepers having to track them all down. "

I glanced at Aislin, who was a witch and a Keeper, and Laylen, who was a vampire and a Keeper. There was one piece missing here—a half-faerie, half-Keeper. So who was the missing link?

My mother stared out at the ocean. "The final step was to seal the portal with the energy of a fallen star."

"So there was another fallen star once that two Keepers had to carry around in them?" I asked, glancing over at Alex. He met my eyes and the electricity ignited. "There were two people just like Alex and me?"

361

My mother tore her eyes off the ocean and shook her head. "No. The star's energy you and Alex carry is the same star's energy the Keepers used those hundreds of years ago. After they sealed the portal, they hid it away because no one knew how to destroy it. The star was also never put in any Keepers. That's one of the things that I've never been able to figure out. I don't understand why Stephan split the star and put its energy in you two." She let out a heavy sigh. "But I do know that in order for Stephan to be able to open the portal, he needs his vampire, his witch, and his faerie that also have Keeper blood in them, so he created them. Then he got his hands on the star, and for some reason he put it in you and Alex."

I felt like I had been hit by a truck. "So if he opens the portal, then what happens? Malefiscus is freed?"

My mother nodded. "He'll be able to enter our world again. Every Death Walker will come out of hiding and even more will come out of the portal. He controls them because of his mark and because of his blood, which is the same reason why Stephan has control over them." She paused. "Anyone who has the Mark of Malefiscus can communicate with the Death Walkers."

I thought of when Nicholas had been talking to them in the forest, and how it had sounded like a one-sided conversation. But it had been because he was talking to a Death Walker, and since Alex and I didn't have the Mark of Malefiscus we couldn't hear anything the Death Walker was saying.

"And along with the Death Walkers, every witch, faerie, and vampire who are the descendants of those who followed Malefiscus during his first reign of terror will be under his control if he gets out of the portal," my mom added in a heavy tone. "So what you saw in the vision, Gemma, was probably the end of what's going to happen to the world. What you saw is probably what came after the massacre."

"Massacre," I said aloud, and then we all just sat there. This was so much worse than what we originally thought. Yes, the world would end in ice, but people would be slaughtered first, and by witches, vampires, and faeries.

"But I don't get it." I said loudly, startling everyone. "How does Stephan know how to do all of this? And why on December 21, 2012?"

"Because that's when he was told it would be possible to open the portal—a Foreseer told him. The same Foreseer who told him he needed to create all of you."

"Is my father the Foreseer?" I asked, shocking both her and everyone else.

My mother jumped up from her chair. "No, it's not your father!" she screamed, and I hovered back in my chair.

She stood there for a moment, her bright blue eyes wild with rage. Then she composed herself and sunk back down in the chair. "I'm so sorry, Gemma."

"It—it's okay," I said, sucking back the tears threatening to leak out of my eyes.

She shook her head. "No, it's not."

Aislin slowly stood up from her chair, her golden blonde hair blowing in the wind. "I think I need to go lie down. This is a lot to take in."

My mother nodded, and Aislin scurried out. Laylen hopped off the railing and followed after her.

My mother glanced between Alex and me. "And you two. I have no idea why he needed to separate the star. Or why he detached Gemma's soul and raised you to be emotionally shut off. It's the one thing we really need to find out, because I have a feeling it might be the key to stopping it all."

"But why did he create Aislin and Laylen?" I asked. "I mean, I understand why he needs them, but why did he create them? Why not just find a vampire and witch who are also Keepers?"

"Because their kind are not easy to find," my mother answered. "And I think it was also so he could keep an eye on them and make sure everything turned out the way that he wanted."

Suddenly, the electricity started to surge even more than it had, almost to the point that it was suffocating me.

"Alex, are you okay?" I asked.

He looked at me. There was a fire in his bright green eyes. Then he stood to his feet, threw the chair over the deck, and stormed inside. I almost followed, but then thought better of it.

I turned my attention back to my mother. "So, that's it, then? Stephan will open up the portal and the world will end, just like I saw it?"

My mom leaned toward me and placed her hand on top of mine. "There are always loopholes, Gemma. You just have to find them."

I took her words in. There were always loopholes; you just had to find them. But what if we couldn't find them?

Then what?

Chapter 41

After my mom had dropped the bombshell on us, everyone scattered around the house. Aislin and Laylen were in
their rooms and Alex had gone outside. My mom said she
needed to lie down and rest—she was still recovering from
being in The Underworld for so long—but she made a re-
quest first. She asked me to go check on Alex.

Yeah, I'm not sure she understood how terrible of an
idea that was, and I tried to explain to her that he and I
tended to argue a lot, and as upset as he was, I would
probably just make him mad. But my mom was very in-
sistent that I do so.

So I did, but with zero confidence that I would be able
to make him feel better.

I found Alex sitting out on the front steps, the sun
shining down on his messy brown hair. He didn't look up
at me when I walked out, but I knew that he knew I was
there, thanks to the electricity. The electric connection felt
so different now that I knew why it was there. In fact, it
was kind of like a painful reminder of what Stephan had
done to us, and what he was planning to do to the world.

The salty air kissed my skin as I sat down on the cement steps beside Alex. I told myself that I could do this—I could make him feel a little better. I had done it for Laylen after all, when he bit the woman. But with Alex it was different.

"How are you?" I asked him, which seemed like a really stupid question once it left my mouth. How are you? I shook my head at myself.

Alex looked at me with the same look I would have given myself if that were possible.

I kicked a rock with my toes. "Sorry, dumb question."

He took a few deep breaths and the expression on his face softened. "No, it's not a dumb question. I just…I don't know how I am." He ran his fingers through his hair so hard he yanked at the roots. "I feel like I don't know anything anymore. I mean, my whole life has been a lie."

I nodded, understanding how he felt completely.

"Gemma." His voice held such uncertainty. He watched me with his bright green eyes, which were filled with the same uncertainty his voice held. "I'm sorry…for everything."

How was I supposed to respond to this? Because it no longer seemed like I should be putting the blame on Alex for what had happened to me.

"It's okay," I told him. "It's really not your fault."

"It is though," he said, his voice cracking a little. "I didn't have to do what my father told me to do. I had a choice…unlike you."

"It's okay," I told him again, leaning back on my hands. "But can I ask you something?"

He hesitated before nodding.

"Why did you come to my house that day? The day my emotions were released? Was it because of the star? Or was it something else?"

He sat there for what seemed like an eternity, just looking at me, and I could almost see the internal struggle he was having with whether or not he should tell me the truth. I now knew that this was because he had been taught to be this way, and I figured it was going to be a hard habit for him to break. So he startled me when he reached behind me and took my hand in his.

"You remember how Nicholas told you about the Blood Promise the Fey made to Malefiscus, right?" he asked, tracing his fingers across the top of my hand.

I tried not to shiver. "Yeah, I remember."

He turned my hand over and moved his finger across the tiny scar on the palm of my hand. And, as crazy as this is going to sound, I swear the faint scar was becoming more noticeable as he touched it. "And you remember the vision you saw when you and me were kids, and I cut both of our hands?"

Forem. "Yeah...but what does that have to do..." It clicked. "Did we make a Blood Promise?"

He nodded. "We did."

Forem. "What kind of promise?"

"The forever kind."

"The forever kind?" I asked. "What does that mean?"

He cocked an eyebrow at me. "You remember the word we said when we pressed our hands together, right?"

I nodded. "*Forem*. But what does it mean?"

Forever," he said, his breath shaky. "It means we're bonded together forever."

Chapter 42

I wasn't sure what to say. I felt strange and slightly light-headed and a little bit breathless. I mean, he just told me that when we were little, we made an unbreakable promise to be together.

Forever.

It took a minute, but I finally found my voice again. "It seems like a really weird promise for two kids to make," I told him, lightly tracing my finger across the scar on the palm of my hand.

He pressed his lips together, holding back a smile. "That's all you have to say after I just told you that we made an unbreakable promise to be together forever?"

I shrugged. "I don't know. It just seems really strange to me."

He closed his hand and then stretched it open again. "Well, we were strange kids." He paused, a small amount of bitterness creeping into his expression. "And now I know why."

I chewed on my bottom lip, thinking about my child-hood and how, thanks to Stephan and Sophia's lovely gift of being able to detach souls from their emotions, I could barely remember anything about it.

"Did we ever feel it?" I asked.

He gave me a funny look. "Did we ever feel what?"

"The electricity—when we were little did we ever feel it?"

"I'm not sure." He stared off at the quiet street in front of us, the sun shining brightly in his eyes. "I don't really think that we felt what we do now, but there was always a connection there."

I remembered the first time I ever laid eyes on him, and how my gaze had found him all on its own. There was definitely a connection—one deeper than even the electricity went.

Alex looked at me and he had such intensity in his bright green eyes that it made me squirm around uncomfortably. A strange feeling passed through me then, and I waited for the prickle to show up and tell me what I was feeling, because whatever was going on right now had to be something new. But the prickle never came and as I continued to grow more uncomfortable, I changed the subject.

"So, do you think we'll be able to fix everything?" I asked, struggling to keep my voice even. "Do you think we'll be able to stop the world from ending—stop what I saw in my vision from actually happening? My mom said there are always loop holes. But what loop holes would there be? I mean, it doesn't make any... " I trailed off because of the astonished look Alex was giving me.

"I think you might want to at least take a breath between your questions," he said.

I gave him an oh-shut-up look. "But there are too many unanswered ones. I mean, how can you be so...*calm* about everything you just heard?"

He shook his head. "I'm not calm." He looked at me and I could see it in his eyes—the sadness, the pain, the hurt of being betrayed and lied to. I knew how it felt, but it was strange to see it in Alex's eyes because he rarely showed much of anything, which now I knew why.

"Are you sure you're going to be o—" I started to say, but I was stopped by a set of lips pressing against mine. A set of warm and sparkling lips.

Way, way in the back of my mind, right where the rational side of my brain was, I had a thought that maybe it wasn't such a good idea for the two of us to be kissing. It had never been made one hundred percent clear if it was a good thing or a bad thing for Alex and me to be this close to one another.

But the irrational and emotional side of my brain took over, and I kissed him back, feeling effervescent and sparkly. The kiss was so much different from the other kisses we shared. There was so much more trust and foreverness to it. And as his hands wrapped around my back and pulled me closer to him, I temporarily forgot about all the problems we had and would be facing very soon. The key word here is *temporarily*. Because moments after the kiss began it was over as Aislin came running out the front door, the screen banging closed behind her.

I quickly pulled away from Alex, but he didn't seem to care as much as I did that we had been caught making out on the front porch. In fact, one of his hands was still residing on the base of my back. And I think Alex was planning on chewing Aislin out for interrupting us. I could see the annoyance in his expression. But then Aislin spoke, and all irritation disappeared from the both of us.

"Laylen's gone," she said, her words rushed, her eyes wide.

"Gone?" Alex's hand fell from my back.

"What do you mean gone?" I asked, jumping to my feet. "I thought he was in his room?"

She shook her head. "No, he's not. And I searched the house, and I can't find him anywhere."

This was bad. Very, very bad. Laylen had been in such a fragile state already, with the whole first-time biting thing, and now he had just found out that he was created on purpose, to help end the world.

"What do we do?" Aislin cried to Alex.

Alex ran his fingers through his hair, thinking. "No one saw where he went?" he asked, looking at Aislin and then me.

I shook my head. "Like I said, I thought he was in his room."

373

"And I haven't seen him since we were on the deck." Aislin's voice trembled. "And Jocelyn said she hasn't seen him anywhere, but she's out back checking if he's out there." Right as she said it, the screen door swung open, and my mom stepped out, looking worried and worn out.

"He wasn't out back," she said, heading down the stairs toward us.

"Well, we have to find him." I was trying not to panic, but finding it very difficult. "He—he was already upset before he found out everything, and now..." What the hell was this? This massive hole in my chest? And the hole seemed to be sucking all the air right out from me.

"Gemma, calm down," Alex said, and I realized I was breathing rather loudly. "We'll find him, but you need to quit freaking out."

"Sorry." I took a deep breath. "So what are we going to do?"

Alex gave me the strangest look, as if something horrible had just occurred to him, but it vanished from his face before I got the chance to ask him what it meant.

"Okay, we need to split up," Alex said, switching into I'm In Charge mode. "Aislin, you go check that way" He pointed to the left of the main road in front of us. "I'll go up the right side, towards where you and I found him the other night." I nodded, and he told my mom, "You go check out to the right side of the beach, and Gemma check the left."

We all nodded and headed off to our designated areas. Before I'd even been able to take two steps, though, Alex pulled me back.

"Don't go too far," he told me. "After what we were just told—you need to be extremely careful."

I nodded. "And so do you."

He nodded too, gave me this weird look, and headed off down the sidewalk. I spun around and ran up the stairs, feeling the same way I'd felt when I'd been at the top of the rollercoaster tracks waiting for it to fall. But I wasn't sure if what would be awaiting me at the bottom was happiness.

The beach was packed with a mob of people, but I figured that even with the abundance of bodies roaming around, the odds seemed fairly favorable in spotting a six-foot-four, blonde haired, blue-tip banged, vampire wandering around. But what if he wasn't just wandering around? What if he was doing something he would regret? What if he was drinking blood again?

I started to walk faster, the sand making my footsteps heavy as I barreled across the shoreline. Every once in awhile the cold ocean would roll up and hit my ankles. I was trying to keep it together, but the further I went down the sandy beach, the more concerned I became that I wasn't going to find him.

I decided that it might be a good idea to ask someone if they had seen him. So, as a girl around my age with auburn hair and hazel eyes walked by me, I stopped her.

"Have you seen a guy that's about six foot four, with blond and blue hair and has a lip ring?" I asked her.

She thought about this and then her expression lit up. "Is he like really good-looking with bright blue eyes, and has these symbols tattooed on his arms?"

I nodded. "Do you know where he is?"

She pointed up the beach, towards a group of rocks that framed the lip of the shore. "Yeah, he went that way."

"Thanks," I said, and I took off, sprinting like a mad man for the rocks.

By the time I reached the rocks, I was panting for air. The mobs of people were so far away now that they looked like dots. There was a small narrow path that went between the rocks, and I stepped down it and the beach disappeared out of sight. I gradually made my way down the path, stepping over the sharp rocks as I braced my hand on the cliff's wall. A few times I lost my balance and slipped, and by the time I made it to the end of the path the palms of my hands were covered in cuts.

But the cuts were the least of my problems, because there was no one at the end of the path, and nowhere else I could go. I tried to listen for voices, but the sound of the ocean was too loud. Shaking my head, I started to turn around, wondering why the girl had told me Laylen had come back here.

"Beautiful day, isn't it?"

His voice sent me scurrying backwards, and I scraped my back on one of the rock's jagged edges.

"Easy, Gemma," Nicholas said, his hands in the pockets of his tan cargo shorts. "Why so jumpy?"

I didn't answer him, my gaze searching desperately for an alternative way out. But after a few seconds, I realized I was trapped.

"Where's Laylen?" I asked him, keeping my back pressed into the rocks, even though it hurt.

He tapped his finger on his lips, his golden eyes watching me like a cat watching a mouse. "Haven't seen him."

I opened my mouth, about to tell him that I knew Laylen had come back here—that an auburn-haired girl back on the beach had told me he had—but the wicked smile on Nicholas's face stopped the words from leaving my mouth.

"It's amazing what a little faerie charm can get people to say," he said, casting a glance back in the direction of the beach. "Well, except on you. My charm never seems to have any effect over you."

"Charm?" I said snidely. "Is that what you call it?"

Nicholas pressed his hand to his heart dramatically. "Oh, Gemma, how your words hurt me."

I glared at him, and he grinned.

"Well," he said. "As much as I would love to hide out here with you all day—I mean, think of the endless possibilities of the things we could do back here, way out of sight of everyone. But I'm afraid I have a promise to finish." He reached for me, and I jumped back, bumping my head on the serrated wall of the rocky cliff.

"Careful there." Then, the next thing I knew, Nicholas was in front of me, so close I could smell his flowery scent overlapping the scent of the salty ocean air. "Don't worry, I don't bite," he whispered, sliding a finger down my cheek.

I kneed him in the stomach, and he buckled forward. I seized the opportunity to dodge around him, but I didn't make it very far, before Nicholas grabbed me by the shoulder and threw me to the ground. My head smacked against a rock, and the world started to spin like a merry-go-round.

He stood above me, looking relieved, as if a huge burden was about to be lifted from his shoulders. "It's time to go," he said.

I think my head had started to bleed. Either that or I was lying in some other kind of warm, sticky liquid. I still tried to get up, but my legs weren't having any part of it. I tried to use my Foreseer power to take me away, but all I got in return was a headache.

Nicholas knelt down beside me and placed his hand on my arm, and there was nothing I could do but lie there as he retrieved the miniature ruby-filled Foreseer ball out of his pocket. He held it close to my face as if to taunt me, and closed his eyes.

Then we were gone.

Chapter 43

When I opened my eyes again, Nicholas was gone. The room I was in was completely empty. And cold—Wyoming mountain cold.

I was lying on the floor, my face pressed against the hard floorboards. My head felt like it had been split in two, my body ached, and there was dried blood in my hair. I also noticed that my necklace was missing from around my neck, which sent a surge of panic soaring through me. The one thing that could protect me from magical harm, and it was gone.

I sat up slowly and glanced around the room that had nothing more than a door on each side of it, and a single window which was barred shut. I had been here once before. This was the place that I had seen myself, lifeless, curled up on the floor.

This was bad. I thought Nicholas would take me to the City of Crystal, especially since he had taken out the ruby-filled crystal ball. But he brought me here instead. Why, though?

Fearing the answer, I got to my feet, ignoring the painful head rush I had, and took a few wobbly steps toward the door. It took me forever to get there, but I finally made it. Before I could get the door open, though, it was opening by itself, and I was hit with a puff of air so cold it froze my body over in a heartbeat.

And then I saw him and part of me wished that the cold air had turned me to ice and killed me.

Stephan stood in the doorway, dressed in black, Death Walkers towering on each side of him, their ravenous eyes gleaming yellow beneath the hood of their black cloaks. Snow was blowing in from the outside, and I could see snow was everywhere outside, just like it had been in the vision I had seen.

"Oh good, you're awake," Stephan said, entering the room as if he owned it.

I stumbled backward, my heart pounding with terror.

"Nicholas said you were out when he left you," Stephan said, still moving toward me.

Thankfully the Death Walkers didn't enter. But really, could I be thankful about that? Stephan was here and the scar on his cheek reminded me of everything my mom had told me.

"Why am-m I-I here?" I stuttered, my whole body shaking, not only with fear, but from the cold that was swirling through the room.

Stephan's dark eyes stared at me, and they held so much irritation that I wanted to duck under something and hide.

"You're here because I had to create an alternative plan." He walked around the room, glancing at the log walls as if he was searching for something. "Since you and my son ruined my original plan—a plan I worked very hard to create—I had to come up with a new one." He turned and faced me, his hands behind his back. "But I think this plan will work out a lot better. And the best part is, I won't have to worry about my son finding you again. He'll never find you here." His dark eyes pierced into me. "No one will."

My breathing faltered, and the room was starting to sway again. "What are you going to do to me?" I asked, thinking about the *memoria extraho* and fearing he was going to use something similar to it on me.

"Oh, I'm not going to do anything to you, Gemma," he said with a wicked grin. "Except leave you here."

"Leave me here?" I glanced at the barred up window, wondering where here was, but all I could see were mountains and trees and the snow that covered them.

"Oh, yes." He walked over to the window, dragging his fingers along the bars. "See, there is something about the cold that preserves your energy—it's why I sent you to Wyoming. And keeping your energy preserved is the most important thing right now."

"And what about Alex's energy?" I asked, trying to keep my balance as a rush of wooziness whipped through me. "How are you planning on preserving his energy?"

This surprised him. "I see you've been busy." He walked toward me again. "My son will preserve the energy himself. It was what I raised him to do. And as long as he's away from you, the star's energy will be fine." He stopped right in front of me. "All I have to do is keep you from him."

"Alex will find me," I told him, but I wasn't so sure of this myself.

Stephan considered this for a very long time, and then I got the feeling that I was about to experience, firsthand, a villain-confessing-his-evil-plan moment.

"See, here's the thing, Gemma," he said, his already dark eyes shifting darker. "Even if he does find you, it'll never work out. You two were just not meant to be with each other."

I touched the scar on the palm of my hand. *Forem.* "Yes, we are."

He let out a laugh that rang though the cabin and echoed out against the snowy mountains. "The ideas you kids have—always wanting to be with the wrong person."

I wasn't sure what he meant by this. "The wrong person?"

He stood in front of me, the two Death Walkers still hovering in the doorway, blocking my only way out. "You think you're supposed to be with someone because you having feelings for them, but trust me Gemma, feelings are way overrated."

Wow. So that's where Alex had gotten the quote from.

The mention of feelings sent rage surging through me, and without even thinking I kicked Stephan in the shin with my bare foot.

He winced, and then hit me across the face. My ears rang like an out of control bell, and I collapsed to the hardwood floor. He leaned over me, his eyes full of anger.

"You think it's so bad, what I've done to you. Well, let me let you in on a little secret. Life is way overrated—emotions are way overrated. Even Malefiscus—which I'm sure you know who he is by now—was at one point weakened by his jealousy for his brother. Although, he did turn it into something good." He dragged his finger along the scar on his cheek.

I hated this man more than I have ever hated anyone before. I could feel the hate burning inside me—I could feel the hate poking at the back of my neck. "You're the one who's weak."

"Oh, am I?" He considered this. "Well, that's one I've never heard before." He let out an evil laugh. "Well, I think after awhile you'll change your mind. Nicholas has already taken your Foreseer power away from you and when it eventually returns, the *praesidium* will take over."

Praesidium? I glanced around the room and noticed that there were lavender marble-sized crystal balls dotting the edge of the hardwood floor.

"I'd take your power away from you completely if I could," Stephan added. "But I need it too much."

"Need it for what?" I asked, my stomach winding into a billion knots.

He ignored me. "The only way for you to get away from here is on foot." He glanced at the window. "And even I wouldn't try and make that walk. By the time I return to get you, you'll be nothing more than an emotionless soul. Being alone will do that to someone."

I remembered myself in my vision; the emptiness my eyes had held. That's how I would turn out if I stayed here.

No. I would not go back to that.

I started to get to my feet, not sure what I would do when I made it up, but I needed to do something. "This plan won't work," I said, struggling to keep my legs under me. "Just like your last plan didn't."

He'd started toward the door, but stopped and turned around. "Even if Alex did find you, eventually you'd both be dead. Every time you two are close to each other, it ignites the power. If you stay close to each other for too long, the star's power will fade out. And so will you and Alex."

My jaw just about hit the floor, and I stood there shocked. Alex and I would eventually kill each other? How was this possible? I thought about the electric bond we shared and the Blood Promise we'd made to be together forever. But if what Stephan had just said was true, then did it mean that if we did stay together forever, our forever wouldn't be that long?

I felt sick, physically and emotionally drained, my heart sinking in my chest.

"Like I said, Gemma, feelings are overrated." And with that he walked outside and shut the door behind him.

I immediately closed my eyes and tried to summon my Foreseer ability, but apparently Stephan had been telling the truth about my ability being gone, because I felt nothing.

This couldn't be happening.

I limped to the door, and opened it up, hoping I wouldn't come face-to-face with a Death Walker. But there was nothing but miles and miles of snow. And scattered across the miles and miles of snow—at least as far as my eyes could see—were dots and dots of tiny lavender crystal balls.

I let out a scream for help, but the only thing that returned to me was my own echo.

Jessica Sorensen lives with her husband and three kids in the snowy mountains of Wyoming, where she spends most of her time reading, writing, and hanging out with her family.